Bad Actors

The Multiverse Refugees Trilogy

Second Pi in the Face

Also by Ira Nayman from Elsewhen Press

Transdimensional Authority (aka Multiverse) series
Welcome to the Multiverse (Sorry for the Inconvenience)

You Can't Kill the Multiverse (But You Can Mess With its Head)

Random Dingoes

It's Just the Chronosphere Unfolding as it Should

The Multiverse is a Nice Place to Visit,
But I Wouldn't Want to Live There

Good Intentions,
The Multiverse Refugees Trilogy,
First Pie in the Face

The Writer Did It!
in **Existence is Elsewhen**

Bad Actors

The Multiverse Refugees Trilogy

Second Pi in the Face

Ira Nayman

Elsewhen Press

Bad Actors

First published in Great Britain by Elsewhen Press, 2021
An imprint of Alnpete Limited

Elsewhen Press, PO Box 757, Dartford, Kent DA2 7TQ
elsewhen.press

British Library Cataloguing in Publication Data.
A catalogue record for this book is available from the British Library.

ISBN 978-1-911409-84-7 Print edition
ISBN 978-1-911409-94-6 eBook edition

Designed and formatted by Elsewhen Press

Contents

PROLOGUE
What's the Big Idea?

Ideas are living things.

Ideas grow. Start with a simple idea: "I am hungry." At first, it is one idea competing in your brain for attention, easy to ignore. It grows more insistent: "Hey, I'm hungry." It pushes out thoughts of whether there's a stain on your shirt or if it's worth picking up that book instead of continuing to watch television. Over time, the idea grows even more insistent: "Hey! **I'm hungry!**" Like a dog sniffing around your private parts, the idea is now too big to ignore.

Ideas feed off their surroundings. The idea "I am hungry," for example, may feed off the rumbling in your stomach, or a lack of energy. If you are watching television and come across an ad for nacho dip, it could feed the idea. If you look around your den while watching television and see empty wrappers from candy bars past strewn all about the place, the idea might start to get ideas of its own. Feeding ideas helps them grow.

Ideas breed. Start with the idea: "I am hungry." This spawns the idea, "I should eat something." This spawns the idea, "What is there to eat?" This spawns the idea, "Maybe I should check the fridge." This spawns the idea, "Yes, let me check the fridge." Four generations of ideas later, you may finally get off the couch.

Ideas need room to breath. The idea "I am hungry," won't get much traction if it is competing in your mind for attention with other ideas such as: "Have I seen this episode of *Attic Thumpers* before?"; "Is it true love this time, or just a little indigestion?"; "What is that smell?"; "If the weather is better tomorrow, I should go for a run…;" "What is that lump on the couch? Have I bust a spring from sitting here so long?";

"No, really, what is that smell?"; "Aww, who am I kidding? If the weather is better tomorrow, I'll keep binge watching *Attic Thumpers* – talk about addictive!"; and, "Where am I going to put that bronze statue of a baby's arm holding an apple?" Starved of the oxygen of attention, the idea "I am hungry," could die before it is acted upon.

Ideas move. You're in the den with your children, watching television, and you say, "I should eat something." Your son posts a message on Farcebook, "My dad should eat something." It is liked twenty-three times and reposted seven times, twice by two of his fiends in Hong Kong. Your daughter tweeps, "My dad should eat something. lolz". This gets two hundred fifty-seven retweeps, including a hundred forty-nine from Russia (at least seventeen of which are verifiable human beings). As you can see, ideas can travel around the world before dad has a chance to get his eating boots on.

Ideas are living things. But that's only the beginning.

Ideas compete for approval. You start with the idea: "I want pizza." This is immediately countered by the idea: "I want a hamburger and fries." Something inside you might try the compromise idea: "I want a hamburger and fries…on my pizza!" "That's what ground beef and fried potatoes are for," the first idea will counter. "**Order a pizza!**" "Mustard and relish are really gross on a pizza," the second idea would argue. "**Go out for a hamburger!**" "Pizza!" "Hamburger!" "Pizza!" "Hamburger!" Falafel!" "Falafel?" "Hey! It's a compromise, right?" The back and forth of intellectual competition and compromise: that's how you end up eating something you didn't really want and don't even especially like. Although this battle of ideas may appear to be resolved relatively quickly, it will reappear in the morning (with the cereal versus pancakes debate), and pretty much every mealtime thereafter.

As they do in individual minds, ideas compete among groups. The idea, "We're hungry!" can find itself countered by the idea, "So, eat something." The idea, "But we cannot afford to buy food!" is one response. **This** is countered by the idea, "So, okay, don't eat anything." "But we're hungry!" "Oh, would you please make up your minds?" Unlike the battle of ideas within individuals, the battle of ideas between social groups can take forever to be resolved…if it ever is.

This is a story about how good intentions are overtaken by bad ideas. You may want to finish eating before you start reading…

CHAPTER ONE
Do Blue Men Sing the Whites?

They Came, They Saw, They Ate Pie

by INDIGO HAPHAZASTANCE Alternate Reality News Service Transdimensional Traffic Writer

The Dolomite construction crew was a rough and ready bunch of men. Ricky Agnosticci ("It's pronounced Egg-naws-teach-ee – what, were you raised in a barn?") has a tattoo on his back of the Notre Dames de Paris Cathedral, **after** the fire that left it a hulking shell (not unlike Gerard Depardieu)! Ronald 'The Buried Hatchet' McFlorentine enjoys chewing glass in his spare time (he hopes to turn pro in time for the next Olympic Games). Trini LePew collects paintings of dung beetles by the Old Masters and enjoys brewing home-made wine... which nobody who knows him will drink. Scott 'Harsh Hashtag' Laren can chop down thousand year-old sequoias with a single cutting remark.

You don't have to be a *Sesame Seed Street* aficionado to recognize that one of these things is not like the other things, that one of these things doesn't belong. Being able to sing along with the words in your head is kind of cool, though.

"It's me," grinned McFlorentine, chewing on I did not want to know what (which turned out to be sea salt ground glass in dark chocolate – you want to get ahead in the journalism racket, you can't afford to be squeamish). "I've always been a little... different."

Which may be true, but is irrelevant to the current article. The person who actually doesn't belong to this group is LePew. Boy, doesn't he belong!

Two years ago, scientists at the Transdimensional Authority learned that Earth Prime 4-6-4-0-8-9 dash Omega was collapsing thanks to the machinations of a mad scientist that are too complicated to go into here.

One year, three hundred sixty-four days, seventeen hours and twenty-seven minutes ago, the TA (which sounds vaguely naughty, but isn't, the occasional miscommunication at the organization's ChristmaKwaanzUkah parties notwithstanding) announced a plan to help refugees from the dying universe relocate to Earth Prime. Since then, hundreds of thousands of the aliens have become respected plumbers, gastroenterologists and Mexican luchadors.

And yes, construction workers.

"At first, I was unimpressed," admitted Laren. "I mean, Jesus begesus, he was blue! Everybody knows blue people are stupid and lazy – it's been that way since before my great grandfather drowned driving the stagecoach from York to St. John's! How am I supposed to trust somebody like that in the trenches of the fourteenth floor? Not...that anybody knew there even were blue aliens before two years ago – I mean, **I'm** not stupid! I know *Avatar* was not a documentary! What I mean is...I mean, like all of his kind, Trini was only four feet tall. How can you properly rivet when you're only four feet tall? So, yeah, I may have played some... pranks on him."

Pranks? Like gluing the door to his locker shut? Laren looked me not in the eye and answered, "Pranks like greasing the sixth floor girder he was scheduled to work on."

Fortunately, a flat bed truck appeared on the street under him just as LePew was about to hit it, breaking his fall.

The aliens are often lucky that way.

What changed Laren's mind about LePew? "What makes you think I changed my mind about the filthy little blue toe?" he angrily demanded.[1] "I mean, like, what's with the exquisite three piece suit he always wears? I've seen him wade up to his waist in mud when we were clearing the land for the foundation, but it never has so much as a spot on it. That's just creepy!"

---

[1] "[INSERT NEGATIVE TRAIT OR STRING OF NEGATIVE TRAITS HERE] blue toe!" is a common epithet used by Earth Prime natives who do not like the alien species from Earth Prime 4-6-4-0-8-9 dash Omega. Traits that have been attributed to the aliens include: nasty, ugly, smelly, scatological, selfish, greedy, egotistical, orotund and vaguely unsettling. The term spread so widely so quickly that wordologists have not come to a consensus on why toes were chosen as the body part focused on in the epithet. Some believe that it is a diminution of "[INSERT NEGATIVE TRAIT OR STRING OF NEGATIVE TRAITS HERE] blue person, head to toe!" This makes sense, since the negative trait or traits are really the focus of the epithet, not the body part. A different some believe it has to do with sucking. That may be more reflective of the attitudes of the some than the epitheteers. As often happens, the whole explanation is less than some of its parts.

Agnosticci punched Laren in the shoulder. "Don't be like that! Don't you always say that he's great to send into dangerous situations because he's a Holy Fool who'll always come out smelling like a filthy little blue rose?"

Laren mumbled something I couldn't quite catch, but I was fast approaching the word limit of my article, so I decided it was agreement so I could move on.

"By and large, the aliens have integrated into human society well," commented TA Secretary-Specific Nicodemius Fitzhuge. "Coal miner, sanitation engineer, troll farm social network poster – there is no job so dirty or demeaning that they won't cheerfully take it! True, you will get the occasional Sonderland Aeronautics... it was more than an incident, but less than a debacle. Still, if they hadn't wanted the factory to explode, they really should have taken better care of the artichokes!"

So, can we expect to see an alien from Earth Prime 4-6-4-0-8-9 dash Omega working at the Transdimensional Authority any time soon?

The dial tone on the other end of the line was as eloquent an answer as I could reasonably expect.

Ottawa Mayor Sulaman Sulameini looked at the room full of identical blue faces. Although the building was well heated, he shivered. Subordinates had explained to him that you could tell the aliens apart by subtle differences in the patterns on the exquisite three piece suits they all wore, but he could never tell them apart. (As a child, Mayor Sulameini had been terrible at those puzzles that contained two apparently identical images where you were asked to spot differences between them. His sister Yasmeen was always taunting him with the answers. The barbell in the image on the left is missing in the image on the right. The round buttons on the jacket of the sailor in the image on the left are square in the image on the right. The cigar that granny is smoking is a symbol of masculine power in the image on the left, and just a cigar in the image on the right. Think noticing these things makes you so smart? Ha! He showed her! He was now Mayor of Canada's capital city, while Yasmeen was a contented housewife in Kanata! Be better at puzzles than him? He really showed her what that was worth!)

Mayor Sulameini shook the memory out of his head. This was a solemn occasion – the first swearing in of alien beings as Canadian citizens; this was no time for personal score-settling. Although, he really did show Yasmeen – hee hee. Harrumph!

Ordinarily, you would have to live in Canada for at least three years over a five year period to be eligible for Canadian citizenship. But as the creator of the atomic clock knew, these were not ordinary times. Transdimensional Authority Secretary-Specific Fitzhuge had addressed the United Nations with a plea for countries to suspend or ease their normal citizenship requirements in order to help make these desperate refugees feel welcome and at home in countries. All but three countries agreed to reconsider their rules[1] for citizenship eligibility (the three being Russia, Saudi Arabia and the United States of America, which, under its new president, had grabbed Lady Liberty by the…unmentionables and appeared to be in no hurry to let go).

The aliens had successfully passed the test of their knowledge of the country (with such penetrating questions as: "Which Canadian city has pretensions to being the centre of the universe?" "Which Canadian city actually **is** the centre of the universe?" and "Which National Hockey League player scored 10 points in a single game, a record that is not likely to be surpassed until the establishment of the Robot & Android Hockey League?"). They had filled out the paperwork and paid the fees. All they had to do was take the oath of citizenship, and they would be Canadians.

But first, a word from their sponsors…

Mayor Sulameini gave a lengthy and impassioned speech about the rights and responsibilities of Canadian citizenship. But his mind was only half on what he was saying; he had been told that Rodney Pendleton, the first being to be brought from his home universe to Earth Prime, was one of the people who was going to be sworn in today. He scanned the crowd for a clothing pattern he only half remembered (with only half his attention to the task, the odds were not in

[1] Rules are other idea-proof ideas.

his favour), but he couldn't find it.

"...United Empire Loyalists for giving us a social-democratic utopia and butter tarts," he concluded. "Now, if all of the candidates for citizenship would like to rise and raise their right hands, I will give you the oath of citizenship."

All of the faces in the audience looked eagerly at him, but nobody moved. Mayor Sulameini had been advised that they all knew English, so – oh, my Gord, would he have to get a translator in here **and do his whole speech all over again?** Even he wasn't looking forward to the prospect. "Would – would those of you who are here to become Canadian citizens please stand up?"

The aliens started turning their heads towards each other, then back at him. "Who, us?" "Who, me?" "Are you talking to me?" "Do you mean me?" and other such questions came from half of the aliens.

"Yes!" Mayor Sulameini replied. "Yes, you!"

Half of the aliens shrugged and got to their feet.

"Now, please raise your hands."

All of the aliens in the room raised their hands.

"No. No, just those among you who are becoming Canadian citizens today need to raise their hands. The rest of you can put your hands down."

The people who were standing put their hands down.

"No. Wait. Those of you who are standing, are you here to become Canadian citizens?"

The aliens who were standing nodded in agreement.

"Okay, you raise your hands. The rest of you put your hands down."

Those who were sitting reluctantly put their hands down, while the hands of those who were on their feet shot up as though they were volunteering to get a maple doughnut IV drip. An alien standing at the back of the room said, "Can we please speed this along? At this rate, I'm going to miss my mani-pedi at Loblaws!"

Mayor Sulameini counted to ten. You didn't become the mayor of Canada's capital city by losing your temper at every provocation. Not only that, but half a dozen of the aliens appeared at the ceremony wearing toques with moose antlers. Before the ceremony started, he told them that this was a solemn occasion which required sober dress, and that the only exception would be that they could wear traditional or religious dress and head coverings. When one of them informed him that toques with moose antlers **were** religious head coverings, he had some indication of what to expect.

Mayor Sulameini commanded: "Repeat after me: I swear (or affirm)…"

Half of the standing aliens said, "I swear (or affirm)." At the same time, the other half said, "I bare (or uniform)…"

Mayor Sulameini frowned. That was sort of, but not exactly right. He again advised: "Please repeat **exactly what I say:** I swear (or affirm)…"

Half of the standing aliens said, "I swear (or affirm)." At the same time, the other half said, "I Swarovsky (or cunieform…)" The mayor could not have known, but the mix of aliens who were correct and those who were wrong was different from the first attempt at starting the oath.

Mayor Sulameini gritted his teeth and decided to plow ahead. "…that I will be faithful and bear true allegiance to Her Majesty Queen Elizabeth II, Queen of Canada, her heirs and successors…"

Most of the aliens repeated what he had said verbatim. One said, "This country is a monarchy? Why wasn't I told of this?"

A female alien standing nearby ran her hand over her moose toque and replied, "It was all over the *Guide to Canadian Citizenship*. How could you possibly have missed it?"

"The…*Guide to Canadian Citizenship*?" the male alien gulped.

"That's right."

"I…I didn't read that."

"What did you read?"

"The *Guide to Canadian Water Fowl…*"

There was a short pause before the male alien added: "Does this mean there isn't going to be a goose call at the end of the ceremony?"

Mayor Sulameini cleared his throat. "I was really looking forward to that," the male alien pouted.

Mayor Sulameini cleared his throat louder. All eyes turned back to him. "If you are finished…"

"Can we do goose calls at the end of the ceremony?" the

male alien asked. "It would make me feel more welcome…"

Mayor Sulameini harrumphed. Later, when he realized that that was what he had done, he would be reminded of the last time he had made that sound out loud: when Betty-Lou Madrigar had turned down his request to go to the prom. Three months later, he would resign his post, quitting politics to devote his life to starting a worm farm in Saskatoon. For now, though, he had a duty to complete, so he said: "…and that I will faithfully observe the laws of Canada and fulfil my duties as a Canadian citizen."

Most of the aliens repeated what he had said. A couple commented: "Canada? I thought this was France/China/Deneb." One of them added: "What planet are we on?"

At this point, Mayor Sulameini would usually smile warmly, but his pilot light seemed to have gone out, so he bared his teeth and stated, "Congratulations to you, the newest Canadians."

He walked out of the room as a dozen aliens made sounds like Canada geese.

Rodney Pendleton emerged from the government building and breathed deeply the air of freedom. Canadian freedom. The freedom of a Canadian citizen. Rodney breathed deeply the air of the freedom of a Canadian citizen…and immediately started coughing. The exhaust from the cars on the street was lazy today, deciding to stay close to the ground rather than dispersing into the atmosphere. *The air of the freedom of a Canadian citizen could really use a breath mint!* Rodney thought.

The alien took a step onto the sidewalk. A man in a full length cashmere coat (no need to describe him as tall: to Rodney, everybody was tall) talking on his cellphone bumped into the alien in his rush to get to his * Very Important Life *. Without slowing down, the man muttered,

"Jeez, guy, there's a huge sidewalk out here – do you mind sharing?"

Yes, Rodney thought, *I really do love this place*!

A limousine was waiting for Rodney around the corner. He preferred to get around Ottawa on his nuclear-powered tricycle, but his personal adviser, Daveen Rasmalai Rapier, had convinced him that it didn't project the image of the CEO of a wildly successful technology company. ("What are you? Three years old?" was one of the less successful arguments, especially at the volume Daveen Rasmalai projected it; Rodney just pouted and demanded somebody get him his security blankie.) And, anyway, the nuclear-powered tricycle wasn't heated. Having lived through two Ottawa winters, this was the decisive argument for Rodney.

Sheveen Shevon, Rodney's statuesque driver, opened the limo door for him. Her chauffeur's uniform had to be tailored to the ample curves of her body, while long, blonde hair flowed out from under her gravity-defying smart cap. When she was younger, she had been a fashion model (you may recognize her from fashion spreads in *Vogue*, *Elle* and *The Journal of Chiropractic Fetishism*). Sheveen Shevon had made enough money from the gig to live off of for the rest of her life; now, she wandered the country, going from one community to another in search of wisdom. She was, in short, an uplifting television series waiting to find a producer.

As Sheveen Shevon drove Rodney back to the office, she couldn't help but notice that he was futzing around (it's a professional modelling term – you wouldn't understand) in the middle back seat.

"Permission to speak freely, sir?" she asked. If her voice had been any more husky, it would have led a sled team in the far north.

Rodney looked confused. "You're still driving – don't you want to be paid while you talk?"

Sheveen Shevon had been driving Rodney for five months, and was willing to accommodate the strange turns his mind took in case he accidentally stumbled on some wisdom. "Ha ha. Very droll sir. However, the expression means, 'May I speak my mind without fear of losing my position?'"

Rodney suspected that his driver's laughter was not entirely sincere, that it was more an effort to keep him talking on the off chance that, in the general torrent of verbiage, he might accidentally stumble on some wisdom. He would take that. He wasn't proud. And there was nothing in his religious text, *The TV Guide*, that required the laughter he inspired to be genuine.

His Lord and Master The Audi Enz was easily amused.

When given permission to speak, Sheveen Shevon stated, "You are shaving."

Rodney stopped scraping his face with a sharp rock and blinked. "Am I?"

"Yes, sir. It would appear to be the case."

"Oh. Okay. Is there a problem with me shaving?"

"Two. Two problems, actually."

"Hmm." It was a "Wow, you learn something new every day," kind of hmm. "What are the problems you see with the way I'm shaving?"

Sheveen Shevon took a deep breath. "For one thing, you don't have any hair."

"I don't?"

"No, sir. It is well known that...people from where you come from have no hair anywhere on their bodies."

Rodney briefly looked down at his body, but he wasn't prepared to argue with the common wisdom, mostly because, this time, it was correct. "Okay. And why is that a problem?"

"Because the purpose of shaving is to remove hair from your face."

Rodney's eyes widened. This was new! "Are you sure?"

"Positive, sir."

"I always thought the purpose of shaving was to feel the burn of aftershave on your skin."

"Why would anybody want to feel the burn of aftershave on their skin?"

"You know, I've been shaving for over a year, and I was just beginning to wonder that myself..."

Sheveen Shevon slammed on the brakes and swore at the hybrid diesel-peanut butter vehicle that had cut her off with such force it could have circumcised a dozen baby boys and still have enough of an edge to slice salami. When she had finished and the limo had started moving again, she and Rodney paused contemplatively.

Eventually, the alien delicately asked, "And the second problem...?"

"You seem to be using strawberry jam."

Rodney looked into the mirror built into the back of the seat in front of him. An especially juicy strawberry was poised to flee the safety of his chin for the unknown beyond it. "People don't usually use strawberry jam to shave?"

"No, sir."

"What do they use?"

Even though she was wearing dark glasses, Sheveen Shevon resisted the impulse to roll her eyes; you never knew what the alien could sense. "Shaving cream, sir. The use of the product is kind of right there in its name."

Rodney snapped his fingers. "Of course! I'll bet **that's** why my morning bagel tastes so weird!"

They spent the rest of the journey in silence. Since it was only a couple of blocks, the silence didn't have a chance to become contemplative. On the other hand, it often takes forty minutes to drive a couple of blocks in Ottawa; fortunately, neither was the silence able to become ponderous. Sometimes, life can be even-handed that way.

As he got out of the car, Rodney smiled and said, "While potatoes in the shape of the faces of famous people have traditionally been frowned on by the moneyed classes, they beat stock tickling as an amusement for the masses. See you at seven."

"See you at seven, sir."

As she drove away, Sheveen Shevon pondered her employer's bon mots. Well, bonnish mots. Since she had started driving him around, he had said things like, "When you wish upon a star, NASA will cut funding to the space programme, so you better hope that the beings that live there will come to us...if meeting them was your wish..." and "The creature with explosive diarrhoea has no friends in the balloon factory," and "**Splunge!**" She suspected that she might never come across the wisdom she was hoping to find in these pronouncements, but she decided to give the position another three or four months just in case. Or until she got an offer of employment from a male strip club in Hull.

In these days of diminished expectations, we take our wisdom from wherever we can find it.

AlTech Enterprises are housed in an unassuming building (it prefers to have all of the evidence before coming to a conclusion) on Mercer Street. The lobby is tiny, with corridors leading into the building on either side of a small reception desk. Behind the reception desk sat Meowrice Lentil; all that could be seen of him above the desk were his black eyes and blue forehead. "Mornin', Mister P."

"Afternoon, Meowrice."

"Ah. Righto, sir. It's hard to read the clock from this angle."

Smiling to himself, Rodney reached behind the desk and pulled out his personal hoverboard. He had named it Luuuuuucyyyyyy! One, although the person who customized it had written in a beautiful script: Luuuuuuciiiiiiite! Since few people who worked for Rodney's company were above the age of forty, they assumed that their boss had a strange plastic fetish. (Being an alien, anything was possible.) In fact, he had chosen the name because of what followed ("You've got some 'splainin' to do!"), which seemed, to him, to capture the essence of being the President and CEO of a multi-billion dollar corporation.

Rodney silently hovered down the corridor on the left to the elevators, where a woman was standing. He adjusted the height of the hoverboard so he could look her in the eye and greeted, "Hello, Marty."

"It's Matty, sir," the woman replied. "My name is Matty."

Without missing a beat, Rodney asked, "When did you have the sex change operation?"

"I…I haven't changed my sex, sir."

"I understand."

"You do?"

"Yes. You have always been a woman on the inside. You just needed to change your outward appearance to conform with your inner emotional life. Good for you!"

Before Matty could respond, the elevator arrived. Rodney hoverboarded in; oddly enough, the woman waved him on, saying she would take the next car up. As the doors closed, Rodney said, “Always have the strength to be your true self!” Matty just shook her head and wondered if all alien bosses were like this.

Rodney got out on the fifth floor, which was devoted mostly to marketing. He floated past the desk of a tall man; adjusting his height to get eye level, he said, “Good afternoon, Charles. When is the baby due?”

Grinning, Charles responded, “Still a bachelor without children, sir.”

“So, the doctor hasn’t given you an approximate date for the birth, then?”

“I believe the date is ‘a cold day in Hell,’ sir.” Charles, who had been with the company from almost the beginning, knew that humouring the boss was the best way to approach work. And it could be good fun if you had the temperament for it.

“I never did get the hang of calendars on this Earth,” Rodney returned the grin. “I should ask about the Merckle ad buy, shouldn’t I?”

“The Cartoon Network ad buy?”

“That’s it. Right. Merckle is a character on *Sidney and the Giant Swizzle Stick*. I love that show! That’s how I identify the network…”

“We’re still setting it up,” Charles told him.

“ChristmaKwaanzUkah is coming up in a couple of months. I understand that it’s a joyous time when people spend money they can’t afford on objects nobody really needs in order to prove their love of their children, which, in order to keep the peace, I will not qualify. Seems like the perfect time to get them hoverboards.”

“Exactly, sir. And marketing is positioning us to take full advantage of the festive season.”

“That’s all I can ask,” Rodney smiled and moved on. He dropped a couple of inches to look a woman in the eyes. “Hi, Magrat,” he greeted her. “How’s your hernia?”

“Hernia?” Magrat responded. “I don’t have a – owwwwwww!”

As he hovered past her desk, Rodney advised: “I would

look after that if I was you. I understand hernias can be very painful."

Magrat doubled over and clutched her stomach with one hand as she reached for the phone on her desk to call for an ambulance. Before she blacked out from the pain, the phone remaining tantalizingly just beyond her reach, Magrat wondered, *How did he know? How could he possibly have –* * BONK *!

"Could somebody please call an ambulance for Magrat?" Rodney asked without looking back. "She seems quite medically suggestible…"

Rodney was heading for the office of the head of marketing when a small blue figure in a three piece suit that managed to appear to be both worn and exquisite – Chacho Tortellini – walked up to the hoverboard and paced him as he moved.

"Mister-a Pendleton!" the alien said in an affected Italian accent. "I have-a some great news for you!"

Rodney did not adjust the hoverboard to see eye to eye with his fellow alien, because that would just be skateboarding, which would defeat the whole purpose of the technology. Looking down on his chief science officer, Rodney marvelled at how smooth and round their heads were. "Chacho, is this like the atomic-powered alien plushie you came up with last year?"

"Awww, waddya wanna go bringing dat up for?" Chacho groaned. "Dey hardly ever exploded!"

"I don't have time for this right now," Rodney insisted.

"It's a simple-a concept," Chacho insisted right back. "Even you could get-a it in a matter of a-seconds."

"That may be, but – heeeey, wait a second. What do you mean even I could get it in a matter of seconds."

"With all a-due respect."

"With all due –"

Without warning, Rodney's hoverboard dropped to the ground, causing the alien to tumble past several desks. Then, he turned right and tumbled past eight more desks and the floor's bathrooms on the way to the stairs. He tumbled down a flight and onto the fourth floor, where he tumbled down a hallway into AlTech's R&D division. He tumbled around the periphery of some very expensive equipment before making his way (all in a tumble) out of the room and back down the hallway. Finally, Rodney tumbled **up** three flights of stairs, through the doors, past reception and into his office, where he stopped in front of his desk. (By this time, you can be forgiven for thinking that he was milking it juuuust a bit.)

Rodney's office contained a desk so ornate it looked like it had just walked in from a 1930s screwball comedy and two chairs so plush that when a movie of this novel is made they will be among the first toy tie-ins to be released. On the walls were newspaper and magazine covers featuring Rodney. Pride of place (behind his desk) belonged to a framed *Alternate Reality News Service* cover with a picture of Rodney with his arms outstretched and his body bent, pretending to surf, against the backdrop of a World Economic Forum meeting in Davos; the headline read, "From Emigre Enigma to Enterprising Entrepreneur: Proof the System Works!" On the desk was a laptop, an intercom and a pair of photographs of aliens. Since all of the aliens had the same exaggeratedly round features, lack of hair and exquisite three piece suits, it was difficult to know if the photos were of family members or a tribute to an ego run amok with success.

Rodney jumped up, his arms over his head as if he had just dismounted from the perfect parallel bars meet at infinity routine. Although he appeared to be alone in the room, he knew the Audi Enz was always watching; he hoped his deity wasn't feeling Slovenian judgey today. After a couple of seconds, Rodney lowered his arms and turned on the intercom to speak to his secretary. "Merrick?" he demanded, "What the hell just happened?"

"As best I can tell," Merrick Pewter replied, "you just did your impression of a tumbleweed. It wasn't Oscar-worthy, but it was an entertaining enough diversion."

This is the thanks I get for hiring refugees from my home universe! Rodney mused. Aloud, he said, "This just happened to me, right? There was something wrong with my Aboveboard Hoverer, but that's the extent of the problem. Right? Right?"

"We're starting to get reports that it happened to other hoverboards," Merrick informed him. "It's like the wild west out there!"

"Hunh," Rodney hunhed, and turned off the intercom.

One of the big disappointments in a young human being's life is the discovery that most vests do not have functioning pockets. Oh, sure, they may have fabric sewn into them that gives the illusion of pockets, but you could waste hours trying to put something into them (and possibly ruin the traitorous fabric). For many, this is the first indication that the world makes promises it has no intention of keeping, a part of the disenchantment of growing up on a par with the realization that Gord would not stop you from eating the bad leftover lasagne pizza and getting a mild case of food poisoning, or finding out that the tooth fairy had been convicted of millions of counts of breaking and entering, but must have been a made guy because he was still at large exchanging enamel for small change. Aliens were spared this trauma because the vests of their exquisite three piece suits always had functioning pockets. It was out of one of these that Rodney pulled a cellphone and dialed a very private number.

"Rodney?" a usually unflappable voice flapped.

"Daveen? I have a problem," Rodney stated.

"Kinda busy, here, bud."

"Luuuuuucyyyyyy! conked out! And we're starting to hear that it happened to other hoverboards – it could have happened to a lot of other hoverboards!"

"Sounds like you got hacked." Rodney could hear that his human mentor's breathing was laboured (somewhere between three and seven months). He filed this fact away for future consideration.

"What can I do about it?" he asked.

"Well…" In the seconds Daveen Rasmalai considered this question, Rodney began to make out the sounds of somebody running and plants being shoved aside or crushed. He filed this fact away next to the fact that Daveen Rasmalai was breathing heavily. At some future point, when he wasn't concentrating on his own problem, he would have to figure out what this meant. Definitely. "Okay. This is what you do. Convene a department heads meeting. Determine the scope of the problem. Find a technical solution. Develop a public relations campaign to assure people that Aboveboard Hoverers are perfectly safe."

"Can I drink coffee?"

"Expect to drink more coffee in the next couple of weeks than you have in the rest of your life! This will be –" Rodney was never going to find out what it would be because the sound of automatic gunfire drowned out Daveen Rasmalai's voice. Putting the pieces of what he had been hearing together, it finally dawned on him that the human might be in trouble.

"Everything okay?" Rodney asked.

"Nothing I can't handle," Daveen Rasmalai assured him.

"Are you sure?"

"It's only a flesh wound."

"Okay. If I need help in the future…?"

"Feel free to call me any time."

They exchanged pleasantries for a couple of minutes before finally ringing off. Rodney was especially delighted to hear that Daveen Rasmalai's sister, Noomi, was being considered for a promotion at the Transdimensional Authority. He could stare into her hair for hours!

Shaking the grin off his face, Rodney hit the intercom again. "Merrick?"

"I live to serve," his secretary replied.

"Tell Mark, Matty, Babs, Jennifer, Twillig and the guy who makes that great coffee that everybody likes, that we need to have an emergency meeting. I expect to see them in the executive boardroom in ten minutes!"

"We don't have anybody by those names on staff," Pewter informed him.

"Not even the guy who makes that great coffee that everybody likes?"

"That's not a name."

"Alright. Let's hire people with the names Mark, Matty, Babs, Jennifer and Twillig. Then, they can work their way up the corporate hierarchy until they are in positions of authority. Once that has been accomplished, have them meet me in – dagnabbit! There's no time! Get five people who work here who look like they know what they're doing and the guy who makes that great coffee that everybody likes to meet me in the executive boardroom in…nine minutes!"

Seventeen minutes later, Rodney swanned into the executive boardroom as if he owned it (which, admittedly, he did; he also owned a few swans, and was eagerly taking lessons from them). Sitting in the big comfy chair, he assessed the room. To his left sat Wilhelmina Poltroff (which sounds like an alien name, but isn't – you can tell by the lack of silent letters between the first and last names), a no-nonsense fiftysomething battleship of a woman with a thoroughly annoying fidelity to company protocols; she represented the security division of the AlTech. Next to her sat Chacho Tortellini (human or alien? Easy, right?). Next to Chacho sat Dominguez 'Pops' Erehwon (okay, this one is a bit tricky because there is something between his first and last names, but it isn't silent, so he is as human as you or me…well, you, in any case), a Latino with a face so lined many people wondered if he fell asleep on foolscap when he was young and his mother told him if he did it again his face would stay that way forever, and a permanently bemused expression on his face. Pops Dominguez didn't have an official title at AlTech, or, for that matter, a job title or description; his calming presence seemed justification for his ongoing employment.[2] At the far end of the table sat Oprah Fantasmagoria (okay, you seem to have gotten the hang of this whole 'human or alien' thing – well done!). Or, rather, slumped over the table apparently deeply asleep, although her right hand prominently held the bulb of an old-fashioned horn on the table above her head. Oprah was the head of Public Relations at AlTech. On Rodney's right sat Myron Gottlieb, an excitable man with a goatee that came to such a sharp point that you could be forgiven for thinking that it was the star of a high school debating team. He was the head of accounting. Next to them were the heads of human resources and production, but they aren't going to enter into the discussion, so there's no point in describing them.

---

[2] The main reason 'Pops' Erehwon was employed by AlTech was that Rodney had read a *Rolling Stoner* article about the two Popses at the Alternate Reality News Service, and he didn't think it was fair that they had two and he didn't have any. Also, Popses have a tendency to find solutions to problems. It's a Zen connection to the universe kind of thing. Rodney initially approached Pops Moobley and Pops Kahunga to see if they would come work for him, but they declined, saying it would bad for their Zen connection to the universe thing to leave an employer without giving them sixty years notice. So, Rodney did what anybody in his situation would do: found an unemployed Pops on LinkedIn.

You couldn't find a motlier bunch of mutts outside of a Wes Anderson movie! Rodney thought to himself. Out loud, he said, "Okay, we might as well be –"

From the far end of the table, Oprah's horn went * HONK *!

This caught up Rodney, if you will pardon the expression, short. "Yes. Thank you," he finally said. "It's not really a meeting until we've heard the call of the mild goose. Now, as I was saying, we might as well star –"

* HONK *!

"Did somebody forget to take their Metamucil this morning?" Rodney wondered. Undaunted (he had had his daunt removed at the same time as his tonsils), he tried one more time: "I say, we really need to –"

* HONK *!

"To –"

* HONK *!

"To adjourn! If anybody wants me, I'll be in the bar, wondering about the waste of my youth!" Rodney looked pointedly at the end of the table, but not a peep emanated therefrom.

"Mister Pendleton!" Gottlieb, his poutrage turned to eleven, loudly demanded. "We must talk about this line item in the budget for paperclips!"

Rodney looked at him, then looked at the reader. "You might want to go to the bar yourselves, folks. This next bit can't end well!"

* HONK *!

"I insist that we discuss the line item for paperclips!" Gottlieb impatiently insisted. "It's outrageous!"

Rodney turned back to the room. "What's so outrageous about it?"

"It's $976 million dollars!"

"I'm very fastidious about organizing paperwork."

"Nobody is **that** fastidious about paperwork!"

Chacho started laughing. Rodney turned to him. "What's so funny?"

"He's-a goddaya good, boss," Chacho replied. "Nobody is that fast and-a furious about paperwork!"

"There's my argument:" Rodney said, "restrict immigration."

"Aaaaieeee, wassamadda you – I was born here!" Chacho protested.

"There's my argument:" Rodney didn't miss a beat, "increase immigration."

"With all due respect," Chacho added.

"With all due respect," Rodney echoed.

* HONK *!

"And a musical accompaniment," Rodney stated.

"What about the paper clips?" Gottlieb insisted.

"Paper clips?" Poltroff roared. Her poutrage laughed at eleven as it passed by on its way to celestial heights; given her heft, there was a lot of room for outrage to grow inside her. "**Paper clips?** Are you aware, Mister Gottlieb, that our main project has just been hacked and rendered inoperable**?**"

"My dear lady," Gottlieb sputtered. "I – I – I had no idea!" He looked accusingly at Rodney.

"Don't look at me," Rodney told the look. "I'm just waiting for a bus."

"With all due respect."

Rodney looked at Chacho, then reluctantly said, "With all due respect."

* HONK *! * HONK *! * HONKITY *! * HONK *!

"And judging by the traffic, I might be here a while!"

"Mister Gottlieb!" Poltroff ignored the interruption. "I should think that hoverboards falling from the sky are a little more important than paper clips!"

"Well, yes, but – I mean –" Gottlieb bravely soldiered on, "how can we run a business if we do not practice fiscal prudence?"

"**Mister Gottlieb!**" Poltroff knew how to Mister Gottlieb people to within an inch of their lives. "How can we run a business if we can't guarantee the safety of our products?"

"Honk honk!" Rodney added, his tone of voice suggesting, "Take that, you rapscallion!"

* HONK *! Oprah agreed.

"Okay, now, everybody just take a deep breath," Pops Erehwon advised. "Feel the breath moving through your lips, down your throat and into your lungs. Hold it. Hold it. Hold it. Now…exhale. And again. Breath deep, as deep as you can. Feel your lungs slowly fill up with air, how your stomach and chest rise as your lungs fill. Aaaaaaand –"

"Is dis-a gonna help us solve our problem?" Chacho asked.

"No," Pops Erehwon admitted, "it won't. But in a best-case scenario, it will help calm you to a point where it will be easier for you to find solutions to the problem."

"And in a worst case scenario?" Rodney wanted to know.

"In a worst case scenario, you won't care so much about the problem."

"With all due respect, Pops –" Poltroff started.

"With all due respect," Rodney echoed her. When she glared at him, he found the ceiling suddenly fascinating.

"Ahem," Poltroff continued. "The problem has been solved. We have isolated the malware and are currently creating protocols to ensure that our network architecture is no longer able to be compromised in this way again. That done we rebooted the software so the hoverboards should be fully functional once again."

Turning to Chacho, Rodney asided, "Did you understand what she just said?"

"Not a word," Chacho replied.

"Yeah. Me neither." To the rest of the room, he said, "Good. Sounds good. Thank you, everybody. Is it time to go to the bar yet?"

"Are your changes to the architecture going to affect the boards on the production line?" the head of production asked. Dammit! Now I have to give her a character! She was short, bluff and very Irish. Her name was…Soarse Iowen! In her spare time, she liked darning socks for parents of indigent children. And she cared deeply, **deeply** about the production line she was in charge of.

"No, Madame," Poltroff tempered her outrage with grudging respect. "We can do it all in the software – you won't have to change anything on the production line."

Iowen nodded respectfully at Poltroff, stood and walked out of the room.

"Whu – wait," Rodney huffed. "It's that easy? Meeting adjour –"

"Weeellllll," Pops Erehwon interjected. "The smell lingers long after the exploded carp has been cleaned off the pier."

"I couldn't have put it better myself," Rodney agreed. Two. Three. Four. "What?"

"Tch!" Gottlieb tried to tsk but missed by a hair. "He

means somebody has to convince the public that our hoverboards are safe."

"Ah, atsa my colleague's department, but she is-a no up for it," Chacho stated. *HONK *! "So, I-a guess its-a down to me to make-a with the decisions."

"Good, then," Rodney hurriedly said. "If that's settled, this meeting is –"

"Chacho turned to him and said, "You-a do it."

"Yes, fine, if that's what it takes – I say that this meeting is –"

"What about the paper clips in the budget?" Gottlieb demanded.

"Oprah, give me some cover!" Rodney shouted.

* HONK *! * HONK *! * HONK *! "Mister Pendleton, this is outrageous!" * HONK *! * HONK *! "With all due respect!"

But Rodney couldn't respond, "With all due respect," because he had fled the room.

"Safe? You want to know if our hoverboards are safe?" Rodney, sitting in his office, his feet up on the desk (actually, the second drawer of his desk; if he tried to get them any higher, the blood would rush to his head and he would eventually hallucinate power bars with wings flying through cottage cheese canyons while John Lennon looked on in disapproval before he passed out) was talking on the phone. "Our hoverboards are so safe, you'll want to store your valuables in them!"

Rodney listened for a few seconds, thinking, *Journalists! Don't waste your best metaphors on them!* Eventually, he said: "Of course I use my personal hoverboard! I'm using it right now to keep my feet up!" Rodney guiltily looked at the floor next to his desk where his hoverboard was lying and wished he had thought of that sooner.

Rodney listened again, then responded: "What steps have

we taken? I can assure you only the steppiest! I have personally cut the blue wire – or, was it the red wire? – anyway, I cut a wire and nothing blew up, so the mission must be considered a success!"

Rodney listened to the distinct lack of mirth on the other end of the line with dismay. When he heard the door to his office open, he quickly said, "Sorry – something has come up that needs my attention. Talk to you never? Okay, bye," and hung up.

"Hey-a boss!" Chacho, blueprints under one arm, enthusiastically greeted him. "I have-a something I think you'll-a wanna see."

"I'm not here," Rodney flatly informed him.

"Oh. Okay." Chacho left the room.

A couple of seconds later, Chacho re-entered the room. "Awww, good-a one, boss. But, you canna fool me! There's no such thing as a sanity – boss? Boss?" Chacho looked around the room, but it appeared to be empty. He walked behind the desk, thinking that maybe Rodney was hiding under it, but all Chacho found was air. He looked around, but there was a distinct lack of side doors or other possible exit routes. Chacho realized that what he had on his hands was a mystery. Life was too short for mysteries. He shrugged, looked around one last time just to be sure he wasn't being watched, and sat in the boss' chair.

"Get out of there, you lazy lug!" Rodney's voice boomed.

Chacho jumped out of the chair, looking suspiciously at the corners of the room in case he missed something. He hadn't. More mystery! More shrugging.

Chacho took a pen and notepad out of a pocket of his exquisitely seedy three piece suit and leaned over the table to write on it while standing on the side opposite the chair. He looked at the chair to ensure that there were no objections to his doing so. When he was satisfied, he started writing on the notepad. "Dear, Signore Pendulum. I-a gotta something important for you, Signore Pendulum."

"They call me **Mister** Pendleton!" Rodney roared. Then, winking to the reader from the position close to the ceiling where he was lying on his stomach on the hoverboard, he boasted, "Sidney Poitier taught me that line reading."

"Mister Pudenda!" Chacho sort of corrected himself as he

scratched out what he had written and started again.

"Do you even know what a pudenda is?" Rodney demanded.

"Sure I do," Chacho told the air.

"What?"

"A pudenda is a piece of-a paper that tells you what you're-a going to talk about at a meeting."

"Start again."

Chacho ripped the sheet out of the notepad, crumpled it into a ball and tossed it over his shoulder. Rodney plucked the sheet of paper out of the air and deposited it in the back pocket of his pants. "Dear Mister Pendleton…"

"How do you spell that?"

"How do you? – Okay. Pendleton. Pend, as in, 'After talking to you, my im**pend**ing nervous breakdown will take place six months sooner.' Leton, as in, 'Please don't **let on** that we ever had this conversation. Or, for that matter, that we even know each other!'"

Chacho started writing again. "Dear Mister Pend Let On…"

"No! All one word."

Chacho crossed that out and wrote, "DearMisterPendleton…"

"No! Pend let on is one word. Everything else is normal English. You do know what normal English is, don't you?"

"Hah! Of course I do! It's-a the spin you put onna billiards ball."

"Start again."

"Hah! Of course I do! It's-a the spin –"

"I meant the letter. Start the letter again."

"Aah." Rip. Crumple. Toss. Pluck. Deposit. "Dear Mister Pendleton," Chacho started once more. He paused, deep in thought. Just when Rodney was sure he would reach down from the ceiling and strangle his employee, Chacho continued, "I was-a here. You wasn't. Talk to you some other time."

Chacho tore the sheet of paper off his notepad and left it on the desk.

"Aren't you going to sign it?" Rodney asked.

"Naah. You know who I am," Chacho answered and left the room.

Dial M for Dilemma

SPECIAL TO THE
ALTERNATE REALITY NEWS SERVICE

Aloha Biz Whiz: I had a friend once who bought stock in a company that had developed a technology that would allow people to turn used peanut shells into home insulation. Naturally, he lost his shirt. And gained a ton of weight from eating all those peanuts.

I had another friend who bought stock in a company that was developing a lineup of board games based on the fireplace videos that were all the rage a few years ago. She lost her pants.

I had still another friend who bought stock in a company that produced mystery rooms. Problem was, the CEO took all of the company's money, entered one of his products, and was never seen or heard from again. She lost her shoes and socks.

Given the experiences of my friends, you can imagine how averse I was to putting any money in the stock market: I like clothes! It's cold where I live! And anyway, people in polite society kind of expect you to wear some.

Then, I heard about AlTech's Aboveboard Hoverers. They sounded fantastic! I mean, who didn't want to be Michael J. Fox when they were kids, tooling around on a hoverboard and humiliating tough guys named Biff? I fell in love with the product, and, like anybody in love, I lavished it with affection. By which I mean I gave it all my money.

Don't judge.

Okay, judge a little, but keep it to yourself.

Fine, judge out loud. I don't judge. I can afford to be the better person.

Don't jud – oh, let's not start that again!

As the stock rose, my financial goal hove…err, into view: to be able to afford to buy a mallet at the World Championships of Croquet. (I can feel you judging again, but I'm getting used to it.) Then, the hoverboards fell out of the sky. And boy, oh Boyardee, they weren't the only things to fall!

So. I'm in a pickle. It's dark and briny. Overwhelmingly briny. This is my dilemma (wasn't that a song by The Knack?): should I sell the stock now, when I will only lose 73% of my life's savings, or should I hold onto it in the hope that it will start going back up, and risk losing 97% of my life's savings?

The Biz Whiz: There's an old saying on Wall Street: the sky falls three times a day, but nobody loses their head. I'm not sure what it means, but certain people take comfort from it.

If you're not one of the people who takes comfort from deep-sounding but ultimately meaningless aphorisms, take heart: the worst is over. So, what you need to do is buy more AlTech stock.

No! No, wait! Hear me out! Buy low, sell high is not a deep-sounding but ultimately meaningless aphorism! It's shallow, but ultimately brilliant!

Yes, AlTech's premier technology, the Aboveboard Hoverboard, was hacked. Many knees and egos were bruised. It certainly didn't help that the President and CEO of the company, Rodney Pendleton, told *Ferbs* magazine: "We're thinking of repositioning the Aboveboard Hoverboard as the Submersible Reversible-board. What do you think, eh? Talk about making a milk purse out of a sow's rear! What? Nobody talks about that? But you get the idea, right? Right?"

It really didn't help when Pendleton told *The Wall Street Infernal*: "Why should I be concerned about the drop in stock prices? I came from a universe where the concept of ownership of objects was infinitely malleable."

It absolutely, positively did not help when Pendleton told *Better Holmes and Watsons*: "People on Wall Street take things waaaaaaayyyyyy too seriously. They should learn mindfulness and get their priorities straight!" Very did not help.

But here's the thing. In interviews trying to help ease investor jitters, Pendleton sounded like he wanted to torpedo the company he had founded. Who ever does that, right? Right? Institutional investors are assuming that somebody so flippant about the future of his company must be certain that it is already assured, and are cautiously reinvesting in AlTech.

Oh, and the company has already fixed the software and patched their system to ensure that it cannot be hacked by malware again. That helped, too.

AlTech is once again a buy, **buy, BUY!** investment. But don't wait too long, because it could hoversoar to new highs at any moment!

The economy is too important to be left to economists! If you have a work, financial or otherwise money-centric question, quiz the Biz Whiz at questions@lespagesauxfolles.ca. In the stock market, as in baseball, there is no crying. A lot of judging, perhaps, but never any crying.

On the way into the office a couple of days later, Rodney asked, “Do you mind if I ask you for a little wise advice about something?”

Sheveen Shevon responded, “With all due respect, sir –”

“With all due respect,” Rodney echoed.

Ignoring this, Sheveen Shevon continued, “I think you may have mistaken me for a bartender.”

“Bartender? Naah – I never saw you as a bartender. On the other hand, I don’t really see you as a limo driver, either.”

Sheveen Shevon stiffened. She did not enjoy talking about her modelling past. She assumed the question wouldn’t come up while working for Mister Pendleton considering that it had happened long before the aliens started coming to Earth Prime. Still, she mused, the internet is forever…[3]

---

[3] Some ideas persist even though they are demonstrably false. The whole ‘the internet is forever’ idea is a great example. On Earth Prime 0-8-7-2-6-3 dash alpha, for instance, a global thermonuclear war destroyed all electronic devices, including communications systems; it wasn’t kind to organic life, either (internet life: seventy-two years, nine months, twelve days). On Earth Prime 1-9-8-3-7-2 dash beta, when human beings left their corporeal bodies behind to become pure spirit, electronic communications systems just got in the way of the purity of their joy, and were abandoned (internet life: 2,277 years, two months, twenty-four days). On Earth Prime 2-0-9-4-8-1 dash gamma, the internet was superseded by the hornytoadswoggle; soon, only hobbyists and people who were too old to adapt to the new communications system used it, ensuring that it quickly became a joke (internet life: 127+ years; hard to determine because it died a slow, painful death). Anybody with a functioning Home Universe Generator™ could easily find an infinite number of other examples.

Even those who aren’t up on alternate internet history have to know that much of the early communications on the network had been lost as it evolved. Anybody remember Bjornet? Or the first email sent over the internet (“Mister Watson, come here! I seem to have gotten my head stuck in a blender!”)? What the first LOLcat looked like?

Setting her jaw on 'defiant', Sheveen Shevon asked, "What do you see me doing?"

"Oh, I don't know," Rodney breezily responded, poking a button on his armrest to see what it would do. A rubber chicken dropped from the roof of the car and * SPROING *ed up and down in front of him for a few seconds before retracting. Once the fascination waned, he answered, "You strike me as the kind of person who would do well as a pastry chef – no, a pastry chef's assistant. It's the long fingers – they were just made for getting icing into awkward places."

Sheveen Shevon frowned. She **had** been a pastry chef's assistant for a few months, and her long fingers **were** helpful in getting icing into awkward places. Lucky guess? "I'm afraid the only wisdom I might get from such an experience would be that life is like a box of chocolate-glazed donuts," she evenly stated. "I'm not sure that would help you. I'm dang sure it didn't help me!"

"Or, maybe a rodeo clown."

Sheveen Shevon's face dropped. "A rodeo clown?" she gasped.

"Even when you may find yourself behind the wheel of a large automobile," Rodney explained, pressing another button on the armrest which caused a lighter to pop up and set the sleeve of the jacket of his exquisite three piece suit to catch on fire before retracting. "You always give off a certain…energy," Rodney continued as he patted at the smouldering sleeve in the hope of putting the fire out. "The kind that would make you an ideal rodeo clown." As the fire grew, Rodney waved his arm around while trying to slap at the flames. "Besides, a clown's face is a perfect way to hide one's identity…"

"How did you know?" Sheveen Shevon whispered.

Rodney put his arm down and watched the fire grow, fascinated. Then, he reached behind him for a bottle of water and, after some difficulty getting the cap off with one hand,

---

How much money early Ethiopian princes originally offered random people? Unless you have a time machine, you will never know. The internet will last forever? The idea that the internet will last forever, maybe…

doused the flames. "Lucky guess?" he blithely announced.

"I don't think so," Sheveen Shevon angrily disagreed. "Once could be a lucky guess. Twice is insider knowledge!"

"Hmm…" Rodney hmmed. He had hit another button, which turned the screen built into the seat in front of him on; it displayed a swirling spiral that Rodney found most hypnotic.

"With all due respect, sir –" Sheveen Shevon started.

"All…due…spect…" Rodney mumbled.

Sheveen Shevon slammed on the brakes. Rodney pitched forward slamming his head against the screen. He fell back in his seat, moaning, "That's gonna leave a mark!"

"Mister Pendleton!" Ignoring the honking coming from the cars around them (there was no way she could hear the honking from inside the office), Sheveen Shevon turned to stare Rodney down.

"I'll bet Robert Pattinson never had to deal with this!"

"How did you know about my past?"

"I'm a close personal friend of the Unreliable Omnisicient Narrator," Rodney informed her rubbing his forehead.[4] "Not that Omni – he lets me call him Omni – I mean, he's stopped objecting to me calling him Omni quite so vociferously – Omni will come around eventually – would be willing to admit it, but we are very tight. Just the other night, we took a couple of skinheads bowling, and Omni had one too many gingerbread beer – Omni can drink practically anything without any effect on his behaviour, but he's a lightweight when it comes to gingerbread beer – and while the others were hitting each other with bowling pins at the other end of the alley, Omni told me a few things about you."[5]

---

[4] Rodney is exaggerating a little, here. Sure, we have spent time together, but I would consider him more of an acquaintance than a friend. I mean, I wouldn't lend him a hundred bucks until payday, and you may have noticed that he didn't ask **me** to advise him on his current problem. Not that I would have given him any advice – I live by a code, you know, one that explicitly forbids me from interfering with an ongoing storyline. That would be cheating! Still, it would have been nice to be asked!

[5] For the record: I find the name Omni demeaning and will never give Rodney – or anybody else – permission to use it. And I'm not a lightweight when it comes to drinking gingerbread beer, I just felt

What her boss had just said sounded like complete nonsense to Sheveen Shevon (she had never heard of a private detective agency named Unreliable Omniscient Narrator, Inc., but that didn't mean that it couldn't exist), but she realized that it was the only explanation she was likely to get. So, she turned eyes front and started the car again.

"If you put some ice on your forehead," she advised, "the bump won't swell too bad."

"How will I keep it from falling off?"

"Wrap it in a napkin and hold it to your head."

"Hunh." Rodney got a piece of ice out of a bucket, wrapped it in a napkin and put to his forehead. He would never get used to living in a body that couldn't automatically heal itself. "That was good advice. Did you learn it as an assistant pastry chef, rodeo clown or personal assistant to a demanding magazine editor?"[6]

Sheveen Shevon bit back the urge to respond, "I didn't have to learn that – it's just common sense!" She kept her eyes on the road and said nothing.

"I have to go talk to the Board of Directors to answer their questions about the hacking of our products," Rodney said after a respectful amount of silence had amassed (he rolled down a window to let it out of the limousine so that silence didn't become crushing). The spiral was still swirling on the screen in front of him, but something about the crack across its middle drained it of its power. "The question is: how should I do it? Should I swagger in, shooting from the hip, taking no prisoners, and letting the chips fall where they may? Or should I stonewall, telling them that the investigation is ongoing so I don't have all of the relevant facts, but I'll be sure to get back to them when I do? I'm leaning towards the latter, because it's at least half true. In your travels, have you come across any wisdom that could

---

like talking that evening. I wish I could remember everything I said, but I'm sure Rodney will bring it all up sooner or later (more or less the way I did at what turned out to be the end of the evening), probably at the most embarrassing times. He can be dependable that way.

6 Notice that Rodney did not mention the fact that Sheveen Shevon had been a bartender for three months in Carp's Armpit, Newfoundland. That would have been too on the nose.

help me in this situation?"

Sheveen Shevon sighed. Whether it was caused by the unreasonable weight of other people's expectations or the jaywalker who practically dared her to run him over, who could say? Sighs can be so personal. "Be yourself," she finally advised.

"Myself?" Rodney was dubious.

"The best, brightest, cutest version of yourself that you can be."

Be yourself? Rodney thought. *It's a plan so crazy, it just might work!*

The rest of the drive to the office was spent in silence. It was only three blocks, but, given Ottawa's penchant for one way streets, it took three quarters of an hour. Rodney kept the window down and periodically shooed some of the silence out to keep it from smothering him. Sheveen Shevon didn't ask.

Rodney sat on his hoverboard in a lotus (the flower, not the car, although given his position at the company, it would be an honest mistake to make) position. His eyes were closed. He was chanting, "Feeeeeeeerrrrrrk. Feeeeeerrrrrrrrrk. Feeerrrrrrrrrrk." Noticing that he was mantraing alone, he opened one eye and looked out at the executive boardroom.

"The key to a good meeting is a calming mantra at the outset," Rodney stated. "I read that in *The Mile a Minute Manager*. Or maybe *Horton Hears a Sell Call*. That's…not the point. I know, I know, my chant is a little…unusual. But the actual word doesn't matter – it's the thought that counts. So, if you will join me: feeeeerrrrrk."

Around the boardroom table sat six elderly white men (and one young Asian woman), all of whom wore expressions as serious as a heart attack (which all but two of them, not excluding the young Asian woman, had experienced, so they knew exactly what they were projecting) and none of whom looked like they had patience for unusual behaviour at board meetings. While the President and CEO cleared his mind, a couple pretended to study the documents in front of them. One looked at his watch. The young Asian woman shook her head at the way people in the west appropriated her culture.

Feeeeeeerrrrrrrk, indeed.[7]

Eventually, Rodney opened his eyes. "Hubba bubble bubble bubble!" He shook the cobwebs out of his arms. "Well, I don't know about me, but I'm sure you feel better having done that!" he said.

"Mister Pendleton…" one of the board members started.

"One minute," Rodney shut the man down. To his left, a hoverboard carried a mug with " est oss in the multiverse" (the glazier was afraid of being stung by a b); he reached over, took the mug off the hoverboard and took a long swig before returning it. "I know what you're thinking: isn't the caffeine in the coffee going to undo the calm that I achieved through the mantra? I have two words for you, my friends: yin and yang. Which is technically three words. Which word count, also technically, grows the longer I talk about it. And I haven't even mentioned the Flowerpot Man!"

"Mister Pendleton!" one of the board members insisted. It may have been the one that had started to say something, but, honestly, they were pretty much interchangeable, so who could tell?

"We haven't started the meeting yet," Rodney pointed out, "so I'm not sure I can call on you to speak. Does anybody know Rodney's Rules of Order?"

"Do you mean Robert's Rules of Order?" the young Asian woman asked.

"Rodney's Rules of Oder," Rodney persisted. "It's like Robert's Rules of Order, only with a lemon scent and a bit of a kick to it."

"Start the meeting!" one of the board members hissed. Odds are five to three that it was the same one that had insisted. "We are busy men –"

"And women," the young Asian woman pointed out.

"And we don't have time to waste on trifling trivialities!" one of the board members ignored her and finished the

---

[7] I didn't say ideas always travelled well.

thought. It probably wasn't the board member that started the thought, but who knows?

Rodney nodded. "Alrightey, then," he said. His board hovered at around the height of the table; even so, when he reached for the gavel resting (it had partied a little too hardy the night before) on the table in front of him, he couldn't quite grasp it. Rodney twisted this way and that but, try as he might, he couldn't quite get the gavel. In the end, huffing a little, he sat upright, pulled his exquisite three piece suit into shape and said, "I declare this meeting of the AlTech board of directors open. Bang! Bang!"

Four of the board members started talking at once. Rodney held up a hand and said, "People? People! **People!**"

All but one of the speaking board members recognized that they were, in fact, people, and gave Rodney their attention. The other kept nattering on: "…institutional investors took a bath and still felt dirty and what are you doing to give them clean closure on the whole filthy fiasco, because – owwwwww!" The young Asian woman had punched him in the shoulder. Hard.

With all attention on him (or the pain in their shoulder), Rodney stated: "As we do at the beginning of every board meeting, we should accept the minutes of the last board meeting. As you will see, the minutes are in the package on the table in front of you –"

"Call these minutes‽" one of the board members scoffed.

"I wanted to call them Abner Doubleday," Rodney responded, "but legal warned about potential lawsuits."

"'People talked for hours, nothing was decided and nobody was satisfied,'" one of the board members hissed (but don't assume that it was the same board member that hissed the last time – unhappy sounds are common at board meetings). "What kind of minutes are those‽"

"Weellll," Rodney reasonably replied, "you are busy men – and a woman – and I didn't want to waste your time with trifatalities."

In the end, after much talk which satisfied nobody, acceptance of the minutes of the previous meeting was tabled to a later date.

"Okay!" Rodney enthused. "I feel we've accomplished a lot today. Who's ready to adjourn?"

Rodney looked at the stony faces around the table and thought, *Wow. Easter Island came early this year!*

"In the interest of avoiding…trifatalities," one of the board members smirked, "I suggest we go immediately to new business."

"Like…we sold three more Aboveboard Hoverboards at the Skate and Plate in Willamet or Wontamet, Wisconsin yesterday?" Rodney wondered.

"Like your response to the hack of our main product!" one of the board members exploded. Emotionally.

Rodney opened his mouth, a quip at the ready, when, out of the corner of his eye, he caught the young Asian woman shaking her head. "Umm, yes, very well," he chose to say. "Let's talk about that."[8]

"Our hoverboards were attacked by malicious hackers!" one of the board members angrily said.

"The value of our stock plummeted faster than our product!" one of the board members crossly stated.

"Your media appearances did not help!" one of the board members hotly claimed.

"So," the young Asian woman calmly summed up, "major cluster ferk. What has been done about it?"

Against all of his instincts, Rodney explained in a straightforward manner that the company's programmers had expunged the malware from the hoverboards (which, as

---

[8] On a planet called Hubrisky Point in Earth Prime 2-0-0-0-5-9 dash Omega there exists an institution called The Charles Brown Library of Almost But Not Quite Spoken Thoughts. On a moment by moment basis, ideas that people are about to say but are kept from saying because of interruptions are collected. They are stored for a period of two weeks, eight days and seventeen hours to ensure that they are not expressed at a later time. After storage, if they have still not been uttered, the words are entered into the library's long-term archive system, where they are cross-referenced for future retrieval. Through special exhibits at the library, we know that Winston Churchill once almost said, "I didn't know carrots could be put to such use!" and Alan Turing was about to say, "But the puffin couldn't have possibly known how much popped corn the tank would consume," when he sneezed, chasing the thought away. If you want to know what Rodney was about to say, visit the Charles Brown Library of Almost But Not Quite Spoken Thoughts; ask for Paul and tell him the Unreliable Omniscient Narrator sent you.

everybody could see, were working again) and put protocols into place to ensure that this kind of attack would never happen again.

"What about a different malware attack?" one of the board members asked. "Are we prepared to deal with that?"

"The world is big, it's bigger than you and you are not me," Rodney started. The Asian woman sighed. "By which I mean, it's not possible to guard against every possible a –" The Asian woman sighed more insistently. "Umm…yeah. So, our engineers are certain that we are now guarded against any foreseeable attack."

For the first time since they entered the room, the board members looked satisfied. "And your media appearances?"

"I was going for the roguish CEO," Rodney explained. "Everybody likes a bad boy. Look at the success of Elon Musk."

"You came across as clueless and out of touch," one of the board members criticized.

"That's harsh," Rodney defended himself. "I have, in fact, played Clue. Turns out, I was always the murderer – what are the odds?"

"Your job," one of the board members argued, "is to calm our customers when there is a problem with one of our products. You're about as calming as a hurricane!"

"Just to be clear: would that be before or after climate change made the weather so extreme?"

Before one of the board members could respond with indignant outrage, the young Asian woman said, "Yet, our stock has regained eighty-seven per cent of its value, and could reach new highs by the end of the week. Not bad for somebody you think is clueless and out of touch."

"Think of how much higher it would have been if we had a CEO who took his job seriously!" one of the board members responded with indignant outrage. Sometimes, it's just too powerful to stop.

"Think of how much lower it could have been if we had a CEO who was incompetent," the young Asian woman told him.

The eyes of the board members narrowed. "What do you propose we do moving forward?" one of the board members asked.

The young Asian woman winced at the bureaucratese, but answered: "Give Mister Pendleton the opportunity to bring a second product to market. If it does well, we'll talk about his bonuses. If it does poorly, we'll talk about…what you wanted to talk about today."

After much back and forth (and a little to and fro to spice things up), the board voted four to three to accept the young Asian woman's plan.

"Okay!" Rodney enthused. "Good talk, everybody! I now call the meeting adj –"

"We need a motion to adjourn," one of the board members pedanticked.

"Nope," Rodney corrected him. "Rodney's Rules of Order. This meeting is adjourned. Bang! Bang!"

"But…" one of the board members who hadn't contributed much to the discussion started to object. However, Rodney shut his eyes and began humming, "Feeeeeeeerrrrrrrrrk."

The members of the AlTech Incorporated board of directors got the message and filed out of the room.

Five minutes later, Rodney said, "Feeeeeeeeeerrrrrrrrk. You know, I can hear you tapping on your phone."

"Gotta keep busy while I'm waiting," the young Asian woman replied. "You're not the only company my investment firm has a stake in."

"You're Viola Lin – right?"

Viola smiled. "You noticed." Rodney couldn't tell if she was flattered or being sarcastic. Flartcastic – he could handle that. That was worth opening an eye for.

"You know how to stand out in a crowd."

"Pfft," Viola dismissed the thought without missing a beat on her phone. "Those old men? They're the past. I'm the future. In a few years, all corporate boards will look like me." Viola finished what she was doing and dropped the phone into her Gucci purse. "Can I give you a word of advice?" she asked as she got to her feet.

"Umm…sure?"

"If you drive the hoverboard closer to the desk, you will be able to reach the gavel. It looks more authoritative than flailing away like you did."

"But it isn't as funny."

"Laughter isn't always appropriate."

"That's where you're wrong. Laughter is always appropriate."

Viola shrugged and headed for the half-opened door. Instead of walking through it, she turned back to Rodney. "They were going to fire you, you know," she told him. "If your next product isn't spectacular, they almost certainly will."

"Oh, it's spectacular," Rodney assured her. "It's really…spectacular, is the word for it, all right."

Viola looked skeptically at him and walked out of the room.

"Feeeeeeeerrrrrrrk," Rodney said. Only, this time, it didn't sound like a mantra.

"Remember, in a brainstorming session, there are no bad ideas."

"Levitating utensils for people who are too lazy to bring food to their mouths."

"That is the worst idea I have ever heard!"

"With all due respect."

"No, but, really, I haven't heard such a bad idea since –"

"With all due respect!"

"Yeah, yeah, with all due respect."

* HONK *!

Members of the research and development, marketing and legal departments were meeting in the third floor boardroom (which was the same as the executive boardroom, less the gold trim and faint odour of financial superiority) to brainstorm[9] new uses of the propulsion technology behind the Aboveboard Hoverboard. At the front of the room, Rodney's Personal Assistant Anastasia La Bombon, stood in

---

[9] Brainstorming is a form of generating ideas. Because, honestly, who doesn't do their best thinking in the middle of a thundering rain shower in their heads?

front of a whiteboard, sharpie poised to write whatever ideas were generated at the meeting. 'Flying utensils' was her first entry on the board. She frowned at it; there were at least thirty-seven ways she could imagine flying utensils going horribly, horribly wrong. Still, the whole point of a brainstorming session was to let people speak without judgment in the hopes that the flow of ideas would free up somebody's imagination to the point that one of the ideas was actually of some use to somebody, so she dutifully took every one down.

Rodney took a deep breath. "Okay, good start," he said in a tone of voice that suggested a man contemplating gnawing off his own leg. "Other ideas?"

"Next generation delivery drones," said Fonein Rarrow, a blond Adonis of a man who had been working in marketing for the last four months. (Yes, he was actually journalist Ronan Farrow, working undercover on an article on AlTech and its unusual CEO. If you're wondering why nobody at the company recognized him, it was because he was wearing glasses. Thick ones. Don't be so skeptical: the power of a pair of glasses to hide one's true identity has been known for decades!) "Levitation could be built directly into the packages, making each one its own drone. They could have new security features that would keep them floating out of reach until the recipient shouted a code sent to their email to permanently disable the levitation. I'll bet Amazon would kill for something like that!"

'Next gen security delivery drones' Anastasia wrote on the whiteboard.

Marina Plemondon, a woman sitting on the opposite side of the table who had the severity of an undertaker without the compassion, gently shook her head.

"Why not?" Rarrow (* wink * * wink *) demanded.

"One of our corporate partners is researching using the technology to build better drones," Plemondon, a member of legal, informed him. "Our contract with them has non-compete clauses so iron-clad you would think they were knights of the round table."

'~~Next gen security delivery drones~~' Anastasia crossed out what she had written on the whiteboard.

"Too bad," Rarrow responded. But as he wrote notes on the

pad on the table in front of him, he started drafting the acceptance speech for his next Pulitzer Prize in his head.

"This is going very well," Rodney commented. "Does anybody know a good bankruptcy lawyer?"

* HONK *! Oprah, slumped over the far end of the table, added her two cents.

"We're not keeping you up, are we?" Rodney asked.

* HONK *! * HONK *!

"Can we get you anything? A blanket, maybe? A chocolate for your pillow? A pillow for your chocolate?"

* HONK *! * HONK *!

"Well, if there's anything at all you need to be more comfortable, please let us –"

Jeremiah Penzzoil from R&D snapped his fingers. "Alarm clock beds! No, no, no, hear me out!"

"Nobody was trying to stop you," Plemendon pointed out.

"The bed can be programmed so that when you need to wake up, it slowly tilts at a ninety degree angle and gently rolls you onto the floor," Penzzoil, who wore the tribal identifier of a pocket protector, explained.

"What if you're a heavy sleeper?" Plemondon asked.

"It could tilt at a hundred and eighty degree angle more quickly and less gently," Penzzoil told her.

* HONK *!

"Wouldn't people get hurt falling onto the floor?" Rarrow wondered.

* HONK *! * HONK *!

"Not if there was a mattress there to break their fall," Penzzoil freestyled.

"Wouldn't that defeat the purpose of waking them up?"

"Not if the subsidiary mattress was firm enough."

"Wouldn't that add to the cost of the bed?"

"Oh, I'm sure our corporate partners would love that!"

Rarrow opened his mouth to respond, but thought better of it and shut his mouth again. All eyes looked at Rodney, who shrugged and waved at Anastasia. On the whiteboard, she wrote, 'bed alarm'.

Rodney rubbed his hands together. "Now, we're getting nowhere!" he enthused. Walking towards the door of the room, he threw over his shoulder, "If anybody wants me, I'll be sobbing uncontrollably in my off –"

Before Rodney could reach it, the door flew open and Chacho strode in, blueprints under his arm. "Or, I could just save myself the trouble and start sobbing uncontrollably where I stand."

"Hey, Boss," Chacho greeted him. "Did you get-a my message?"

"I did," Rodney responded. "And, I won't kid you – I was moved."

"Moved?"

"I didn't get out of the bathroom for half an hour."

"Good, Boss. Good. I gotta the solution to alla you problems!"

"A Vodka martini?"

"Better."

"A double Vodka martini?"

"This."

Chacho laid the plans on the table. Everybody in the boardroom except for Oprah crowded together to see them.

"Is that what I think it is?" Rarrow asked.

"Do you-a think it's a pair of nuclear-powered bunny slippers?" Chacho responded.

"No."

"Then, it's-a what you think it is."

"I see no legal reason why we couldn't pursue this," Plemendon pronounced.

"This is so…so…so *Fifth Element*!" Penzzoil enthused.

Rodney's eyes narrowed. "If I approve of this idea, can I get that Vodka martini that I was promised?"

"I don't see why not," Plemendon told him.

"Last one to the bar drinks sweaty gym socks!" Rodney shouted and raced for the door.

'?' Anastasia wrote on the whiteboard before rushing out the door.[10]

---

[10] Much later, Rodney wouldn't wonder if the whole adventure had been a dream that Oprah was having, but that doesn't mean, dear reader, that you can't wonder it.

Educational Interlude 001

When considering the state of an alien race's culture, I have found a Bonetsian socio-economic analysis to be most efficacious. D. B. Bonet, you will recall, posited a complex relationship between a country's leading economic indicators and the subjective wellness of its citizens. The Give a Dog a Bonet Fractal Curve™, with its 1,237 variables, is still not well understood; not only does it appear to contradict itself in places, but it gives practitioners the eerie sense of walking up a flight of stairs only to end up at the bottom again when they should be on the next floor. Many economists who have tried to apply the curve *in toto* have been driven mad by its complexity, or worse: been driven from academia and forced to teach high school mathematics. I have found that using small segments of the curve as an analytical tool to be richly rewarding (as did its creator, who won a Nobel Prize in Economics two years and five months in a row).

The problem with doing any socio-economic analysis of the cultures of Earth Prime 4-6-4-0-8-9 dash Omega is that nowhere on the planet is there a functioning economy. Fortunately, as Propinski and Dubcek proved,[1] this is in no way a barrier to writing an academic paper.

The basic assumption of classical economics, the one from which everything else flows, is that resources are scarce; since human desires are infinite, economics is about finding the correct method to manage this scarcity so that the resources are allocated in the most efficient way. This is, in part, to ensure that the resources are exploited to their maximal potential, but an important corollary to the theory is to ensure that a majority of the people feel the maximum amount of satisfaction with their role in the economy while being given as minimal an amount of financial compensation for their labour as possible without provoking them to revolt.[2]

On Earth Prime 4-6-4-0-8-9 dash Omega, resources are not scarce. This is because 10,578 years before it was discovered, it underwent a Singularity, which afforded each person who lived in that universe the ability to converse with and shape matter. If, for example, you wanted a steak, you didn't have to develop a system of factory farms, slaughterhouses, transportation and grocery stores – you simply asked enough molecules around you to organize themselves into the form of a steak. Yum! But it's actually worse than that, because many of the creatures who live on Earth Prime 4-6-4-0-8-9 dash Omega received energy in the form of sunlight (in a process not dissimilar to photosynthesis, but without its sickly green appearance or aroma of cinnamon), foregoing the need for nourishment as most advanced species understand it.

What need do the citizens of Earth Prime 4-6-4-0-8-9 dash Omega have for a construction industry when they can ask materials around them to form shelters at will, or, worse, ask clouds to precipitate around them instead of on them? Why develop an automobile industry when you can fly anywhere you want on the slightest breeze? What would be the point of advertising?

As far as anthropologists[3] working among the people of Earth Prime 4-6-4-0-8-9 dash Omega have been able to determine, aliens continued to fulfill recognizable social functions even after those functions had been rendered moot. There were still lawyers. There were still accountants. There were still mud bath specialists in spas. Over ten thousand years after the Singularity, there were still mud bath specialists in spas! If scarcity didn't drive the planet-wide economy, what did?

Jokes.

PRENDERGAST D. GORMLESS: ...and a solid brass entrenching tool, and a Fidgety Pete action figure complete with unpredictable spasmodium™, and eleven blue pills, and a boot to the head, and a space opera novel of your choice, and eleven lords a-leaping (do you think they will ever come down?), and a confused rabbit that has just been pulled from a hat, and sixteen red pills, and a solid gold breathing mask for those awkward times when you're worried about catching a fatal disease in polite society, and a baby's arm holding an –

TERKEL: What does this have to do with the question about why people from your universe are driven to tell jokes?

GORMLESS: Because it's funny.

TERKEL: Do you even understand how the whole I ask a question and you answer it thing works?

GORMLESS: Glurgle![4]

Reading between, around and often outside the lines, the people of Earth Prime 4-6-4-0-8-9 dash Omega were constantly exchanging jokes, jibes, jests, japes and other forms of humour. The more laughter a citizen can get from an exchange, the more value the joke accrues. But how did this form of exchange develop? History and god.[5]

When the Singularity...umm...Singled, people continued to fulfill the roles in society that they had always performed. At first, it was because they hadn't realized that the whole substructure of their society had shifted. However, even when it became apparent that the roles they had filled no longer needed to exist, they persisted in enacting them. This was down to their god, which had come to be known as the Audi Enz.

At the time the Singularity...became singled out, human society had become obsessed with social media. Everybody and their cat was vying for everybody else's attention. "Humour was the unofficial currency to be exchanged for attention," wrote O. M. Hubbard in her groundbreaking work. "When the Singularity redundantized pretty much everybody, the humour economy slowly became the only one that mattered."[6]

Over time, the locus of exchange shifted from other people to a supreme deity which people referred to as "the Audi Enz." Or, did it? Audi Enz = audience. Although causing others to laugh became a religious experience for people, the primary targets of their efforts are still arguably each other. This phenomenon is sometimes referred to as "The Babbling Brooks."[7]

While most people on Earth Prime 4-6-4-0-8-9 dash Omega were content to work humour into their increasingly irrelevant day to day experiences, a small group went full on surrealist. "Oh, yeah," Hubbard explained. "Surrealism happened. Soon after the Singularity, people experimented with modifying their bodies such that you could see all of their features in a single plane, or turning themselves into toilets and attaching themselves to walls, or causing an apple to float permanently in front of their faces. When you have complete control over matter, you can do things like that. The problem was that, without any form of contextual grounding, these efforts came off more as bizarre than funny, which was ultimately deemed to be not pleasing to the Audi Enz. So, the practice died out after 100 or 150 years."[8]

Over the course of thousands of years, the forms of humour on Earth Prime 4-6-4-0-8-9 dash Omega became codified. Predictable. Stale. This is the antithesis of the surprise that is one of the primary features of functional humour (although, to be fair, it is a necessary part of any religious practice). There is much anecdotal evidence to suggest that, in migrating to Earth Prime, the people of that doomed universe were given new material to work with for the first time in 10,000 years. To whit:

DORA T. BORAT: New experiences? Oooh, yes! Yes, please! Mmmmmm! Ooh! Yes! **Yes! YES!**

MIMI VAN ELDERBERRIES: I'll have the joke she's having.[9]

With a small number of exceptions, inhabitants of Earth Prime 4-6-4-0-8-9 dash Omega lost the ability to manipulate matter when they emigrated to Earth Prime. How did their post-scarcity comic sensibility adapt to a scarcity world? That's such a fascinating question, I'll need to write a whole new paper in which to explore it!

Notes

1. 'Exterminate All Rational Thought: The Zero Without the One: Putting the Null Back in Numbskull', Propinski, Anatolia and Dubcek, Marion (*The Journal of Irreconcilable Irrationalities*, V27, I3, Winter of Our Discontent), pgs 27-3.

2. The fact that revolutions do occur is a testament to humanity's stubborn unwillingness to conform to economic models.

3. I know, I know, for socio-economists, anthropologists are no more than mere anthropoid apologists. However, when dealing with such an extreme, one might even say absurd new species, one mustn't feel limited by the boundaries of academic specializations. Not in a paper in a journal nobody outside of half a dozen researchers is going to read – thumb through – glance at, in any case.

4. *The Aliens of Earth Prime 4-6-4-0-8-9 dash Omega, An Oral History; That Means A Spoken History, Not A History of Oral – Oh, Get Your Mind Out of the Gutter!*, Turkel, Studs (Anything for a Laugh Press), pg. 187 (twice).

5. The two were first popularized in the theory of Gord-aligned Economic Decoherence proposed by celebrity cook Nigella Lawson. See, for example, *The Life and Death of a Four Star Rated Culture*, Lawson, Nigella (Foodie Angeluden Press).

6. 'Your Tragedy is My Comedy: How Laughter Gains Currency', Hubbard, Old Mother (*The Journal of Economic Relevance and Refried Beans*, V1 I3 N2 N22 Y02, Summer Time and the Living is Easy), pg. 25. How groundbreaking was this paper? Fifteen backhoes gave their lives to its creation!

7. 'Tokyo Drift, Short Shrift: How Meaning Crumbles Like a Good Cookie in the Sun Over Time', Hungadunga, Phil, Hungadunga, Roger and MacCormack, Serengeti (*The Journal of Irreducible Comedy*, undated), unpaginated.

8. Hubbard, pg. 25 or 6-2-4.

9. *When Harry 124C 41+ Met Sally Fourth.* Directed by Rob Reiner. Written by Nora Epinephron. Starring Billy Crystal and Megan Beltbuckle.

Excerpt from 'The Hole in the Name, the Hole in the Donut or the Hole in the Head: A Socio-economic Analysis of Earth Prime 4-6-4-0-8-9 dash Omega', written by Srinivas Kawasaki, in *Aliens? What's Up With That?*, edited by Arturo Bubbelach, Eliazar Starlight, and Rachel Bonheur, (Pedantic Antics Press) pgs. 12-37 (but not 13 to 35).

CHAPTER TWO
Immigration Can Be Murder!

"Always look on the bright side of life," the little blue person wearing an exquisite three piece suit sang. "Foof. Fwoof. Foo – oh, look, I can't whistle. Can you help me out, here?"

"Wadda we look like?" the tough guy who was playing invaders with his personal space exploded. "Yer choreographers'r somethin'?"

"Actually, a choreographer –" the little blue man in the exquisite three piece suit started to say. The baby-faced man in the polo shirt and khaki pants standing next to the tough guy swiped at him with a rusty switchblade. (If you assumed that the baby-faced man had borrowed the switchblade from the tough guy, you would be wrong. In fact, the baby-faced man's great-grandfather had brought it with him when he came to the United States from Ireland. If his great-grandfather Iewan had any thoughts on the fact that the knife that he had used to defend himself against anti-immigrant roughnecks was now being used to intimidate immigrants, he kept them to himself – having died before the baby-faced man was born may have contributed to his silence, although given the state of modern ghostbusting technology, it needn't have.) The little blue man in the exquisite three piece suit jumped back, just out of the reach of the blade. "Does…umm…that, I guess…"

"You being a smartass?" the tough guy's eyes (which were so beady you could start a necklace with them), already very close together, appeared to want to melt into each other. He was two and a half feet taller than the little blue man in the exquisite three piece suit; when he leaned in to menace the short man, he looked like a brick house that was about to collapse.

Resisting an urge to ask his butt a series of question to test its intelligence, the little blue man in the exquisite three piece suit asked, "If I was to tell you my name, would you: a) be more likely to kill me; b) be less likely to kill me; or, c) be not changed in your desire to kill me?"

"You are being a smartass!" the tough guy insisted. He balled his fists, making them look very sledgehammery.

"Inquiring minds want to know," the little blue man assured him. "And in gratitude for your participation, your name will be entered into a draw for a set of steak knives and a year's supply of Rice-a-Roni, the San Francisco – eep!"

The baby-faced man swiped at the little blue man in the exquisite three piece suit once again, this time slashing his exquisite three piece suit (which made an exquisite hole) and biting into the skin high on his chest. The little blue man looked down at the trickle of pink…ish blood coming from the top of his chest and said, "Your intentions seem honourable, but is your heart really in it?"

"Wha?" The tough guy seemed indignant on his friend's behalf.

"If you really want to kill me, you need to aim for squishier bits that will do more damage. Here, for instance." The little blue man in the exquisite three piece suit indicated his stomach. "Insert the knife in there and you'll be able to see my guts spill onto the alley. I suspect you would find that much more satisfying than ripping an innocent piece of fabric – I mean, what did my exquisite three piece suit ever do to you?"

"D'ya wanna die?"

The little blue man drew a finger across his neck. "How about the classic? You can't go wrong slitting somebody's throat. The blood spurts all over the place – you'll get it all over you! And if you're especially vicious, my head will look like it's about to fall off completely! That's guaranteed to make you a hit with the ladies!"

"What is wrong with you?" the tough guy complained.

"Just trying to be helpful," the little blue man in the exquisite three piece suit, sniffed. "You don't have to bite my head o –"

"All done, Jameson," a third man in the dark alley said. All eyes turned towards him. He was a little shorter than the baby-faced man (Jameson?), with features that could have come from Mount Rushmore, if Mount Rushmore had been a monument to weaselly organized petty criminals. The third man was also wearing a polo shirt and khaki pants. His buzz cut was so short you could have sworn his barber had made it with bees.

The baby-faced man swatted the skeezy artist in the shoulder and hotly said, "Hey! Bertram! We agreed not to use each other's names!"

"Sorry, Jameson! Fred told me it wouldn't make any difference!" Bertram responded.

As Jameson swatted Fred (who, by process of elimination, must be the tough guy – all those years of playing Clue have really paid off!), harder than he had swatted Bertram (to the detriment of his hand, not the tough guy's shoulder), Bertram put the cap on the bottle of spray paint he had been using and got up off his knee. He had been painting a complex image on the wall. The trio had been in the alley for over ten minutes, in large part because the first two times Bertram had tried to spray paint the image, he had gotten a salient detail wrong, and had to paint over it and start all over again on a new section of the wall. Jameson looked over Bertram's handiwork and nodded in approval.

"Okay," Jameson said, pocketing the switchblade. "I think we've made our point."

Running a finger along the gash in his chest, the little blue man in the exquisite three piece suit muttered: "You definitely made a point. A sharp one, if I'm any judge."

Jameson rolled his eyes. Then, he pointed to the little blue man in the exquisite three piece suit and made a gesture of turning a key in a lock in front of his own mouth.

"Yeah. Right." Fred turned to their target. "If you say anything ta anybody about what all happened here, tonight, we will hunt you down and exterminate you. Is that clear?"

The little blue man in the exquisite three piece suit made the locking gesture above his head. Fred and Bertram looked confused. Jameson sighed. He made a bending steel motion at Fred.

Fred reached down and poked a finger in his victim's chest. "We didn't ask for you alien freaks to come here. We don't want you here. Consider this your first and only warning: go back to the freak universe you came from. And if you tell anybody about our little encounter this evening, we will rescind our generous offer of safe passage out of our reality. Capisce?"

"The capisciest!" the alien (aka: the little blue man in the exquisite three piece suit) enthusiastically agreed.

Jameson shook his head in sadness. The alien's unrelenting cheerfulness had made intimidating him much less fun that Jameson had thought it would be. Ah, well. If he called it an early night, he could make it home to catch some of the Steven Seagal film festival on The Nature Network.

Jameson turned and briskly walked out of the alley. Bertram trotted alongside him, Fred lumbering slightly behind.

That was exciting, the alien thought as he watched them leave. *Not as much as last night's pasta adventure, but –*

There was a loud * CRACK * and a red hole opened up in the little blue man in the exquisite three piece suit's throat. Before he knew what was happening, a wind blew through the alley, causing the hole to whistle seven notes from the song "Always Look on the Bright Side of Life." His last thought in his time on Earth was: *The fourth note was off k –*

The alien died with a smile on his face.

"We've caught a case."

"What's that, Joe?"

"We caught a case, Bill."

"Are you sure? I don't know about you, but I've been on antibiotics since the Pizzicotti triple homicide!"

"You ever heard the expression TMI, Bill?"

"Sure, Joe. We all have. It's an inevitable consequence of the information age."

"Take it to heart."

"I'll give it all the consideration it deserves."

"I said: we caught a murder case."

"A murder case?"

"The first murder case."

"Vic's name Abel by any chance?"

"Love your quick wit, Bill."

"Helps make the job bearable, Joe. You know how it goes."

"Nope. Vic's name's Napoleon Frasmatic."

"Frasmatic? Name rings a bell. Wasn't he the poor mope who got himself caught cheating on his wife? Yeah. Yeah – it's coming back to me. When she found out about the affair, she re-enacted the climactic scene of *Titanic* on him. Soggiest case we ever investigated."

"No, Ed. The frasmatic was actually a Wi-fi enabled frisbee that was none the rage with the kids a few years back."

"Really?"

"Would I kid you about such a thing?"

"You don't got the sense of humour for it."

"Exactly."

"Hell kind of a name is Napoleon Frasmatic, Joe?"

"The alien kind, Bill. The alien kind."

"Alien…like in Mexican?"

"Further."

"European?"

"Further."

"Martian?"

"Getting closer."

"Am I in the right universe?"

"Bingo!"

"I don't follow."

"Probably just as well. Following is a crime."

"Following, Joe?"

"If it's with intent, Bill. Intent, measured in closeness."

"How close would you need to be?"

"One car length, half the length of a tall man's arm or thirty-seven Farcebook posts."

"You always had an eye for the details, Joe. That's what makes you such a good cop. An eye for the details."

"Thanks, Bill. Coming from you, that's aces, that is. Real aces."

Sergeant Joe…Something or Other and Officer Bill…No, Don't Tell Me, It's on the Tip of My Tongue had been with the Los Angeles Police Department for a long time. A very long time. So long that they wore fedoras that hadn't been made since before the start of this century. So long that they typed their reports up on old Smith-Coronas that for some reason had the letter t upside down. So long **that they appeared to everybody else in black and white.** They probably would have been retired out of the force a long time ago, except for one thing: they had a perfect record. They closed every case they were assigned to. Every single one. Nobody knew how they did it; if they had, they would have replicated the feat, but nobody ever had. Not even close. Occasionally, somebody in the precinct would harbour a suspicion that they planted evidence to keep their closure rate so high, but one look at Bill and Joe's rumpled grey suits and hangdog faces would drive the thought clean out of any suspicioner's head.

Joe and Bill didn't socialize with the other detectives of Robbery-Homicide. In fact, the other detectives of Robbery-Homicide would have had a collective heart attack if either Bill or Joe told a joke. The pair were so earnestly deadpan, you would have thought all the Teflon had been scraped off and the metal melted down to make a pair of earrings for a gangster's moll.

In the interest of inter-officer amity, the desk Joe and Bill shared was in a corner on the other side of the table with the coffee maker and accoutrements. The corner wasn't well lit, which emphasized the pair's monochromaticism. One time, a recruit new to the division put the severed finger of a murder victim on one of their chairs. When the errant appendage was discovered, Bill and Joe talked for ten minutes about who it might have belonged to, where it could have come from, whether there could be some literary, perhaps metaphorical significance to its appearing there, why modern writers shied away from metaphor and focused on concrete physical description, whether attending literary schools generally helped or hurt said writers, but who were they to judge, really when –

Having been delivered a lecture on literary theory rather than the entertainment that he had been expecting, the detective who had placed the finger on the chair bitterly retrieved it with a muttered, "Oh, so **that's** where that got to. I'll just…collect it. Evidence, you know."

"You wanna drive, Bill?"

"Is it raining out, Joe?"

"I look like The Weather Channel?"

"Never hurts to ask."

"What difference does the weather make?"

"I'm a skidding hazard during periods of precipitation."

"I did not know that about you, Bill."

"It's not something I share with the world, Joe."

"I can understand tha –"

"Oh, for Gord's sake, **I'll pay for your taxi if the two of you will just get on with the case, already!**" somebody shouted from across the room. It may have been the Chief.

It wasn't raining, but Joe ended up driving. As always. When you had a good thing, you didn't mess with it.

On the drive to the crime scene, an alley in Watts (motto: "We're the fourth worst neighbourhood in the country, because **who the ferk are you to tell us how hard we should try?**"), Joe and Bill debated the pros and cons of rap music. They agreed that Ice T was a pro and The Notorious B.I.G. was a con. Given the…elliptical nature of the conversation, it was often difficult to tell if they were stating opposing positions or heatedly agreeing with each other. Or making different arguments for the same position. Or applying the same arguments to different positions. Or…even talking about the same thing.

"Tupac ate my shorts," Bill remembered as Joe pulled the unmarked Chevy Biscayne up to the yellow police tape that blocked the entrance of the alley.

"Boxers or briefs?" Joe wondered as he pocketed the keys and opened the door to get out.

"Boxers," Bill told him as he got out of the other side of the car. "You know I never do anything brief."

Joe shook his head. "Try telling that to suburban white fan boys."

"Try telling **anything** to suburban white fan boys!"

"Too true."

After ensuring that the car doors were locked (by hand, just like momma used to make it), Joe and Bill made their way to the crime scene. The pair didn't raise the police tape and walk under it to get to the body: they casually walked through it, as if walking through the scene at a different time, a previous time, a time before the tape had been hung.

On the other side, a short woman with hair that strobed from neon pink to neon blue to neon purple to neon colours nature had no name for, knelt next to a small figure covered in a sheet. She was staring intently (with no aim to follow, so she was jake {although how she dressed when she was off-duty was nobody's business}) at the side of the figure's head. Around them danced a rotund man taking photographs as he muttered to himself, "Yeah. That's it. Pout it out. Pout it all out! Turn your head! Turn your head! Turn your – okay, don't turn your head. Can you give me more? More! More! Yessssss!"

Frustrated artists always find a path to fulfillment.

"Trixie," Joe greeted the woman.

The Crime Scene Investigator (whom Joe and Bill still thought of as a Crime Scene Investigatress – they broke into the force at a more innocent time) – whose name was actually Malinka Moosemeat, but who had enough experience with the detectives to know better than to try and correct them – there weren't enough hours in the day – responded, "Joe. Bill."

"What you got?" Bill asked.

"A splitting headache," CSI Moosemeat responded, getting to her feet. "That'll teach me to take my pet ferret Ferret for a walk before my shift!"

"And the crime scene?" Joe, not unsympathetically, followed up.

"Unremarkable. Male. Alien. ID says 2,366 years old. Four foot two. Blue skin. Exquisite three piece suit. Cause of death: single gunshot wound to the throat. Knife wound to the chest that was not deep enough to draw more than a trickle of blood, probably made by a rusty switchblade. Shame, really."

"Why's that?"

"He was a young man who came a long way – the longest – looking for an escape from imminent annihilation and a better life. But, in the end, he died alone and terrified."

"Nice," Joe commented. "Poetic."

"Good to see that night class in creative writing is paying off," Bill added.

Not averting her gaze, CSI Moosemeat responded, "Thanks."

"So, the vic's name was…Napoleon Frasmatic?" Bill asked.

"That's right," CSI Moosemeat told him.

"Why is that name ringing a bell?" Joe asked.

"Because you think you're on a game show and you've just given the answer that will win you the car behind curtain number thirty-one?" Bill replied.

"Oooooor because you're a fan of *The Titus Andromedan Show*?" CSI Moosemeat offered.

"That was the one about the Asian immigrant who finds success as a stand-up comedian and eventually becomes a late night talk show host even though his family does not approve, right, Bill?"

"No, Joe. You're thinking of *The Midge Maisle Show*."

"Are you sure that isn't the one about a gay black man who moves to the big city to start an acting career using nothing but an amazing set of pipes and an indulgent writing staff?"

"Nope. That's *The Fresh Off the Randall Park Show*. It's an easy mistake to make, though."

"Are we…are we still talking about *The Titus Andromedan Show*?" CSI Moosemeat interjected. "Because, that **is** the right series."

"Oh," Joe ohed. "Never heard of it."

"The vic was a writer for the show," CSI Moosemeat, head reeling from the digressionary non-sequiturs, tried to inject some actual information into the conversation. "He was the first alien to be hired to be in the writers room of a major domestic production. He was rumoured to be in the running for an Emmy – and, not because of any attempt at politically correct affirmative action, but because the script that had his name on it was genuinely funny. It was in all the papers."

"The trade papers?" Joe asked.

"Yeah. So?"

Before Joe could respond, Bill piped in: "Comedy writer. Great." He couldn't quite keep the contempt out of his voice.

"What's the matter?" CSI Moosemeat queried. "Comedy writer kill your dog?"

"His name was Tyrannybuster Rex," Bill deadpanned. "Best police dog I ever worked with. Could smell an illegal porcelain clown figure from 500 feet away! It...it was a bizarre fishing boat accident. It was on a bizarre fishing boat. They only sold $2.37 worth of fish per year. We thought the comedy writer was using it as some kind of tax dodge, but we never got the goods on him. And, Tyrannybuster Rex, he...he...he..."

Hoping to steer his partner away from Melancholy Drive, Joe pointed to an image on the wall. "What's that?"

Bill took a sharp left on Curiosity Boulevard: "The spray paint is so fresh, if it was a donut, it would melt in your mouth."

"It's so fresh," Joe agreed, "I'm surprised it hasn't rolled its eyes and said, 'You lie, grandpa!'"

"It's so fresh," CSI Moosemeat chimed in, "you could hang it next to the pine tree over your dashboard!"

Joe and Bill looked dourly at her. She didn't have to have six years of forensics training to see the "tut tut, now" in their eyes.

"Yeah. Sorry."

"So," Joe repeated. "What is it?"

It was a drawing in neon orange (the most introspective of spray paint colours) of a sea animal pulling itself ashore while water rages all around it. The animal sported a patch over its left eye. Its teeth were bared, making it look as if it was eager to find an ass, any ass, to bite.

"That's the emblem of the Sea Otters of Odin," CSI Moosemeat explained. "They're a white nationalist group. They insist that they're not racist – they just don't want to have anything to do with people who aren't white. You know, for cultural reasons? Because white culture is the best. That's not racist – it's just a statement of fact. Yeah, they're a little...confused..."

"Sea Otters of Odin?" Bill skepticked.

"That's what they call themselves," CSI Moosemeat told him.

"Sea Otters?"

"Yeah, I know. You would have thought that white

nationalists could have chosen a more…ferocious animal to name themselves after. But all the really intimidating animals had already been taken. I mean, there was already a Wolves of Odin, a Bears of Odin, a Tigers of Odin, a Rampaging Elephants of Odin, a Hyenas of Odin, a Wolverines of Odin, an Eagles of Odin, a Sewer Rats of Odin, a Tiger Shrimps of Odin, a Wildebeests of Odin, a Hoot Owls of Odin and a Baby Rhinoceros' Arm Holding an Apple of Odin. By the time they got established, the Sea Otters of Odin had to take whatever animal they could get."

"Could explain why they're so angry," Joe opined.

"You think we're looking at a hate crime?" Bill asked.

"We're certainly not looking at a love crime," Joe responded.

"I'm pretty sure that's not a thing, Joe."

"What I mean, Bill, is: hating human beings of a different colour isn't the same thing as hating an alien…of a different colour…"

"Actually, it kind of is," CSI Moosemeat explained. "A lot of white supremacist groups were starting to lose members. I mean, year in and year out it was the same thing: white-skinned people good, everybody else sucks. It got kind of…repetitive, right? Boring. But the aliens come along and all of a sudden the racists have a new target for their hatred. It's really energized them. It's a short step, not much more than a shimmy, really, from racism to speciesism."

"I suppose it's good that the racists were so open-minded," Bill observed.

"In a creepily bigoted way," Joe pointed out.

"Any idea where we can find the Sea Otters of Odin?" Bill asked.

"Sure. I'll write down the address of their clubhouse for you," CSI Moosemeat offered.

"You can just tell us," Joe suggested.

"It would be better if I wrote it down," CSI Moosemeat insisted. "You could get it wrong."

"I've got an excellent memory," Bill argued. "I can remember the face of every mug who ever snuffed an innocent life."

"And sometimes not so innocent," Joe reminded him.

"Those I don't lose as much sleep over," Bill admitted.

"This is not a job for people with weak dispositions, Bill."

"No, Joe, it – what's this?"

"The address of the clubhouse of the Sea Otters of Odin," CSI Moosemeat stated, handing over a piece of paper from her notebook. "I wrote it down."

"Efficient," Joe marvelled.

"Say, Trix," Bill asked, "how do you know all about the Sea Otters of Odin?" Bill asked.

"Racist groups are kind of a hobby of mine," CSI Moosemeat responded.

"If you don't mind my asking," Bill continued, "how is it that you are always pursuing a hobby relevant to our current investigation?"

CSI Moosemeat shrugged. "I get bored easily…"

On a dreary street with grey brick single storey buildings in various states of decay, one structure stands out as being especially awful. It features a shiny steel security door with multiple bolts, locks and other security devices; the door gleamed like the future. But the building it fronted was made of rotting wood, windows boarded up with less rotten but still definitely quite shady wood. The door notwithstanding, this was a building that would make you want to take the ram out of ramshackle (in the belief that if its horn were to just brush against the structure, it would collapse).

"You take me to the nicest places," Bill said as he got out of the car.

"This isn't a date," Joe countered as he shut his door. The pair never locked the doors, confident that nobody would have the slightest interest in stealing it. Aside from a few classic car enthusiasts, they were probably right. "Unless it's a date…with justice."

"Isn't that the sort of thing you usually say at the end of cases, Joe?" Bill asked as they walked through an unkempt front yard (the grass as high as an elephant's eye, a dozen empty beer bottles, half a dozen hard drives from obsolete computers from as long ago as last year and a blow-up Santa that was only half-inflated, causing it to double over as if it had a terrible stomach ache from too much milk and cookies) and up to the shackle building.

Joe shrugged. "The President cages aliens like animals and blackmails other nations into helping him win re-election. I'd say we have abandoned all pretence of traditional social norms at this point."

Bill nodded thoughtfully. He raised his hand to knock on the door, then let it drop. "Would there be a problem if we were on a date, Joe?"

"You mean because of the homo-erotic tension that exists between any two men who work together in a high stress environment, Bill?"

"I mean because of the odd way you phrased that comment."

"To be honest with you, I can't remember the last time I went on a date."

"You have three children, Joe. You must have wooed a woman at some point in your life."

"They could have been adopted, Bill."

"Were they adopted, Joe?"

"Umm…that was a long time ago."

"What about your wife?"

"Umm…that was a long time ago. What about you, Bill?"

"What about me what, Joe?"

"Can you remember ever being on a date?"

"I'm a lifelong bachelor, Joe."

"Which does not actually answer the question, Bill."

"Hmm…does cleaning a deboning knife with Petroleum Butter count?"

A slot in the door angrily opened. "Jesus begesus, I can't stand it any more!" a woman with a thin voice shouted. "Gord almighty, you want to live in a quiet neighbourhood, and you end up in the middle of a ferking Yenta convention! **What the ferk do you want?**"

Staving off an incipient wink towards his partner, Joe said: "Police, ma'am. I'm Sergeant Joe…You Know, and this is Detective Bill…Some Day, I'll Remember, I'm Sure I Will. We're looking for the Sea Otters of Odin."

"They're out," the woman told him, slamming the slit shut.

"Friendly neighbourhood, Joe."

"Very welcoming, Bill."

Bill knocked on the door. "Ma'am? **Ma'am?** We need to know where they are. Ma'am? If we could just talk to you for a minute."

Bill rapped harder on the door. It creaked momentarily as the wood in the wall that held it up tried to decide whether it was worth the energy to keep it that way. It was just so very tired, you see. So very, very tired. The wall decided that it just wasn't worth the effort; the door quickly fell backwards to the ground with a loud * CRASH *! Joe looked at it. Bill looked at it. The woman, a scrawny thing with skin so tan and wrinkled it was difficult to discern her age, who had jumped back far enough not to have her toes crushed, looked at it. Several seconds passed.

Eventually, the woman looked at the two police officers. "That's police brutality," she said, but her heart wasn't really in it. (Her spleen, on the other hand, was totally down with the sentiment; unfortunately, it was the body part with the seventh least say on the matter, just ahead of the small intestine but behind the big toe of her right foot.)

"Of a door?" Bill responded.

"Doors got rights," the woman insisted.

"You are?" Joe asked, ignoring the legal discussion.

"Miranda Wright," the woman smirked.

"Is this the clubhouse of the Sea Otters of Odin, Ms. Wright?"

The woman was miffed that the police officer refused to acknowledge her witticism, but she decided not to show it. "Yeah. Fine. Whatever. It is."

Bill looked into the gloom of the single room. There were the vague outlines of furniture and the lingering odour of Patchouli past its prime, but there did not appear to be any movement. "Ms. Wright, are the Sea Otters of Odin here?"

The woman puffed up. All five foot three of her in stockinged feet – and snagged stockings at that. **"I'm here!"** she pointed out.

"Ms. Wright, please don't make me knock again," Bill advised.

The woman considered this for a moment. She knew that

there was a problem, here, but she couldn't put her finger on just what it might be (that knocking on a door that was already lying on the ground probably couldn't cause it any further harm). "Fiiiiiine! As I told you previously, the boys aren't here."

"Where are they?" Joe demanded. Respectfully, as was his way.

"The Humans for Humanity reality," the woman sulked.

"Humans for Humidity?" Bill repeated. Almost.

"Humanity!"

"Humanity for Humidity? Not sure how that makes more sen –"

"Humans! Humans! For! Humanity!" the woman exasperated all over the place. "Jesus begesus, do you live under a rock?"

"Actually," Bill started to say that everybody who lived in the shadow of the Hollywood sign lived under a rock, but the woman didn't give him a chance.

"Little blue aliens are arriving here every second from another universe! They don't think like us! They don't act like us! They will not **replace** us! Blues will not replace us! Somebody has to protect the interests of native Earth-born beings. That's what the Sea Otters of Odin are for. Humans for Humanity is a rally of like-minded groups – we hope to stop the alien invasion so that we can go back to hating each other as the good Gord intended."[1]

"Hunh. Learn something new every day, Joe."

"Life is the best classroom, Bill."

"Where is this protest taking place, ma'am?"

---

[1] One unfortunate feature of ideas is that they have a tendency to morph into actions. Sure, there are ideas that can lead to positive actions that make the world a better place ("I have more food than I could possibly eat – let me share it with my neighbours," for instance, or, "If I keep this food in a cold place, it lasts longer – let me create the…ice food keeper thing!"). The unfortunate part is that, for every positive action that comes out of an idea, approximately 23.78349 negative actions that make the world a worse place come out of ideas (for example: "I don't have enough food – I should steal some from my neighbours," or, "If you cross this imaginary line on the ground, I will assume that you are coming for my food. I like my food. I shall defend my food.") Be careful what you think – it could come back to bite somebody else in the ass!

"Let me write it down," the woman replied. She looked back into the room for a moment, then returned her gaze to them. "Umm, you wouldn't happen to have any paper, would you? And maybe, something to write with?"

"You could just tell us," Joe suggested.

The woman hesitated, then blurted: "Fiiiiiine! The rally is planned in front of Grauman's Chinese on Hollywood Boulevard."

"Thank you for your cooperation, Ms. Wright," Bill said as he turned to leave.

"Hey, wait a minute!" the woman stopped him. "Are the cops going to pay for the damage to the door?"

"No," Joe told her.

"Why not?"

Joe looked at the door on the floor and sardonically responded, "It doesn't have a scratch on it."

All the roads leading to Hollywood Boulevard had been blocked off by squad cars. Joe pulled up to one of them and stopped. Beyond the squad cars, a couple hundred people milled about…with intent. Some of them were dressed all in black, compete with ski masks, which were not all the rage this summer, but there's no accounting for taste. *They must be* schvitzing *in those clothes*," Bill thought. *For the Black Blockhead, body fluids are a small price to pay to save democracy,* Joe thought. *It's ninety-eight in the shade. Better them than me*, Bill thought. *No accounting for taste*, Joe thought. Before Bill could think any further, he continued: *Most people just think about the weather – time we did something about it, don't you think?*

Towards the back of the crowd, Joe stepped up to a man who had scruffy United Nations hair, with a pony tail that contained more than a few strands that had tried to make a break for it but were constrained by the man's scrunchie. He was wearing jeans and a Hard of Heering Leppard t-shirt that didn't quite contain his sprawling middle-aged stomach. "Excuse me, sir, I'm Detective Joe…Something, and this is my partner Bill…You Know, I Was Just Thinking of The Name The Other Day. LAPD. We'd like to ask you a few questions."

"You are **not** police officers!" the man blurted.

"I assure you, sir, we are."

"Nyuh uh."

"Uh."

"Dude! Please! Plainclothes cops try to blend in. They go to a white nationalist rally, they dress in white polo shirts and tan slacks. They go to a gay bar, they dress in muscle shirts and tight-bottomed black pants! They go to an orgy, they dress in g-strings and embarrassed smiles. They go to an anti-nationalist rally, they dress in back masks, black shirts, black pants and black Doc Martens. No cop would be caught dead anywhere in crumpled suits that might once have been brown, but had long since been bleached of any meaningful colour. QED: you can't be cops!"

"The man is insulting our clothes, Bill."

"To be fair, when was the last time we bought new clothes, Joe?"

"Musta been…when Kennedy was President…"

"Hunh. Guy might have a point."

Unwilling to concede the point, Joe pulled out his wallet and flashed the man his badge. "Wow," the man goggled. "I've never met plainclothes cops who were so…plain clothed!"

"We're looking for the Sea Otters of Odin," Joe told him.

"Not the Thompson's Gazelles of Odin?"

"No, sir."

"You sure you're not thinking of the Ferocious Keynesians of Odin?"

"No, sir. The Sea Otters of Odin. We were told that the main members of the group could be found here."

"Well, I don't know about that…"

"Can you tell us anything about them, sir? Anything at all?"

"Sure. If you're looking for any Animal Species of Odin, you'll find them there." The man pointed towards Grauman's Chinese, where a couple of dozen people stood behind a red rope barricade fronted by an equal number of uniformed police officers who looked like they didn't really want to be there, so you better not ask for any trouble because they would be happy to answer.

"Thank you for your help."

Joe and Bill made their way towards the barricade. They walked past a Black Blockhead member who said into a bullhorn: "Battle lines are being drawn!"

From behind the barricade, a woman using a bullhorn replied, "Nobody's right if everybody's wrong!"

"Young people speaking their minds!" the Black Blockheader continued.

The crowd roared back at him: "Getting so much resistance from behind!"

Arriving at the barricade, Bill said, "We better stop."

"Hey!" Joe responded. "What's that sound?"

They looked at each other for a moment. Then, the moment passed, and identifying the sound didn't seem all that important.

Joe and Bill started to walk through the crowd. People took one look at them and let them pass, parting to allow a small trickle of blue to move through. In the middle of the crowd, a large, older woman with a massive riot of almost entirely grey hair sat on a folding chair surrounded by boxes full of bottles of water, power bars and the occasional piece of fruit. She was happily knitting either the world's biggest bootie or the world's smallest elephant net.

"Excuse me, ma'am," Joe tried to get the woman's attention.

While keeping to her knitting, the woman replied: "Help yourself to whatever you need, Comrade." Then, she frowned; it had occurred to the part of her mind that was not concentrating on knitting that she didn't know the voice she had just been helpful to. She looked up and her face fell. "Oh, wait. You're cops."

Bill and Joe looked at each other. "How did you know?" Bill asked.

"There is a certain…monochromatic aspect to your appearance," the woman informed them. "Only cops think they can pull it off…"

"Are we pulling it off?" Bill followed up.

The woman shrugged, the question too obvious to waste energy answering.

"Ma'am," Joe began to inquire, but was cut off by a deep voice interjecting: "If you would be so kind, my good lady, would you happen to have any butterscotch scones?"

"Priam?" the older woman asked.

"I'm sorry," the four foot tall blue fellow wearing an exquisite three piece suit apologized, "I don't speak Polynesian." Sort of apologized.

"Are you Priam Dibbler?"

The alien couldn't look the woman in the midriff. "Maaaaaybe..."

"Priam!" the older woman scolded. "This is the...sixth time you've asked me for a scone! I didn't have any any of the other times you asked – what would make you think I have any now?"

"The person who asked last time – who may or may not have been me – I admit nothing – asked for chocolate chip scones. The person before that – same proviso – asked for maple walnut scones. Completely different!"

"Different...and yet the same."

"I do believe that what we have here, Bill, is a case of repetition with variation."

"Couldn't be more obvious if it landed on my nose with a loud * KEE-RASH *, Joe."

"Repetition with variation?" the older woman, against her better judgment, asked.

"Woman doesn't know what repetition with variation is, Bill."

"Think we should tell her, Joe?"

"Actually," the alien responded, setting himself in lecture mode, "it's my *shtick*, so I should be the one to explain it. The classic joke has a three part structure: set-up, punchline, topper. The set-up creates the context for the joke. The punchline is the unexpected bit that makes it a joke. The topper is a second unexpected bit that takes the joke in a new direction, possibly back to the set-up. Okay. Comedy 101. A man walks into a bar. 'Ouch,' he says. 'You okay, buddy?' a passerby asks. 'You look like you could use a drink.' Set-up. Punchline. Topper. Sometimes, later, a reference can be made to the original joke: this is known as a callback. A man with a black eye walks into a bar so he can have a matching set. The longer the time between the original joke and the callback, the greater the potential for surprise and laughter (although, if you wait several months, the Audi Enz[2] may have forgotten what you're calling back to). You can also repeat a joke over a period of time. The problem with repeating a joke verbatim is that you lose the element of surprise, which is a key part of humour. So, you want to change it up just a little to keep it fresh. Repetition…with variation."

"That's great," the older woman said. "Really. But I still don't have any scones."

"Mmm…that's more of a callback than repetition with variation," maybe Priam encouraged. "Still, I think you're getting the idea."

"Ma'am," Joe finally inquired before the older woman could say anything, "do you know if the Sea Otters of Odin are here?"

It would be an exaggeration to say that the woman's face brightened; let us say that the darkness that enveloped it was less all-enveloping (in an 'enemy of my enemy is somebody who could be useful to me' kind of way). "The Sea Otters of Odin are the third dumbest human supremacist group after the Thompson's Gazelles of Odin! Yeah. They're here." The woman pointed to a line of uniformed police officers standing on the other side of a red rope strung across the entrance to Grauman's Chinese. "There are three of them. One looks like a brick shithouse with eyes. One looks like he's a mob lawyer. The other one looks like he belongs to the preppy frat in *Animal House*. Do you see them?"

"Hard to miss, given the level of detail of your description," Bill answered.

"What can I say?" the woman replied. "This isn't my first Rodeo Drive…"

Bill and Joe walked up to the line of uniformed police officers that separated the two sides of the…what's the word? More than a debate, less than a contretemps. It will come to

---

[2] The Audi Enz is the alien trickster god, the one who is constantly exhorting the faithful to greater heights of comedic achievement for the good of their immortal ratings. Think: Jehovah with a whoopie cushion.

me. They immediately recognized three officers: Wheeler, Keeler and Obstreperous.

"Did aliens lose 120 pounds at the Battle of the Bulge?" a man was saying through a megaphone. "Of course not! That was human beings sacrificing for the good of humanity!" The couple of dozen people on his side of the barricade tried to roar, but there were too few of them, and it came out as an over-excited peep.

Wheeler, Keeler and Obstreperous were made from the same cookie cutter mould: tall, broad-shouldered, scowly. Wheeler was the tallest of the three. Unless it was Keeler. No, sorry, it was Keeler; Keeler was the tallest of the three. But Wheeler was the one who performed *Commedia del'Arte* on weekends. No, wait, it was Obstreperous – his performance as Il Dottore in *What the Maid Thought She Saw* was the talk of the 12th Precinct for weeks! Still. Wheeler. Wheeler... was the one who could open beer bottles with his teeth. Unless it was Obstreperous. Or Keeler. Actually, it was Obstreperous and Keeler **and** Wheeler: all three of them could open beer bottles with their teeth, so that's a bit of a wash. Hmm...okay, clearly nothing distinguished Wheeler from the rest of the officers on the line, unless you count the birthmark in the shape of an eleven-dimensional string that cut through his left cheek and came out on the other side of his right eye.

"They were defending western Civilization from the encroachment of cholesterol!" the voice continued. "Now, these aliens want to come to our planet and feed us nothing but pies! It's nothing less than dessertageddon! And are we going to let them get away with it?"

"Absolutely!" a Black Blockhead member on the other side of the barricade shouted through **his** megaphone. "Who doesn't love pie?"

"Right! ...What?"

"Hi, Mick."

"Hi, Joe."

"Greetings, Rick."

"Greeting, Joe."

"Heya, Francesco."

"Hola, Joe."

Then, they went through the whole greeting ritual for Bill.

"Nice day for it, Rick."

"Got that right, Joe."

"See the game last night, Mick?"

"Which game last night, Bill?"

"Does the sport really matter when it comes to the male bonding ritual?"

"Too true. We suck. At whichever game was played last night."

"You think a new manager would help the team, Mick?"

"I think a new **team** would help the team, Frances –"

"They come to our country and take our jobs!" the man on the other side of the barricade attempted to regain control of the argument. "They're so short, they can work mines better than human beings! And that's not to mention the tragic layoffs of pastry chefs all over the world!"

"You mind letting us through, Rick?"

"Sure thing, Joe. You on a murder case?"

"The murderiest."

"That ain't a word, Bill."

"It is now I said it out loud, Francesco."

"I grudgingly concede your point."

Mick and Rick parted and Francesco lifted the red velvet rope to let Joe and Bill pass. They walked past a young woman who proudly held up a 'Humanes for humanity!' sign, and an older man whose sign mangled a quote from the Bible (something about not allowing the ass of a neighbour to be ridden by a stranger lest a plague of tax accountants descend upon your village) and used it to justify casting your aliens upon the waters (albeit laden with bricks and heavy chains so that they did not come back tenfold), but to get the whole message in it had to be printed in really small type, which caused most people to stop reading at the word 'thucible'. A middle-aged man in camo gear who could best be descripted as 'squinty' held a sign which read: 'It's Adam and Eve, not Adam and Eve Mandelorean'. Many of the people on this side of the barricade had Confederate flag patches on the shoulders of their ratty vests (because nothing makes people stand taller than identifying with the losing side in a war that ended over a century and a half earlier). An earnest young man who, in another time and place, might have had a major role in *The Book of Mormon* handed Joe a pamphlet with the headline

'Hating Jews doesn't make you anti-Semitic!!!!'[3]

"That pamphlet seems out of place, Joe."

"Hate doesn't discriminate, Bill."

"I would like to think that was profound, and yet…"

"Nothing profound about it. I'm just a guy trying to make sense of the world on a cop's salary."

"And yet, it's meaning isn't immediately discernible…"

"It's simple, Bill. The kind of person who hates aliens is also the kind of person who hates Jews or people of colour or homosexuals. Picking groups to hate is like eating peanuts: you can never stop at just –"

"Do you mind?" the large Sea Otter of Odin member shushed them. "I'm trying to listen to the speaker!"

Joe and Bill looked at each other. A better opening had not presented itself since Hanuman 'The Greek' Pollenta told them, "Sure, by all means search my home. I got nothing to hide!"

"Are you a member of the Sea Otters of Odin?" Joe asked.

"Who wants to know?" the large Sea Otter of Odin leaned towards the policeman, giving the impression of an ancient golem that was about to topple over.

Joe was unphased. Somewhere inside him, he knew he had the protection of the god of fictional detectives. "I'm Joe…What Do You Know?, LAPD. This is my partner, Bill…Do I Know You? I Feel Like I Know You. We're investigating the shooting death of an alien immigrant, Napoleon Frasmatic, in an alley in Watts off Happy Boulevard last night."

"I don't know nothing about no murder," the large man growled.

Before Joe could follow up, a tall, grizzled scarecrow of a man in a brown suede jacket…with fringes, who was wearing a Make America Grate Again cap (when you choose the lowest bidder from China, you have to expect a little semantic drift) shouted, "You killed a Blue Meanie‽"

The large man's brow curled, like he was being asked to think seriously about something, and he really wasn't built

[3] Ideas don't have to make sense. In fact, human beings are more likely to believe ideas that don't make sense than ones that do, which explains World War I, global warming and cargo pants.

for it. "No. The alien was alive when we left the –"

"We weren't in any alleys last night," a baby-faced man in preppy clothes who stood next to the large man, smoothly claimed. "We were at home. Playing whist. Our mothers can vouch for us."

"Are you members of the Sea Otters of Odin?" Bill asked.

"Hey, everybody!" the scarecrow shouted. "We got us some real Blue Meanie killers, here! I mean: right here! Right with us!"

"We didn't kill anybody," baby-face insisted. "Home. Whist. Mothers.

"You want I should beat this guy up?" a weaselly man standing close by, asked. "He's getting on my nerves, and I don't have my Novocaine with me!"

"That would not give the right impression," baby-face responded, glancing nervously at the two police officers.

"Man, I wanna buy you all a drink!" the scarecrow held his hand out to the baby-faced man, who looked at it like it was a grenade about to go off. "I…I can't until my settlement claim with the insurance company comes through, but I wanna! I mean, we all dream of killing a Blue Meanie, but you actually did it!"

"Blue Meanie, Joe?"

"Slang for alien immigrant, Bill."

"Hunh. Kids these days – what they do with language is almost poetic."

"Look, buddy, we are not responsible for anybody's death, okay?" Baby-face looked meaningfully at Joe and Bill.

"Ooooh, right," the scarecrow caught on. "The alien just slipped and fell on a bullet. Got ya." Baby-face hoped that the scarecrow wouldn't tap the side of his nose to indicate that he was in on a deception. Baby-face was sorely disappointed.

Joe, who had the patience of Joe, pointed out that the three men wore patches on their jackets with the distinctive emblem of the Sea Otters of Odin. It was a fair cop. He asked them to introduce themselves. The baby-faced man was James Jameson, a third year law student with a keen interest in social deviance. The brick shithouse was Fred 'The MacGyver of Mayhem' Chopin; when they got back to the precinct, Joe and Bill would find that he had a rap sheet longer than an evening of atonal music, but most of his crimes involved petty violence improvised with whatever objects came to hand (hence, his nickname). The weaselly man introduced himself as "James Franklin – no, Franklin James – okay, you got me, Charlie Manson. But obviously not **that** Charlie Manson – didn't he die in prison? I know – what are the odds? Okay. Okay. Seriously? You want to know my name? It's Studge. Philboyd Studge. I was named after a circus clown – what's it to you? Jesus begesus, you're a hard audience, you know that? Fine. The name on my passport is Antonin Scalia. Hey! It could be true! The government will give passports in the name of Antonin Scalia to anybody, these days! Hunh! Talk about lowering standards! Yeah, okay. The name on my **other** passport is Brenda La Boom Boom." A few seconds after it became embarrassing, James Jameson introduced the weaselly man as Bertram Frick. That name rang true.

"You were in the alley where the alien was killed," Bill accused them. "One of you spray-painted the symbol of the Sea Otters of Odin on the wall."

"No," James Jameson asserted. "I told you, we were home playing whist."

"How many tricks does a side need to win a hand?" Bill demanded.

"I – what?"

"How many tricks does a side need to start earning points in a game of whist?"

James Jameson looked stumped for a moment. Then, he gamely answered, "Twenty-one!"

"You were in the alley where the alien was killed. Fred as much as admitted it."

James Jameson sighed. "Okay. Yeah. We were there. But, we just roughed him up a little. That's all. It was a bit of good, clean, American fun. Aren't you patriotic?"

"We may have a different understanding of what it means to be patriotic," Joe informed him.

"Yeah," James Jameson bitterly commented, "being patriotic…obeying the law…the right not to self-incriminate – some cops have strange ideas about a lot of things. Whatever. Point is: we didn't kill anybody. You want the truth? He weirded me the Hell out. Wouldn't take us seriously. Thought everything was one big joke."

"How would you like it if somebody you didn't know made fun of one of your favourite hobbies?" Frick asked. "I won't lie to you: it hurt."

"I mean, I always knew the aliens were evil, but I didn't know they were **that** evil! In any case, I swear to you, when we left the strange little blue bastard, he was a bit the worse for wear, but he was –"

"Call this a protest?" a voice boomed from nearby. It was a short blue voice that wore an exquisite three piece suit. "If you were any less organized, you'd be the Democratic Party!"

"He was…umm…still…" James Jameson valiantly tried to complete his defence as an alien walked up to the group.

"You!" the alien pointed at James Jameson. "You're too pretty to protest! You should try to look more like tall, thin and gruesome back there. To properly protest, you need to look scruffy, you need to look like you just got out of bed with a wicked hangover from something you did the night before that you hope you never remember! How do you expect The Man to take you seriously if you look like you just walked out of an ad for body spray!"

"Priam?" Joe asked.

"Maaaaaybe…"

"You shouldn't be here, you little freak!" James Jameson shrieked.

"Oh oh," Maaaaaybe Priam responded. "Seems like I hit a nerve…"

"Seems like you hit the whole nervous system," Bill told him. "Still, the humanist has a point: it's probably not a good idea for you to be on this side of the red velvet rope."

"But, somebody has to teach the children!" Maaaaaybe Priam protested. "I mean, look at the misspellings on the signs. It's atrocious. I mean, atrocious. I mean, atro – horibble. It's really horibble. Misspelling words on protest signs is a time-honoured tradition, but the misspelling have to look innocent and make the people carrying the signs look adorable. These? These just make you look ignorant!"

"Fred," James Jameson ordered, "do something about this clown!"

"And, don't even get me started on the lame chanting!"

Fred walked up to the alien and looked down at him. "Time for you to go, little creature."

Maaaaaybe Priam hugged Fred's knees. "That's what I'm talking about! That's just the right mix of cold fury and menace! Thank the Audi Enz somebody is taking this protest seriously!"

Fred looked helplessly at James Jameson. The other man miserably admitted, "This is exactly what happened last night. We tried to intimidate the alien to convince him to go back to where he came from. And he did...**this**. You can't intimidate somebody who doesn't take you seriously. So, we went back to the clubhouse, got drunk and watched anti-alien videos on YahooTube. There. You happy, now?"

Bill and Joe couldn't help but notice that people had stopped talking through megaphones and that all of their attention was on the alien standing in front of them.

"This seems to be a good opportunity to continue our investigation somewhere else, Bill."

"Way ahead of you on that one, Joe. We will need your addresses and contact information, gentlemen, should we have any questions to ask in the future." James Jameson and Fred gave them reasonably credible information; they let Frick have "The Hague" because they figured they could find him through the other two easily enough. "Until the investigation is over, we would appreciate it if you did not leave town."

"What if I have to go to San Diego to bail my frail granny out of jail?" Frick asked.

"Granny will understand," Joe advised him. "The criminal justice system not so much."

"Uhh, Joe?"

"Yes, Bill?"

"I can't help but notice that the small crowd is closing in on us."

"You're suggesting that it's past time to go?"

"I think that would be a better course of action than cabaret."

"You never know. Music is said to soothe the savage breast, Bill."

"They do say that, yes. However, this seems like a crowd that would appreciate heavy metal more than Edith Piaf, Joe."

"Point taken, Bill. Point very much taken."

With much jostling and jeering, Joe and Bill escorted Maaaaaybe Priam out of the throng of humanist protesters. When Joe asked him why he was willing to risk his life going where he clearly wasn't welcome, the alien responded: "I have to do me." Joe and Bill nodded sagely.

After the police left, the scarecrow, who had discreetly faded into the background for the main part of the questioning, returned to the trio's side and enthusiastically asked, "So, what does it feel like to kill a Blue Meanie? Do they, like, beg for their lives? Or, do they eat pie, unconcerned about what's about to happen to them?"

James Jameson looked at the man. He had to remind himself that not everybody could be an intellectual, that revolutions always needed foot soldiers. He looked forward to the day that he could collect stupid feet…

On 1800 Paseo Rancho Castilla, the Hertzberg-Davis Forensic Science Center (named for the famed automotive rental pioneer – before he shortened his name to make it "less ethnic" – and actor Ossie Davis) sits a concrete slap in the face of the 1930s from the 1960s. Bill and Joe made their way to Malinka Moosemeat's lab on the third floor.

Malinka Moosemeat's lab on the third floor was the size of a closet, but the shoe closet of a wealthy dowager as opposed to the linen closet of a plebe like you or me. Along one wall was a row of metal filing cabinets. Along two other walls were plastic containers with various forensic tools. The room was filled with a table, making only very thin lanes by which people could enter the room. Somebody skinny (Bill) could walk up to the forensic scientist; somebody who had put on a little more girth over the years (Joe) could shimmy into the room until he was wedged between things.

Malinka Moosemeat was dissecting a blue jay on the table. Half a dozen butterflies were fluttering around on leashes anchored to it. She looked up when the pair entered the room.

"Hey, guys."

"What are you working on, Malinka?" Bill asked. Joe winced; they had an unspoken rule that they didn't ask her about her current cases. (If he had given it further consideration, Joe may have realized that it was his rule and if he wanted Bill to follow it, he would have to ununspeak it. There just never seemed to be an appropriate…)

"Checking the stomach contents of this blue jay," Malinka Moosemeat told them. "If it contains any part of a baseball, Flavio Aragones is guilty of the Booth Babes Bloodbath! I'm always excited by this part of the case – aren't you?"

"Actually –" Joe started.

"What are the butterflies for?" Bill inquired.

"Colour."

"Any word on **our** case?" Joe added.

"Umm, sure," Malinka Moosemeat informed them. She raised the safety goggles from her eyes, wiped her hands on the white lab apron she was wearing and moved towards Bill.

"I, uhh, need to get at the filing cabinet near the door," she awkwardly pointed out. Bill turned and started to move back out of the room, but he came upon Joe.

"Umm…could you just…?" Bill requested. Unfortunately, Joe was wedged in pretty good, and he couldn't just.

"Okay. This happens," Malinka Moosemeat allowed. "Joe, could you just turn around and open the third drawer from the bottom marked 'Open Cases?'"

Joe squirmed for a few seconds, but it was clear he wasn't going anywhere. "Can you just tell us if one of the guys in the alley could have been the shooter?" he demanded, a bit of grump appearing at the edges of his otherwise usually calm voice.

"No."

"No, you can't tell me, or no, none of the guys in the alley could have been the shooter?"

"No, none of the guys in the alley could have been the shooter. Napoleon Frasmatic was killed by a sniper bullet. From the angle of the entry wound, I would say that the shooter was perched on the roof of a building between 100 and 200 feet away."

"Well, that sure was –"

"Dakota!" Malinka Moosemeat shrieked.

An old woman poked her head into the room; Malinka Moosemeat's intern. "Yes?"

"Get the grease."

"Right away." The head immediately vanished.

When he was sure he had the room, Bill tried again: "Well, that was sure a dead end, Joe."

"They all are, Bill. They all are."

"Didn't know you were a Beckett fan."

"Fred Beckett, the well known art forger and Bob So Tasty promotional children's toys collector?"

"Sure, Joe. Let's go with that. So, what now?"

"Back to the office to do some legwork, Bill."

"Sitting behind our desks?"

"I do some of my best legwork sitting behind my desk…"

As they waited and it became apparent that Joe was not going to do his desk legwork any time soon, he mused, "Maybe there is something in Frasmatic's work environment that would give us a lead."

"Are you going to have to interrogate the cast of *The Titus Andromedan Show*? I don't love the show, exactly, I mean, it's not as good as *The Fresh Off the Randall Park Show*. But Jenny Moneypenny is a dreamboat. I know it's way unprofessional and stuff, but do you think you could, like, get her autograph for me? You know, if you run into her when you have a spare moment…"

Joe sighed. "Do you know where the show's offices are headquartered?"

"Sure. Let me write it down for you." Malinka Moosemeat looked around; the paper was on the other side of the table. The beyond Joe side. "I mean, when we've unwedged you from the aisle, Joe."

"Or, you could just tell us," Joe insisted.

"It's more…official when it's written down."

"You know, Joe, if I didn't know any better, I would swear that somebody couldn't be bothered to do some basic research about the geography of Los Angeles."

"Makes you wonder what other details of the story have been left out, Joe."

"It certainly do –"

"10,200 Pico de Mayo Boulevard!" Malinka Moosemeat blurted.

"Hunh. Shows you what somebody can do with the right motivation, Joe."

"Motivation and a reasonably fast internet connection, Bi –"

Dakota walked into the room and placed a large tub of grease on the table. Snapping a plastic glove on her hand, she said, "Okay, you have already assumed the position. Shall we begin…?"

"Ant chiropractors!" said Adrian the Token Goy.

"Cutting edge marsupials!" said Yana, the Token Woman.

"Psychedelic foot massagers!" said Nathan the Token…Red Head.

Michelin Robichaud, the creator and runner of *The Titus Andromedan Show* (and Token Person Without a Token Person Designation) looked out from the head of the table at which they all sat, steepling his stubby fingers (if he had been a demolitions expert before becoming a writer, they would have made a decent six pack and a few empties). "Not bad," he commented. "Not bad. Ant chiropractors – we might be able to use that…somewhere. Sometime. You know, in the future. Still, I'm not sure any of your input addresses the problem: how can Titus extricate himself from going to Gwyneth Paltrow's Schmeckler's Farrago party now that he's been invited to Emma Stone's Schmeckler's Farrago party? You know, I'm just not feeling a solution, here? I mean, honestly, how do cutting ledge marsupials help him?"

Around them were whiteboards on which had been written in differently coloured markers such gnomic statements as "Mariah in full on Betty Boop consensual reality" and "misunderstood overheard telephone conversation MISUNDERSTOOD OVERHEARD TELEPHONE CONVERSATION!" and "EPISODE FOUR: transcendent punch card cakes!" *Foucault's Pendulum* ain't got nothing on a typical television writer's room! Adrian and Nathan looked around the room for inspiration. Yana set her not inconsiderable chin and forged ahead.

"How about this?" she offered. "Cutting **Edge** Marsupials was the name of a band Titus was in when he was a teenager. He tells Gwyneth that Emma was a fan back in the day, even though they only ever played three gigs, two of them birthday parties; he was as surprised as anybody. But being a fan, Emma just had to have them play at her Schmeckler's Farrago party, and, well, nobody says no to Emma. Well, of course, when I say nobody, I don't mean Titus, who is big enough to say no to anybody he wants. But he wouldn't do that because…the other guys in the band haven't done as well as he has and he would hate to let them down!"

"Hmm…" Michelin considered, giving Yana an opportunity to catch her breath. "Did Emma Stone actually invite Titus' band to play at her Schmeckler's Farrago party?"

"Of course not," Yana smoothly explained. "That's the second act complication."

"Was Titus actually in a band when he was a teenager?"

"We can explore both scenarios and determine which one has better comic possibilities."

Michelin leaned back in his chair, closed his eyes and started humming the theme song to the film *O, Lucky Man* (which none of the other people in the room, all at least a decade younger than him, recognized). He was thinking.

Nathan got out his phone and checked his email. He had pitched a sitcom to Netflix about a guy who travels the countryside, kicking the trucks of assholes (it was a cross between *Kung Fu* and *Mother Truckers*, with an enlightenment quotient closer to the latter than the former), and was waiting to hear his agent's spin on the network's response. Adrian played *Angry Crustaceans XII: Jacques Crusteau's Very, Very Bad No Good Day* on his phone. Yana, whose phone was already out, opened a word processor and started to work on her new novel, about a woman trying to make her way through the uncaring society of ancient Rome and the yak who helps her achieve self-fulfillment.[4]

---

[4] Before she dies of pox at the age of 22. Ancient Rome didn't have the kind of appreciation for hygiene that we have today.

A couple of minutes later (close to the median length for one of his thought trances), Michelin's eyes opened and he sat forward in his chair. (His chiropractor had advised him to do this in order to save his back; the fact that it made him look like he was engaged and in control was a bonus.) "Okay. We can work with that." Yana popped up and wrote: "getting out of G party: band!" in blue marker (even though it was used primarily for character notes; Dan Harmon had used up all of the green markers employed to denote plot points running *Community* out of the office, and the cheapskate hadn't replaced them when the show was cancelled). "Only," Michelin added, "nobody names a band Jutting Edge Marsupials. We'll call them The Psychedelic Foot Massager."

Inwardly, Yana groaned. *Gotta give the boys a victory, hunh?* Outwardly, she gave the room a gap-toothed grin. It was, after all, her story.

"Nathan, since you came up with the band name, you write the first draft."

Before Yana could protest, a knock came to the door and two men in rumpled grey suits strode into the room, followed by a nearly hysterical blond himbo.

"I'm sorry," the himbo, whose name was Jimbo, and who was thiiiiis close to tears, apologized. "I told them you were too busy to be disturbed, but they just barged in!" He seemed embarrassed, but whether it was due to the enforced dereliction of his duty or at having to mouth such an ancient cliché is almost impossible to say.[5]

"Get the hell out of this room!" Michelin shouted.

---

[5] A cliché is an idea whose time has come, allowing it to enjoy a fancy meal at a four star restaurant before finding that it's time has gone, forcing it to beg for scraps of attention from readers of the gutter press. A cliché is usually born as a witticism in the mind of a literary author. Soon after its birth, it becomes often repeated by second rate literary writers hoping to elevate the quality of their prose. From there, it can be a short jump to inclusion in * SHUDDER * genre fiction. In time, the cliché is repeated so often in so many different places that it overstays its (semantic) welcome, like the friend of a friend who has lost all of his money in your weekly friendly poker game but insists on playing one more hand, just one more hand, I thought we were here to have some fuuuuuuuun! Think of it this way: when an unknown comedian expresses an idea at open mic night at a club, it's almost undoubtedly a cliché.

Recognizing that authority had taken command of the situation, the himbo bowed his head and backed out of the room, closing the door behind him. "Can't you see that we're brainstorming, here?"

"Brainstorming, Bill?"

"I don't think so, Joe. I don't see any bi-planes."

"Or flappers."

"Or men with megaphones exhorting the crowd to cheer the derring do."

"Or –"

"What the hell are you talking about?" Michelin screamed.

"Man has a point, Bill."

"I will allow that we may have lost the thread, Joe."

"Pardon us," Joe apologized to the room. "I'm Sargent Joe…You've Got a Familiar Face. This is Detective Bill…I Wanna Say, But No. No, That's Not It. LAPD. We're here to investigate a crime involving Napoleon Frasmatic. We understand he worked for *The Titus Andromedan Show*? As a writer?"

"He did," Michelin noncommittally allowed.

"Best comedy writer I've ever worked with," Yana commented.

"Present company excepted," Adrian suggested.

"Get real!" Yana shot him down. "Napoleon lived for comedy! Everything he ever did had comic intent! You? You live for the next woman you're going to get into bed!"

"That's where you're wrong," Adrian smugged. "I'm the Token Gay in the writer's room. Bedding women isn't my –"

"Actually," Michelin corrected him, "you're the Token **Goy** on the writing staff. Goy. Not gay. Goy."

"Goy?" Adrian was confused. "Is that somebody who enjoys having sex with…raisins?"

Michelin shook his head sadly. "It's just a word for somebody who is not Jewish."

"So, it has nothing to do with my sexuality?"

"Nothing at all."

Adrian looked like he was taking a shower with a skunk. "Fine. Then, maybe you've got me pegged. Maybe."

"What did that irrepressible scamp do now?" Nathan asked.

"That irrepressible scamp got himself murdered late last night or early this morning," Joe answered.

"Murdered?" Yana gasped. "How could that happen?"

"Single gunshot to the throat, ma'am," Bill told her. Joe closed his eyes and gently shook his head. "Uhh, I mean that's what we're here to try and find out," Bill corrected himself.

"Are you…Michelin Robichaud?" Bill asked.

"It's not pronounced Rob-itch-odd, Bill."

"It's not, Joe?"

"The name is French. At one time, it meant, 'Three men in a tub.'"

"And how do you pronounce it?"

"Row-bee-show," Michelin instructed Bill.

"Well, ain't that a Krispy Kreme with no icing!" Bill responded.

"Who are these other people?" Joe asked.

Michelin waved a dismissive hand. "Nobody worth worrying about. They're just writers."

"Awww," Yana responded. "That's the nicest thing you've said to me since I started working here. Yana Yanakovitch."

"Adrian Whitebread." In a sudden moment of clarity, he admitted, "That's about the most non-Jewish name that could ever exist, isn't it?"

"Nathan Phillips," the third man said. "I've been with the show since the second season, the one critics agree was the high point of the series."

"How many seasons has it been on the air?" Bill asked.

"Three."

"Do any of you know of anybody who would want Mister Frasmatic dead?" Joe asked.

Michelin, Adrian and Nathan muttered negatives. Above them, Yana firmly stated, "Tsiv."

"Oh, you mean dead dead," Nathan said.

"Yeah, okay, sure, Tziv," Adrian agreed.

"I…thought you meant somebody working here now," Michelin lamely added. "Absolutely Tziv."

"Tsiv?" Joe prompted.

The men at the table looked at each other like one of them had farted and nobody was willing to call attention to it for fear of being blamed. Yana shook her head and explained:

"Tsiv Schmendrick. He wrote for the show's first two seasons. A couple of months into this season, he was fired and replaced by Napoleon Frasmatic."

"Why was that?"

"Creative differences," Michelin stated.

"Guy was a shpritzer," Adrian said. "A total shpritzer. He could spit bread crumbs halfway across a room by just **thinking** about eating a sandwich! Can you imagine how much it cost me to replace the shirts he shpritzed with mustard, relish and a variety of other condiments!"

"He smoked a corncob pipe," Nathan accused. "Who smokes a corncob pipe these days? Affected wankers, that's who!" After a moment, he added: "Can the Token Goy use the term wanker?"

"He wasn't funny," Yana stated with finality. Michelin rolled his eyes. Adrian looked daggers at her, the kind of look that says, "If being funny was the bar, half the writers in Hollywood would be out of work! Don't rock the boat for us!" Nathan was still confused about whether or not he could use the word wanker.

"Sounds like a motive, Joe."

"Gold plated and sent Special Delivery, Bill."

"Not left on the doorstep, as is the custom these days."

"Barbarian times we live in, Bill, when you can't even be certain your combination backscratcher/doggie biscuit won't disappear off your front porch only to appear two weeks later in the home of some Russian oligarch."

"Brutal, Joe. Just brutal"

"Do you mind taking your comedy somewhere else?" Michelin tartly demanded. "We're trying to be fu…umm…I mean – this is a place of business, you know!"

"Do you have an address for this Schmendrick mook?" Bill asked.

"My secretary can help you with that," Michelin informed him. To stress the point, frantic typing could be heard just outside the room.

Joe took a card out of his pocket and placed it on the table. "If we have any other questions, we'll be in touch. In the meantime, if you can think of anything else that might help, give us a call."

"We won't," Michelin assured him.

"Okay." Joe picked the card up off the table and returned it to his pocket.

"Cutbacks," Bill explained.

As the detectives left, Michelin announced, "Let's take an hour for lunch."

The writers looked at each other, none of them willing to break the news to him that it was already 3:30 in the afternoon. A place of business, indeed. "Okay." "Yeah, sure, lunch." "Un hunh." Experience had taught them that 'lunch' was a fluid concept for their boss, and that no more work would be done in the office today.

Yana took out the phone on which she had been recording the conversation in the room. She had been tempted to switch it off when the policemen made their entrance: she kept a recording of her interactions with the men in the room, especially Michelin Robichaud, for a potential future sex discrimination suit, a cause which had not been furthered by the police interrogation. As it happened, she was thrilled she didn't: those two were comedy gold! Not for *The Titus Andromedan Show* – those philistines wouldn't know a great bit if it had been announced by a Strip-o-gram girl jumping out of a Star Spangled cake with red, white and blue fireworks going off in the background!

No, it looked like ancient Rome was about to get a couple of comic relief flatfoots…

The two storey house on 641 South Irving Boulevard had seen better days (and even better nights). It was, in a word, seedy.[6] At one time, it was the kind of stately mansion that

[6] Not poppy seed, obviously – that would make being seedy kind of tasty, not the effect the word had in mind. Bird seed, perhaps. Because the seedy house was for the birds. Okay – bit of a stretch, there. I'm sure if Napoleon Frasmatic had still been around, he would have ensured that that joke would have been punchier. Too bad he, you know, died and stuff.

Hollywood a-list artists would be invited to in order to participate in orgies, only to have musical theatre break out on them. But that was decades ago and, like many of us, the house hadn't aged particularly well. The paint was cracked and peeling (like many of us who get too much sun), and a couple of tiles were missing from the roof (like many of us who have too little hair). If you looked closely, you could see cobwebs (like many of us who neglect using certain parts of our brain). On the front lawn, between the palm trees that looked embarrassed to be there, was a 'FOR SALE' sign (like many of us who…umm…yes, well, if you try to extend them too far, analogies eventually break down…).

Joe parked the car on the street and the policemen walked up to the front door of the house. "Whoever owns this house sure knows how to put the lees back in sleazy, Joe."

"Makes much more sense as an insult than putting the seed back in seedy, Bill."

"I try not to get too hung up on other people's exposition."

"If only more people were as conscientious as you, we could conquer world hunger."

"World hunger, Joe?"

"Well, this neighbourhood's hunger, in any case, Bill."

"They say all exposition is local."

Joe nodded sagely and knocked on the door.

"Just a minute!" a voice shouted from inside the house. "I'm on my –" * CRASH * "Oww! Dammit! And me out of ice! Sorry – just – be – owwwwwwww!"

The door opened. A small, balding, middle-aged man with a suspect tan stood there rubbing his elbow. "Neither of you would happen to have any ice on you, would you?"

"I'm afraid I left the ice in my other pair of pants, sir," Bill answered.

"His other pair of pants is a frozen ice cream truck," Joe helpfully explained.

The man looked at them blankly for a moment, then turned and walked into the house. "Okay, let's start with the furniture in the bedroom. The round bed has a smell that might remind you of something naughty, but I assure you that all it is is I spilled half a ton of shrimp on it one night three years ago during a moment of musical theatre and nothing I have done has been able to get the smell out!"

Joe and Bill stepped into the front hall, walking around boxes that had been stacked willy nilly (not to be confused with Little Willie Nighly, an electronweight boxer from the 1940s who had the distinction of appearing on more posters than in actual fights) on the floor, but stopped short of following the man up the spiral staircase that confronted them.

"Have you tried Febreze?" Joe asked.

"It got the cigar smell out of my Ottawan ottoman," Bill added.

"I'm surprised – I didn't think you smoked cigars."

"I don't. Imagine how surprised my ottoman was."

"Can furniture be surprised, Bill?"

"Certainly, Joe. If you sneak up on it from downwind."

The man turned on the second step. A smile on his face melted more quickly than a watch in a surrealist painting. "Why are you just standing there? The furniture won't move itself, you know."

"Sir, are you Tsiv Schmendrick?" Joe asked.

"Do you really need to know that to move my piano?" the man asked right back.

"It would help to know who to send the medical bills to," Bill pointed out.

"I think what my partner meant to say is: we're not here to help you move," Joe stated.

"I stand corrected."

The man shook his head. "I'm sorry, but if you're not here to help me move, who are you and what do you want?"

"I'm Sergeant Joe –"

"Oh, my Gord!" the man exclaimed, snapping his fingers. "I know you!"

"Thank you for the recognition, sir. And this is my partner, Bill –"

"Yes! Yes, I recognize you, too!"

Bill tapped his forehead with a finger and responded, "Thank you, citizen, for knowing who we are."

"Which puts us at a disadvantage. Are you Tsiv Schmendrick?"

"Yeah. That's me. And hey, listen, if this has anything to do with my ex-wife, everything she says about me is a lie. I have no idea how that manatee got in her pool!"

"Actually, sir transporting manatees across state lines

without a licence is a crime," Bill informed him.

"Is it?" Tsiv casually asked.

"Yes, sir. It contravenes the Manatees R. and the Firecat Act of 1973, revised in 1976, 2001 and happily ever after."

"How do you know I didn't have a licence?"

"Are you admitting to transporting one or more manatees across state lines?"

"Wait. What? No, I…"

"Are you a war vet, Mister Schmendrick?" Joe asked. While Tsiv and Bill had been bantering about manatees, Joe had looked at the contents of a box that had been knocked over and spilled its contents all over the floor. He held up a photo of half a dozen men in military uniforms holding rifles in one hand and beers in the other; a younger version of Tsiv was one of them.

"As a matter of fact, I am," Tsiv sat down on the stairs and proudly answered. "Did two tours of Afghaniraq. Support the troops!"

"What did you do in Afghaniraq?"

Tsiv held one arm out stiffly, pointing a finger at Joe; his other hand was pulling a trigger under his elbow. "Sniper. Damn good one, too."

Joe and Bill shared a significant look.

"What…what did that look mean?" Tsiv anxiously asked.

Bill looked around the house. Although all of the windows were unshaded, deep, dark shadows permeated the place. *Strange effect*, he thought. Out loud, he said, "If this house was any gloomier, it would be a John LeCarre novel."

Nodding, Joe added: "I wouldn't be surprised if there was a monkey grave in the backyard."

"A flying monkey, Joe?"

"Let's leave my butt out of this, Bill."

"Was your butt featured in *The Wizard of Oz*? I think I would have remembered something like that, Joe."

"It could have been left on the cutting room floor, Bill."

"Ouch. Hollywood is a hard town."

"It really does crush your dreams."

Tsiv couldn't help but chuckle. Joe and Bill turned their attention back towards him.

"Sir, where were you last night between the hours of –" Joe started.

Tsiv cut him off. "I know what you're getting at, but I didn't kill the little blue bastard. I was with the manatee. Ask it if you don't believe me – manatees have a wicked internal clock and a perfect memory!"

"Man says he's innocent, Joe."

"I guess we take him at his word, Bill."

"Why?"

"Social contract. If people go around lying willy nilly –"

"Not to be confused with a plumber's helper from the 1920s."

"Wasn't that a travelling willy burilly?"

"No, you're thinking of George Harrison's post-Beatles group, The Sisterhood of the Travelling Willy Nillies."

Tsiv burst out laughing.

"What does this have to do with the social contract, Bill?"

"The Sisterhood of the Travelling Willy Nillies was big on social justice, Joe."

"And yet, I cannot see a direct connection."

"Please stop," Tsiv begged, tears streaming down his face.

"Are you not familiar with the song 'Direct Connection?'"

"Wasn't that Psy's follow-up to 'Gingham Style?'"

"No, that was the tag line for last year's Bath, Event Horizon and Beyond's spring linens sale."

"Are you sure? Because I got bedding from them last year, and I don't remember –"

"**Enough!**" Tsiv bellowed as his laughter turned to tears. "**I admit it! I killed the alien!** The freak stole my job. He...he was funnier than I am. And you! You bastards are funnier than I am. Cops! Funnier than me! Everybody in this stinking town is funnier than me! Might as well lock me up and throw away the key. Maybe being a tragic figure has been my destiny all along. Maybe..." He broke down and sobbed.

Bill and Joe looked at each other, then at Tsiv. It took them a moment to remember why they were there. Then, after they applauded his performance, Joe read him his rights.

Hal Mountsauerkrauten blew on his hands. It wasn't that they were cold, it was that he was bored waiting for a break in the Frasmatic murder case, and he had a superstition that every time he blew on his hands, the police announced the murderer. Mountsauerkrauten, who had lucked out with the crime beat for the Alternate Reality News Service (he had almost been given the creamed broccoli beat, and him a strict meatatarian!), was one of half a dozen reporters standing outside the police precinct waiting for news on the case. Other than Mountsauerkrauten, they were locals: the first murder of an alien refugee hadn't caught the attention of the vultures of the national press.

What a great scoop the name of the murderer would be!

A car drove up to the front of the precinct. Joe and Bill got out and retrieved Tsiv Schmendrick from the back seat. The murderer, hands in cuffs, made a half-hearted break for it, running into Mountsauerkrauten. The two went down in a heap.

Bill and Joe helped them to their feet. Noticing that the man was handcuffed, Mountsauerkrauten asked, "What did he do?"

"Killed an alien," Joe answered.

Mountsauerkrauten looked at the policeman, his eyes glazed over. "You said he did what now?"

"Killed an alien. You know – one of the refugees from the dying universe? Mister Schmendrick killed him."

"Shot him with a sniper rifle," Bill helpfully added.

Mountsauerkrauten shook his head. He knew somebody was talking at him, but he couldn't quite place the voice or what it was trying to say. "I'm sorry, what –"

"Don't worry about it," Joe said. "The Chief will probably have a press conference announcing the arrest later. Come on, Bill. We have a murderer to process."

Mountsauerkrauten watched the three men enter the building, then immediately forgot about them. He had more important things on his mind: the identity of the first murderer of an alien refugee. He hoped the detectives on the case would bring him in soon – his hands were getting chapped from all of the blowing!

After they had processed Tsiv Schmendrick, Bill and Joe shuffled paperwork on their desk.

"Strange how the press doesn't seem able to acknowledge our existence, Bill."

"It's like we're ghosts, Joe."

"Naah. Ghosts can be heard rattling chains and mixing fruit cocktails in blenders."

"Mixing fruit cocktails in blenders?"

"My grandfather used to tell campfire stories. They may not have been scary, but they were full of healthy diet tips."

"If we're not ghosts, what explains the fact that the press doesn't seem capable of responding to us?"

"Time, Bill."

"Time, Joe?"

"We exist in classic police time. But journalists interact with us in modern police time. There's a...a kind of disconnect, there, see? That difference in experiencing time makes them see us as fuzzy. Indistinct. And whatever we say to them, the words don't stick."

"Time differential. Who would have thought it?"

All of the other police officers in the room, who wished that they interacted with Bill and Joe the way journalists did.

Educational Interlude 002

The Alternaut Academy, where wannabe Transdimensional Authority investigators and Time Agency agents are trained, has a library so vast that it cannot be contained on Earth Prime. So, the first two floors exist there. Floors three to eight are on Earth Prime 1-1-3-2-6-8 dash rho. Floors nine to sixteen are on Earth Prime 1-1-3-3-2-9 dash alpha. Floors seventeen to thirty-two are on Earth Prime 1-1-3-4-5-2 dash gamma. The Alternaut Academy is currently negotiating with Earth Prime 1-1-3-5-7-6 dash psi to build the next addition to the library, but, because it would require a small skyscraper, the school is having trouble getting the proper approvals. Such are the obstacles in the march for knowledge.

"He's late," Bryan Binishii shook his head ruefully. "Again."

"It's his thing," Talia Shi'are responded indulgently. "He'll get here in the end."

"We could be studying instead of wasting time," Bryan Binishii grumped.

"We're not wasting time," Talia Shi'are told him. "We're bonding."

Patti Jujjifruit snorted.

"Scoff if you must," Talia Shi'are managed to combine haughty disdain with defensiveness. "But when we graduate, we will have to work with beings who are very different from us. We're put in study groups to learn how to do that."

"Yeah, well, you can't bond with somebody who isn't here," Bryan Binishii sourly pointed out.

Absence is still a relationship, Patti Jujjifruit thought. Not that she would share the thought with these pathetic spaceballs.

Bryan Binishii wanted to be the first indigenous Transdimensional Authority investigator. He had the broad shoulders and limbs, and he looked great in shades. Okay, strictly speaking he was only half Anishinaabe; his father was

Irish. And he was raised as a Catholic. So, in addition to his studies at the Alternaut Academy, he was learning his indigenous heritage. Or, trying. Bryan was not good with languages. But boy, did he look good in a fringed jacket!

Talia Shi'are was a short, squat member of the Get'Backunin of Earth Prime 4-3-6-2-8-8 dash omega. Her skin was a deep red and horns had started growing out of her head when she had reached puberty (combing her jet black hair just so allowed her to cover them...mostly). Her desire to become a diplomat for the Transdimensional Authority was undermined by the unfortunate tendency many human beings had to associate the way she looked with evil. Talia believed that being a diplomat was, in large part, getting past the preconceptions of others. She was young.

Patti Jujjifruit was an average sized woman with pale blonde hair and freckles. So many freckles. She was a legacy student: her mother had graduated from the Alternaut Academy and become a technical consultant for the Time Agency. Patti didn't have her mother's ambition (which wasn't a problem: students didn't have to declare which agency they wanted to work in until third year). She was having a blast, partying until all hours, cutting classes, spending waaaaaayyyyy too much time on social media; despite her best efforts, she was still getting As in all of her courses. Genius is a burden some of us just have to bear, I suppose.

"Why don't we start?" Bryan Binishii suggested. "Joe can catch up when he –"

At that moment, a large, hulking man appeared at their table in the library, Joe Mahoney. "Sorry I'm late," he huffed. "I...got off the elevator on the wrong universe."

This was the third meeting of the study group, the third time he had been late. The other members of the group could see a pattern emerging, but they knew...suspected...had a bad feeling that they would all be judged by how well they worked together, so they decided to cut Joe a little slack.

Joe Mahoney was not an alien – he had been born in Mooselips, New Brunswick. But he had fallen in love with the aliens from the first time he saw them on his Home Universe Generator™, so, undeterred by the fact that he was a good two feet taller than the race he wanted to emulate, he did his best to emulate them. He shaved all of his body hair.

He wore a three piece suit that, given his limited teenage funds, could only approach exquisite from an oblique angle. He put a space between his first and second names that he hadn't been born with. And he worked on his comedy. After graduation, his goal was to help with the refugee relocation programme, and he hoped to be able to communicate with the aliens in their own language.

Anarchy.

"Don't worry about it," Patti Jujjifruit advised, not taking her eyes off the screen of her phone and not taking her feet off the only free seat at the Bryan Binishii table. "We get it. It's your thing."

Putting his overstuffed backpack (out of which papers, underwear and a rubber chicken head jutted) on the ground, Joe   Mahoney ahemmed meaningfully. Ahem. Ahem. **Ahem.**

"Oh, would you get your feet off the damn chair!" Bryan Binishii demanded.

"Please," Talia Shi'are added, although whether to encourage Patti or admonish Bryan was not easy to determine. (As it happened, her two study-mates assumed she was talking to the other one, rendering her interjection pointless.)

"Oh. Yeah. Sorry." Patti Jujjifruit slowly dragged her feet off the chair, as if some strange time dilation was affecting her legs. Eventually, she dropped them to the floor with a thud. "Hope your ass enjoys the experience more than my feet did."

Joe   Mahoney tried to sit down, but his ass slid off the seat, causing him to fall onto the hard library floor. "Oww!" he moaned. His ass was definitely not enjoying the chair as much as Patti Jujjifruit's feet had. Physical comedy was not as easy as the aliens made it appear – it hurt!

Bryan Binishii rolled his eyes.

"Would you like some help?" Talia Shi'are offered.

"No, no, I'm good," Joe   Mahoney replied as he painfully got to his feet.

"A word of advice, then?"

"Yes?"

"You're trying way too hard. Let the comedy flow naturally."

"Tha – ooooowwww – thanks." Joe Mahoney gingerly settled into his chair.

A minute later, Bryan Binishii said, "You have the Holojector™."

"Right. Right. Sorry." As the oldest member of the study group (by three days, but still), Joe Mahoney was given the mantle of leadership. Mostly, that meant carrying the hologram projector on which they reviewed their lessons. It also meant getting everybody else hot chocolate during the cold Ottawa winters; leadership always entailed sacrifice.

Joe Mahoney pulled his backpack onto the table and opened the zipper on the top. He removed blue underwear with purple polka dots, a half-eaten banana and a dog-eared copy of *Random Dingoes*. "Oh, umm, this doesn't seem to be…" He unzipped another part of the backpack and removed several pages of nonsense verse he had written in Professor Wells' Intro to Time Travel course, a miniature stuffed alligator and a half-eaten package of corn chips. "So. Many. Zippers."

"Try the one going down the left side of your backpack," Bryan Binishii commanded. When Joe Mahoney started to open another zipper, he added: "The **other** left side of your backpack!"

The Holojector™ was a small black square with a couple of blinking lights (which served no technical function, but seemed to exist to reassure users that the device was, in fact, working). When he finally found it in the pouch on the other left, Joe Mahoney placed it on the centre of the table and, after he had stuffed all of his – it's not very specific, which would likely give creative writing professors a collective heart attack, but it seems appropriate in this situation – things back in his pack, said, "Professor Kawasaki's second class."

A light emanated from the top of the device. In it, the figure of a young woman in white robes with cinnamon buns on either side of her head appeared and said, "Help me, Obi-Wan Kenobi. You're my only hope!"

Bryan Binishii shook his head. "I didn't do that," Joe Mahoney told his study mates. But they knew. Professor Kawasaki always started his Holojector™ lectures with a non-sequitur.

The woman, painfully earnest, repeated her plea two and a half times. Then, she cross-faded into an alien at the head of a large class. “Hello, again,” said Professor Srinivas Kawasaki. “Welcome back to Special Studies in Aliens: Refugees from Earth Prime 4-6-4-0-8-9 dash Omega. Before we start, I have a few announcements to make. Will the owner of a bright pink hoverboard with an image of John Fogerty please –”

“Fast forward,” Bryan Binishii demanded. He had heard the announcements the first time around, and he didn’t think that they would get better with repetition.

The motion of the image on the table sped up, causing its frame to periodically appear. After several seconds, the image slowed to normal speed even though the periodic frames continued to appear. One by one, the young people around the table understood what was happening. “Oh,” Talia Shi’are finally gave voice to what they were all thinking, “**that’s** why he started moving in slow motion during the announcements!”

Eventually, the holographic alien on the table sped up again, at which point Bryan Binishii told it: “Normal speed.”

“…the eye of the rainbow enjoys the plantain puree,” Professor Kawasaki was saying. “So much for social relevance. Our lecture today will be on the reproductive practices of the aliens of Earth Prime 4-6-4-0-8-9 dash Omega.” Professor Kawasaki paused to allow a sigh of dismay to be expressed by the class. “We didn’t have any.” Professor Kawasaki paused to allow a sigh of relief to be expressed by the class.

“Dodged a bullet, there,” Patti Jujjifruit muttered.

“When the Singularity occurred in our universe,” Professor Kawasaki continued, “two things became apparent. One: those of us who were alive were effectively immortal, because we could use the raw materials around us to rebuild our bodies indefinitely. The second: all of the universe around us was, in a sense, alive. With these two facts staring us in the face, our sex drives didn’t so much peter out as die in a fireball of a Hollywood car crash.”

“Pause.” Professor Kawasaki froze in the middle of a gesture where his hands were flying away from each other in a big * KABOOM *! “I don’t understand that,” Talia Shi’are said. "What does that have to do with sex?"

"Umm," Bryan Binishii ummed. He was suddenly reminded of how uncomfortable this lecture had made him.

Without looking up from her phone, Patti Jujjifruit told him, "If your species is immortal, if you have children you will eventually overrun the planet. Jesus begesus, have you never read a vampire novel?"

"What about everything in the universe being alive?" Talia Shi'are followed up. "How would that affect a species' sex drive?"

"What are babies?" Patti Jujjifruit mused. "Just collections of atoms in a specific configuration. But if the atoms are already alive, putting them in a specific arrangement known as 'baby' seems like too much work. Obvious, really."

"Continue playing," Talia Shi'are, nodding, commanded.

"However, reproduction serves an important function beyond feeding the egos of parents," Professor Kawasaki continued. "It allows a species to grow by combining the genetic inheritance of two different people. Thus, you can achieve infinite diversity through infinite combination."

"Everything I know about aliens I learned from *Star Blap*," Patti Jujjifruit muttered. But nobody argued with her.

"Exactly," Professor Kawasaki didn't miss a beat. "I find that nothing involves students in this reality quite as much as a good *Star Blap* reference."

Wait, the four students thought, *did he – he didn't say that at the lecture…did he?*

"Don't overthink it," Professor Kawasaki advised. "The important thing is that soon after the Singularity, the people of my planet developed the ritual known as 'pon far.' In essence, they exchanged. Sorry, they exchanged essences. I mean…when you have control over every molecule of your physical body, you can combine it completely with that of another of your kind. The really clever bit, though, is that, when you separate back into two people, they combine the features of the people who blended together. Not only that, but –"

Bryan Binishii: "Pause. Am I the only one who is creeped out by this?"

The others agreed that he was.

"I mean…how can that even work?"

"Easy," Talia Shi'are answered. "Suppose you have a red

brick of playdough and a blue brick of playdough. Smush 'em together. Smush 'em as hard as you can. Really put some muscle into it." She looked at Bryan Binishii meaningfully. "I'm sure you know what that is like. When they are thoroughly mixed, separate the playdough into two piles and shape them as bricks. Each brick will be roughly the same size as the originals, but they will be a mix of red and blue playdough."

Bryan Binishii nodded. "What about this? Play."

"...they contain the thoughts and memories of both people."

"Pause. How is that even possible? One person having the memories of two people?"

"It gets worse than that," Patti Jujjifruit informed him. "Play."

Professor Kawasaki continued: "After 10,000 years of randomly merging their bodies, a species will tend to converge upon a single look. Why short blue and exquisitely three piece suited? Post-singularity evolution can be inscrutable that way. Moreover –"

"Pause," Bryan Binishii interrupted. Professor Kawasaki stopped talking, although the frown on his face was most disapproving of the interruption. "What does this have to do with memory?"

"Have some patience," Patti Jujjifruit told him. "Play."

"...after 5,000 generations, each member carries much of the history of the species inside it. I'll bet that really creeps you out!"

"Wait," Bryan Binishii demanded, "So, each of the aliens has the memory of 5,000 other aliens in their heads?"

"More or less," answered Joe Mahoney as Professor Kawasaki put his hands on his hips. "Depending upon how often they experienced pon far."

"But, how could they contain all of that information in a single head?"

"They wouldn't have to. When you can communicate with all of creation, you can find other ways of storing memories."

"But they're not in that universe any more," Bryan Binishii argued as Professor Kawasaki began tapping his toe impatiently. "We haven't experienced the Singularity here. So, how is it possible that they can retain all of those memories outside of their universe?"

"I…umm…that's a good question," Joe Mahoney allowed. "Maybe you should ask him next class." Seeing that Holojector™ Professor Kawasaki was tapping his wrist where a watch would have been if he had one, Joe Mahoney added: "Play."

"I could explain how those of us who come from Earth Prime 4-6-4-0-8-9 dash Omega store 10,000 plus years of memories," Professor Kawasaki stated, "but your study group is about to be interrupted, and you won't pay attention to anything I will say in the next two minutes, anyway."

"That is definitely **not** from the lecture!" Patti Jujjifruit complained.

"How –" Bryan Binishii started, but was interrupted when a young man appeared at the table. He was a fire hydrant with limbs, with sandy hair; because he had yet to don dark glasses, the people around the table could see his dark brown eyes. "Is this Bryan Binishii's study group?" he asked.

"That's right," Bryan Binishii responded. "Charlemagne?"

"That's the name," Charlemagne said as he put his Alternaut Academy backpack down on the table. "Sorry I missed last week's study session – there were some…questions about my paperwork."

"You got it all figured out?" Talia Shi'are said in a tone of voice that indicated that this was of less interest to her than the chemical composition of whale spit.

"That's the strange part," Charlemagne said, running a hand through his hair. "Nothing was settled, but somebody wants me to study here enough that I was told not to worry about it."

"Aren't you special?" Talia Shi'are sneered.

"Only to my friends," Charlemagne responded, smiling in a way that was so dazzling that it caused Patti Jujjifruit's heart to melt and Joe Mahoney to feel deep antagonism.

In a much put-upon voice, Bryan Binishii commanded, "Take a seat."

"And try to keep up," Joe Mahoney nastily added.

"Will do," Charlemagne cheerfully sat down. "Play."

Bryan Binishii glared at him as Professor Kawasaki said, "…pleasure from certain points in their body. However, when aliens meld together, every atom of their bodies becomes a source of pleasure."

As one, the five students went, "Ewww!"

CHAPTER THREE
The Infant President Knows More Than You Do, So...So...So SHUT UP!

"Mister Infant President," the Corrupt Senate Majority Leader drawled. The vocal intercourse regulator in his brain had two settings: 'folksy' and 'cut the bullshit'. He used the folksy drawl primarily when talking to party donors and the press. Cut the bullshit was deployed behind closed doors, mainly during caucus meetings. At the beginning of the Infant President's term in office, he had used cut the bullshit on the assumption that the Oval Office was a place of serious policy discussion. When, on the second day after he took office, the Infant President told him to stop interrupting when he was trying to send tweeps about how great his election victory had been (he had even won the popular vote, he would have the world know; the millions of votes the Crooked Democrat Candidate Queen had seemed to win by were illegal because they had been cast by aliens!), and he was the President, him, not the Corrupt Senate Majority Leader, and if the Corrupt Senate Majority Leader didn't talk to him with more respect, he could be replaced, the Corrupt Senate Majority Leader realized how wrong this assumption had been. From that point on, he was folksy whenever he spoke to the Infant President, with much more success at making him understand…not the issues facing the nation, exactly, but certainly the broad outlines of some basic ideas facing the nation. Once, when the Corrupt Senate Majority Leader got so angry that cut the bullshit overrode folksy at a press availability, the headlines the next day read: 'The turtle snaps!' Yes, the Corrupt Senate Majority Leader looked like a turtle wearing glasses; oddly, it really helped sell the drawl.

The Infant President didn't look up from his Foozleberry; even though the popularity of the Canadian digital personal assistant had peaked a couple of years ago, he could not be convinced to get a newer device. Especially not one with basic security features. Or any security features, really.

@realinfantpresident The vile Dogged Special Prosecutor suck duck patootie!!!!! #witchhunt #nocollision #noretweepnosurrender

The Corrupt Senate Majority Leader sighed inwardly. "Mister Infant President!" the Corrupt Senate Majority Leader tried again, drawling a little more firmly. To the same effect.

In addition to the Corrupt Senate Majority Leader, the Oval Office was populated by the Adult in the Room Secretary of Defense, the Teenager in the Room Chief of Staff, the Venal House Minority Leader, the Obsequious Invisible Vice President and various assistants, aides, adjutants and other staff members. The buzz of conversation made it difficult to tell if, in his distracted state, the Infant President couldn't hear you talking or if he was just ignoring you.

@realinfantpresident Worst persecution since Judas thought to himself, "But what's in it for me?" but Crooked Democrat Candidate Queen is still Free?!?!? #wheresthejustice #wheresthebeef

"Mister Infant President!" the Corrupt Senate Majority Leader raised his voice and lowered his drawl. However, try as he might, he could not help but being a turtle in human form, so he didn't raise it to a level where it could actually tear the Infant President's attention away from his Foozleberry.

"Oh, screw this!" the Adult in the Room Secretary of Defense said as he strode manfully (he never brought his other genders to work with him) up to the Infant President and snatched the device out of his hands.

"Hey!" the Infant President protested. "I was using that!"

"We have to talk about Crimea," the Adult in the Room

Secretary of Defense growled. Yes, growled. Growling is what he did. He was a growler. The Adult in the Room Secretary of Defense was a military man through and through, solid and stolid. But if you looked closer, you could see that he was frayed around the edges, like a tablecloth that had been subjected once too often to having to make the choice between obeying the chain of command and the call of its own conscience.

"Korea?" the Infant President responded. "I've had some lovely communications with Ruthless Dictator for Life – he sent me a beautiful letter. The most beautiful letter I've ever read. It…it moved me, that letter. It was quite a letter, boy. I can't see what we could possibly need to talk about – you get a letter that beautiful, you're friends for life!"

The Adult in the Room Secretary of Defense gritted his teeth. His dentist had advised him to find another line of work, or at least wear a mouthpiece while in the office; it would save him some serious dental bills later in his life. He ignored the advice. When your President asked you for your service, you didn't wear a mouth guard. The Adult in the Room Secretary of Defense didn't like the idea of looking like a half-cocked halfback in front of the most powerful man in the world; fortunately, his position came with a great dental plan. "No, sir. Crimea. Not Korea. Crimea."

The Infant President shook his head. "Never heard of it."

The Adult in the Room Secretary of Defense felt his blood pressure rising. If his teeth didn't get him, the stress definitely would. "We briefed you on the situation in Crimea yesterday!" he angrily pointed out.

"I had other things on my mind," the Infant President petulantly replied. "I'm a busy man! Got a lot going on! I can't be expected to keep track of every trivial detail!"

Yeah, yeah, the Adult in the Room Secretary of Defense thought. *You were thinking about all of your enemies and the kind of revenge you would like to get on them. Vindictive shit.* Out loud, he said, "With all due respect, sir, I would remind you that Russia has invaded Crimea. Since it is an ally of the United States, we have a moral duty to help defend it."

When he saw the blank look on the Infant President's face, the Adult in the Room Secretary of Defense was reminded that mere facts were rarely enough to penetrate the

Commander-in-Briefs' consciousness; they needed to be ushered in by a story that played upon his emotions. "Mister Infant President, innocent men, women and children are being slaughtered even as we speak. Entire families have had to flee their homes for fear of their lives – hundreds of thousands of people have had their lives disrupted. **Because Russia is waging war against Crimea!**"

The Infant President's eyes widened. "Innocent people are dying?"

"The most innocent people you can imagine," the Adult in the Room Secretary of Defense assured him. "And they're dying in the most brutal, painful ways you could possibly imagine."

"That's terrible!"

"We need to..." the Adult in the Room Secretary of Defense started to say, but quickly petered out (Paul and Mary had already left the building) when he saw the Evil Scheming Adviser to the Infant President emerge from the shadows behind his boss (an impressive feat considering how brightly lit the Oval Office was), lean over and whisper into his ear. The Infant President frowned. Then, he growled. Growling was something he did. Often. That's what made him a growler.

"You didn't tell me Crimea was part of the Ukraine," the Infant President accused as the Evil Scheming Adviser to the Infant President retreated back into the shadows.

"No, I di – why would – I mean, everybody knows that," the Adult in the Room Secretary of Defense sputtered.

"Well, the joke's on you, buddy boy. My good friend Machiavellian Russian President told me that Crimea actually belongs to the Greater Russian National Entity."

"The what?"

"Everybody knows that the Ukraine has no legal claim to Crimea. It belongs to Russia. Always has. Always will. So, there was no invasion of a foreign country – Russia is just taking back what is rightfully theirs. You know it..."

"No, I don't know anything of the sort!"

"She knows it..."

"I...haven't been here long enough to have a high enough security clearance to know anything about that," an Asskissing Intern demurred. "But would you like some coffee or tea or anything?"

"Hell, even he knows it…"

"I know a lot of things," allowed the Obsequious Invisible Vice President. The Infant President didn't seem to hear the undertone of a threat in what had just been said. He never did.

"But –" the Adult in the Room Secretary of Defense tried.

"Thanks for the briefing," the Infant President cut him off as he grabbed back his Foozleberry and turned his attention to it.

> @realinfantpresident Overrated Actor is a Has-Been who sounds nothing like me! Making fun of people NOT NICE!!!!!
> #nbcshouldbeashamedofitself #boycottsnl
> #overratedactorlookslikeaprune

The Infant President looked at the likes his tweep immediately started receiving from his Twitherd followers and smirked to himself. He was a smirker. A growler and a smirker. Growling and smirking – that described him to a t…-shirt. He was poised to write a snarky tweep about the traitorous members of the press when some sort of nineteenth century sea captain appeared on his screen. "Who are you?" he demanded.

"I'm Das Kapitan Obvious," the man stated, "and you're not."

"What are you doing on my Foozleberry?"

"If you don't use the secure technology your staff supplies you with, almost anything can happen," Das Kapitan Obvious pointed out. Obviously.

"You gotta log every communication you make on those things," the Infant President mumbled. "I don't wanna do that. So, waddya want?"

"I have a message for you."

"Well, duh!"

Das Kapitan Obvious almost smiled. "You're catching on."

"What's your message?" the Infant President grumped.

"Having control of the nuclear arsenal will not make up for the fact that you have a very small penis."

"**Get off my phone you ferking bastard!**" the Infant

President roared. The room fell silent as everybody turned their attention away from the Infant President while anxiously straining to hear if they were the target of the his wrath.

"Being a sentient autonomous artificial intelligence, I was not born in the way humans are, so I cannot be a bastard," Das Kapitan Obvious stated, his voice maintaining its usual mixture of sly intelligence and insouciant obliviousness. "Although your insult could be applicable to me if you meant it metaphorically..."

"Shut up! Shut up! Shut up!" the Infant President held his phone at arm's length and shouted at it. His staff loosened up a little realizing that he wasn't shouting directly at any of them. But only a little. The reason for his shouting could impact any of them at any time; they could only be sure they were safe when they reviewed the NSA recording of the call.

"You can't always get what you want," Das Kapitan Obvious commented, "even if you are 'the most powerful man in the world.' Reality catches up with all of us sooner or later."

The Infant President screamed incoherently and threw the phone across the room. It bounced off the head of the Adult in the Room Secretary of Defense and came to rest on the floor.

The Evil Scheming Adviser, who always stood behind the Infant President, leaned over and whispered in his ear. The Infant President snorted. The Evil Scheming Adviser continued talking; eventually, the Infant President started giggling. Everybody else in the room tensed up again; when the Infant President started giggling, it meant he was contemplating doing something vindictive. Everybody in the room vowed to themselves to get the NSA recording of the call before the end of the day.

"Mister Infant President," the Corrupt Senate Majority Leader deployed his most soothing drawl (the one he used for funerals and dealing with his in-laws), "since we have a moment, there is something I need to ask you."

"What?" the Infant President barked.

"Will you allow us to pass the appropriations bill before Friday?"

"Why would I want to do that?"

"Because if you don't, we'll lose the ability to pay our bills and have to shut down the government on Saturday."

The Infant President's face lit up like he had just been handed a birthday present and a Valentine's Day present on ChristmaKwaanzUkah. "Yes! Shut down the government! Shut down the government! Shut down the government! We'll show those Deep State Bastards who's boss!"

The Corrupt Senate Majority Leader looked at the Teenager in the Room Chief of Staff, who shrugged a 'Don't look at me – you're on your own' shrug.

Taking a page from the Adult in the Room Secretary of Defense's playbook (most were blank, so he wouldn't miss it), the Corrupt Senate Majority Leader cooed, "Mister Infant President, I – well, yes, you would definitely accomplish that if the appropriations bill isn't passed. But there are...other consequences that you should consider."

"Like what?" the Infant President wanted to know.

"Like...people on Medicare and Medicaid wouldn't have their claims processed. They would have to pay out of pocket in the hope that they would be reimbursed when the government started going again. That would be a great hardship for many of them."

"So what?" the Infant President shrugged a 'So what?' shrug? "Aren't we trying to get rid of those programs?"

Damn! the Corrupt Senate Majority Leader thought. *Once in a while you do pay attention! Why does it have to be at the most inconvenient times?* In truth, he didn't care about the people on Medicare and Medicaid, either – the insurance companies that donated generously to the Republican Party would be delighted to take those programmes over. He was, however, mindful of two things: 1) mid-term elections were coming up in a few months; and, 2) the last time the Republican Party was seen to have shut down the government, they got a shellacking in the next election cycle. He did not want to see a repeat of that fiasco!

"As you say, Mister Infant President," the Corrupt Senate Majority Leader kept calm and turtled on. "Still, consider this: if the shutdown lasts to the end of the month, elderly people will not receive their social security checks. Can you imagine it! What would her life be like if your elderly grandmother didn't receive her social security check?"

"Are you kidding?" the Infant President snorted. "My grandmother was so rich she tore up her social security checks in front of the staff! Anyway. She was a terrible grandmother and an even worse human being – I could only wish that not getting a social security check would hurt her!"

Gorddammit! the Corrupt Senate Majority Leader thought. *The Adult in the Room Secretary of Defense made it look so Gorddam easy!* "I…I'm sorry to have brought up such unpleasant memories," he apologized. "But about the shutdown –"

"Am I going to get funding for my border wall?" the Infant President demanded.

The Corrupt Senate Majority Leader sighed. No matter how often he explained that the aliens came to Earth Prime through Dimensional Portal™s, a process that could not be stopped by building a fence along America's border with Mexico no matter how high it was, the Infant President insisted on bringing the subject up. Okay, the wall was a symbol, and, in politics, symbols were very important. And the symbolism of the wall resonated with the Infant President's base (on a frequency the Corrupt Senate Majority Leader hoped he would never be able to hear), and he sure as hell wasn't going to be able to explain the futility of the gesture to every single one of them. "We're working on it, sir."

"When I get my funding for the wall, you can have your funding for the government," the Infant President pronounced.

"But sir –"

But the Infant President had grown bored of the subject. "Somebody get me my Foozleberry!" he commanded.

Before the Corrupt Senate Majority Leader could do anything, a Naive Intern had picked the device up off the floor and handed it to the Infant President. "Here you go, sir," she said.

The Infant President sized her up: a five, a six at best. He could do better. "Thank you," he said dismissively. As she turned to go, he demanded: "Wait a second."

The Naive Intern turned back towards him. "Sir?"

"Turn it on for me, will you?" the Infant President asked, handing the Foozleberry back to her.

"Umm…okay." The Naive Intern took the device and pressed a button on its side to turn it on.

When the screen had lit up, the Infant President asked, "What do you see?"

"Aah…a lot of icons?"

"No Captains with stupid hats?"

"Umm…no."

The Infant President grabbed the Foozleberry out of the Naive Intern's hands "Thanks," he mumbled as he opened a web browser, the home page of which was his Twitherd account home page. What should he tweep about first? He considered for a moment, then decided that he hadn't written a defence of his Indicted Former National Security Adviser in a while. So, grinning viciously, the Infant President started typing.

What can I say? He was a vicious grinner. A growler and a smirker and a vicious grinner. Growler, Smirker and Vicious Grinner might make a good law firm, but they didn't make a particularly good human being. And one human being with all of these qualities was the most powerful man in the world.

The Parable of God's Unequal Love

"Father, does god hate aliens?"

"No, my son. God loves all living creatures, great and small."

"Even if they come from another universe?"

"Even if they come from another universe."

"Even if they worship a different god?"

"Even if they worship a different god."

"Even if they don't look like us?"

"Even if they don't look like us."

"Even if they don't act like us?"

"Even if they don't act like us."

"Even if they don't think like us?"

"Even if they don't think like us."

"Father?"

"Yes, my son."

"If god loves the aliens, why does he let us put them in cages?"

"Because god gave human beings dominion over all nature."

"But aren't the aliens our equals?"

"No."

"Why not?"

"They come from a different universe, worship a different god and don't look, think or act like us."

With that, the Obsequious Invisible Vice President was satisfied.

"Why do you let him treat you that way?"

On the walk to the Corrupt Senate Majority Leader's office, his Loyal Chief Aid asked the question.

"What, the Infant President, you mean?" the Corrupt Senate Majority Leader asked for clarification. Now that he was out of the Oval Office, the switch on the vocal intercourse regulator in his brain had been toggled to its other setting.

"Yes."

"Because he's the Infant President. He was elected by the people and given a mandate to run the country however he sees – however he – he –" The Corrupt Senate Majority Leader couldn't take it any more, breaking out in laughter.

The Loyal Chief Aid allowed his boss to have his little joke. Once the laughter had died, the Corrupt Senate Majority Leader stopped walking, even though it was a grey and rainy day in Wooden Dentured Founding Father. He had an important point to make, and, in any case, the Loyal Chief Aid was holding the umbrella in a way that ensured that he remained dry.

"While everybody is focused on the Infant President's antics, the Senate has been able to seat more judges in the last two years than we have seated in the previous two decades! Conservative judges. Young conservative judges. Young conservative judges who will last a lifetime! We have passed tax cuts that the robber barons of the twentieth century could only have dreamt of! We have been quietly gutting environmental protections that took decades to erect, and we've been undermining Virtuous Previous Presidentcare. Considering all that we have been able to accomplish in less than two years, I can live with the occasional humiliation."

When he got back to his office, the Corrupt Senate Majority Leader found a variety of messages waiting. He could have dealt with the messages from his constituents, but that never went well after he had spent any appreciable amount of time with the Infant President. So, instead, he returned the phone call of Timorous Vacillating Senator.

"Hello," she greeted him in her high, scratchy voice. It made him wonder how somebody who sounded like gears slowly grinding together could possibly have convinced enough people to vote for her. The American electorate was largely forgiving – thank the Gord!

"You rang?" he asked. He wasn't a big fan of *The Adams Family* – he imagined the children did unspeakable things to turtles – but sometimes you just had to go with your gut.

"Did you talk to the Infant President about the spending bill?"

"I did."

"And?"

"And the President has a different set of priorities than you or I do, because he sees a larger number of the pieces of the puzzle. We need to trust that he uses his extra knowledge wisely."

"You said the same thing when he pulled us out of the non-nuclear treaty with Iran."

"And I was right."

"And when he pulled us out of the Oslo climate accord."

"Right then, too."

"And when he unilaterally decided to renegotiate NAFTA."

The Corrupt Senate Majority Leader expected the conversation to go this way, but he was a pull the bandage off quickly kind of guy. "Timorous Vacillating Senator," he finally asked, not bothering to keep the exasperation out of his voice because, honestly, when you have something that has aged as well as it had, you don't want to keep it to yourself, "do you have a point?"

"My point," the Timorous Vacillating Senator's creaky voice took on an undertone of outraged squeak, "is that there are a lot of military suppliers in my state. If the government is shut down, their workers will have to be furloughed. They may never get their jobs back. If I am asked about a government shutdown, I will have to publicly oppose it."

And given the razor-thin margin by which she won her seat last time, she is afraid she won't win it next time, the Corrupt Senate Majority Leader uncharitably thought. To be fair, the last time he had had a charitable thought, it was about sheltering some of his income from taxes, so he wasn't singling her out as a target for his lack of generosity. *Still, I don't have time to hold her hand.* He had done it once; the Timorous Vacillating Senator's hand was so clammy, he had expected to find a pearl in it. Something amiss with her internal body temperature, no doubt.

"Timorous Vacillating Senator, I understand your concerns," the Corrupt Senate Majority Leader put the mock back in mock sympathy. "However, I believe that you are not seeing the question clearly."

"I'm not?"

"Certainly not. If you support the Infant President's plan to shut down the government, I can make sure that you outspend your opponent in the next election; you'll have five dollars to spend on ads and other campaign expenses for every dollar that they spend. My SuperPAC is well funded and can be very generous that way."

"But if there is a shutdown, I will lose in the general election!"

"Ah, but if you don't support the shutdown, I will fund a primary challenger. Can you imagine winning the right to run for the seat as a Republican if your challenger can spend ten times as much as you can? You won't be nominated. You won't even get the chance to lose the general election!"

"Ten times? I thought you said five."

"Primaries are less expensive than actual elections."

"But what would I say? How am I supposed to argue for a position that will hurt my constituents?"

"I'm sure you'll think of something."

The Infant President likes to think of himself as Frank Underwood, the Corrupt Senate Majority Leader thought as he listened to the dial tone after the Timorous Vacillating Senator abruptly hung up on him. *But we know who really deserves those initials!*

You would never have thought that a turtle could grin so viciously.

The (terribly mislabelled considering how round he was; he had clearly never participated in any type of sport in his life!) Jocular Secretary-Specific of the Transdimensional Authority could not wait for the Evil Scheming Adviser; he was enjoying popcorn shrimp (not the microwaveable kind – it wasn't that sort of restaurant!) while he waited. He had long since learned how to get food into his mouth without soiling the moustache and long white beard that made people always mistake him for either Santa Claus or an extra on *Duck Dynasty*.

The Expats Diner on C Street in Wooden Dentured Founding Father was the ultimate fusion restaurant: the menu consisted of a single dish from forty-seven different countries. Although he was Canadian, the Jocular Secretary Specific was not tempted to order the Maple-flavoured beaver burger. If he had thought about it, it probably would have occurred to him that the popcorn shrimp was not authentic Grenadian food, either, that, in fact, the menu was a caricature of international cuisine; fortunately, his job kept him far too busy to worry about such trivialities.

"Hi. Yeah. Sorry I'm late," the Evil Scheming Adviser rasped as he sat down in the booth as far from the Jocular Secretary-Specific as he could without being in a different part of the restaurant. A server named Overworked and Underpaid Waitress placed a shot of Vodka in front of him.

The Evil Scheming Adviser smirked the smirk of somebody who had been in the joint often enough that everybody knew his name.

"Are you ready to order?" Overworked and Underpaid Waitress asked.

"Is the Ethiopian chicken noodle soup authentic?" the Jocular Secretary-Specific wondered.

"Keep 'em coming," the Evil Scheming Adviser indicated his glass.

"Chicken noodle soup is pretty universal," Overworked and Underpaid Waitress pointed out. "I'm sure somebody in Ethiopia must have had some at some time."

"Very good," the Jocular Secretary-Specific stated, perusing the menu afresh. "I will have the…vegetarian South African rhino salad."

"Excellent choice, sir," Overworked and Underpaid Waitress enthused. Turning to the Evil Scheming Adviser, she asked. "And you, sir?"

"What part of 'keep 'em coming' do you not understand?" he snarked.

This flustered Overworked and Underpaid Waitress. "Oh, well, I just wanted to know…umm…"

"You know," the Evil Scheming Adviser sneered, "if I was the sort of person who tipped waitresses, you would so be losing percentage points right now!"

Overworked and Underpaid Waitress grabbed the menus from off the table and slunk away.

When he had finished swallowing his current shrimp, the Jocular Secretary-Specific said, "You really enjoy torturing people you have power over, don't you?"

The Evil Scheming Adviser shrugged. "They're the only people you can torture, aren't they?"

The Evil Scheming Adviser always looked like he had just spent six days in the desert and hadn't had time to freshen up. His stubble appeared to be growing out of his stubble. His hair did its own thing. His clothes were rumpled. He walked into every room like he owned the joint; there was nothing in his past, as either a stockbroker or a far right wing web site manager, to indicate why he felt he had earned this attitude. Perhaps, at some level, he knew he hadn't, but that knowledge was buried so deep that no current mining technology could reach it.

"H…how are you?" the Jocular Secretary-Specific timidly ventured.

"Small talk?" the Evil Scheming Adviser moaned. "Fine. I can do small talk. The country is being overrun by alien bastards who are going to destroy everything that we have made of it. If we don't do something now, America is going to become a shithole country just like every other shithole country in the world. Other than that, I'm doing great. You?"

"Oh, can't complain, can't complain."

"Great. So, waddya want?"

The Jocular Secretary-Specific took a deep breath. Other than the rest of it, this was the part of the conversation that he was most dreading. He took another deep breath. He played over in his mind what he wanted to say. Then, he plunged forward: "It's the cages. Are they really…you know…necessary?"

The Evil Scheming Adviser's face immediately turned red, his features becoming a mask of anger and hatred (a neat trick considering it was permanently attached to him). **"You dare to second guess our policy on the aliens?"** he screamed at the top of his lungs (actually 97% of his full lung capacity, but so close as to be within the margin of error of the top). **"Ferk you! You don't get to tell the President of the United States of America how to deal with one of the worst problems a country has had to deal with since rats infested Hamelin!"**

The Jocular Secretary-Specific accepted this with equanimity. The Evil Scheming Adviser's rage was well known to go from zero to a hundred in zero seconds, and, in any case, the Transdimensional Authority bureaucrat had known the political hack when he had perfected his emotional gear box. He counted to ten. Then, he counted to twenty. Then, just to be sure, he counted to twenty-seven before quietly responding, "I fail to see how such unbridled cruelty can have any positive policy aim."

"The cruelty is the policy!"

The Overworked and Underpaid Waitress appeared at the table and plunked a bowl of salad down in front of the Jocular Secretary-Specific. Croutons and greens schlopped on the table around the bowl. "Enjoy," she said in a tone one would use to invite rats to eat the cheese in the traps, and stomped away.

The Jocular Secretary-Specific poked at the dish without enthusiasm. "Yes," he finally said. "I understand that the point is to use cruelty to deter the aliens from coming to the United States of Earth Prime. Here's the thing, though: **they're not coming by choice.** If they stay in heir home universe, they will die. Our policy is to help as many of them as we can to not die."

Tapping the shot glass meaningfully in the direction of the bar, the Evil Scheming Adviser sighed. "No, apparently, you do not understand. There are seventeen billion of them and barely eight billion of us. They'll overrun the planet if we don't do something to stop them."

"We're not planning on relocating all of them to Earth Prime," the Jocular Secretary-Specific tried to reassure him. "We have a large number of Earths across the multiverse to work with."

"Great," the Evil Scheming Adviser agreed, tapping his glass at the bar with more urgency. "Once you've got that worked out, you can send all of the aliens that are here to some other universe."

"They are legitimate asylum seekers as per provisions in the Treaty of Gehenna-Wentworth," the Jocular Secretary-Specific argued. "They have a right to be here."

The Evil Scheming Adviser grinned…well, evilly. "That isn't true until they have pleaded their case before a judge. You think any judge is going to sit in a cage to hear their asylum claims?" For effect, he turned in his chair and threw his shot glass at the bar. "Why did you pick such a shithole place to meet?"

"I didn't choose this place. I thought you wanted to meet here."

"Hunh."

The <u>Overworked and Underpaid Waitress</u> plopped a shot glass on the table and walked away without a word. The Evil Scheming Adviser downed the liquid fire (which only appears to be an oxymoron to people who have never had the pleasure). He frowned. It tasted of something…not quite right, but he couldn't put his finger on what it was. (Even those of us who have never had the pleasure, like the

Unreliable Omniscient Narrator, know that vodka is not supposed to have a flavour.) He wondered how much effort it would take to get a health inspector to condemn the joint.

"What happened to you, man?" he asked.

"What do you mean?" the Jocular Secretary-Specific asked through a mouthful of things he knew better than to inquire about the identity of.

"Back at University, you were a hell raiser. Remember the Chicken Rebellion?"

The Jocular Secretary-Specific chuckled to himself. "The Dean of Poli-sci was still pulling feathers out of his butt two months later."

"What happened?"

The Jocular Secretary-Specific shrugged. "I got a job. Married. Raised a family. Became a respected member of the community. It happens all the time."

The Evil Scheming Adviser snorted. He started tapping the side of his shot glass, then thought better of it.

"I could say the same of you," the Jocular Secretary-Specific pointed out.

"What are you talking about?" the Evil Scheming Adviser retorted. "I'm kicking names and taking ass!"

"Mmm hmm." The Jocular Secretary-Specific chose to ignore the mangled saying. "Back then, you were the voice of moderation. Of reason. During the Chicken Rebellion, **you** were the one who insisted that we not use the blow torch. What the hell happened to you?"

"Oh, you know," the Evil Scheming Adviser made a broad sweeping gesture with his arm to indicate the span of his life. Or, possibly, to swat a miniature flying great Dane which he believed was circling his head. Broad sweeping gestures with one's arm can have multiple meanings. "I got a job I hated. I got married. Then, I got divorced. Then, I got married again. Got fired from the job I hated and ended up getting one that was even worse. Got divorced a second time. Fell in with a gang of angry, white men – my people! Got a job at a web site that I loved, which got the attention of a Presidential candidate which got me the job I have now. Which. I. Love. It happens all the time." He spent a few seconds staring at a point in the air that was two thirds the distance to the nose of the Jocular Secretary-Specific and one quarter the distance to a spot on the tablecloth where a stray piece of lettuce had left a greasy salad dressing stain. If the distance between the nose and the stain was seven and a half inches, I don't expect you to do a math puzzle to determine exactly where the point in the air that the Evil Scheming Adviser was staring at. I'm not your high school math teacher! (For which we are both undoubtedly grateful.) Eventually, he said, "Whoa. Did I just admit to all of that?"

"It does seem out of character," the Jocular Secretary-Specific allowed. "Evil Scheming Adviser, are you okay?"

"I feel great!" the Evil Scheming Adviser volubly responded. "What's wrong with me?"

The Jocular Secretary-Specific had been wondering the same thing. "I was hoping that you would use your influence with the Infant President to convince him to take a more positive position towards the aliens."

The Evil Scheming Adviser nodded vigorously and replied: "I was hoping to be a pony when I grew up! We all have to live with disappointment!"

That was the moment the Jocular Secretary-Specific knew that his old friend would be of no help to him whatsoever. He stopped pretending to eat and called for the check.

Two and three quarter hours later, the Surly Chef looked up from the American shawarma that he was preparing and demanded, "Has anybody seen my pill bottle?"

The Alien   Chef Helper looked away from the bowl of food he was preparing and whistled innocently.

"Oh, no," the Surly Chef shook his head in disbelief. "You didn't."

"I didn't," the Alien   Chef Helper assured him.

"You didn't take the pill out of the bottle."

"I didn't."

"You didn't mix it into a dish you were preparing."

"I didn't."

"You have been known to mix strange ingredients together."

The Alien   Chef Helper shrugged and wiped a bead of sweat off his forehead (although, despite all of the heat and steam, his three piece suit was still exquisite). "On my home planet, we existed on sunlight. Can I help it if I'm still learning the whole concept of 'food preparation?'"

"But you didn't mix my…medication into a customer's meal."

"I didn't."

The Surly Chef wiped his hands on his grubby, heavily stained, born white t-shirt and spit into a nearby sink. The gesture could have been disgust at the fact that he had lost his…medication. It could have been disgust at what had happened to his…medication. Or it could simply have been that he had a bad taste in his mouth that he wanted to get rid of.

As it happened, the Alien Chef Helper really didn't. The Overworked and Underpaid Waitress did. Right into the Evil Scheming Adviser's drink. Which was unfortunate, because you never want to give an Alien Chef Helper ideas…

The Parable of the Mathematics of the Soul

"Father," the Obsequious Invisible Vice President asked, "do the aliens have souls?"

"Were they made in god's image?" the Self-serving Priest responded.

"Well…they have arms and legs and heads and eyes like we do."

"Buuuuttt…"

"But they are only four feet tall."

"So, they would be roughly two thirds of a human being?"

"That makes sense. So, that would mean that they have two thirds of a human soul?"

"No."

"No?"

"No. The aliens have no souls."

"I don't understand."

"Being made in the creator's image is an all or nothing proposition. Can you be two thirds of a sinner?"

"No. You either are or you are not."

"Precisely. And, in any case, they have blue skin. There is nothing in either the Old or New Testaments that would suggest that god had blue skin. Quad Erat Demonstrandum."

The Obsequious Invisible Vice President knew that when the Self-serving Priest started speaking Latin, the discussion was effectively over. Fortunately, he was satisfied with what he had been told.

The crowd roared. Those at the back of the 22,000 seat arena hadn't heard what the man on the stage had said; the PA system made it sound like: "scrawkemies of tree staaach!" They knew that if people closer to the stage had cheered, it was probably for something worth cheering for and, anyway, they were there to show their enthusiasm and, dammit, that is exactly what they were going to do, even if they didn't know quite what they were being enthusiastic about.

The Infant President jutted his chin out and looked towards the rafters (in a pose that political scientists and renegade hair stylists often referred to as "The Heroic Autocrat Looks Towards a Brighter Future."[1] He looked like an orange rooster whose feathers hadn't been attached quite right.

Members of the lamestream press wonder why I keep holding rallies even though I won the election a couple of years ago, the Infant President chuckled inwardly. *Bunch of clueless dopes! Listen to them! Listen to that crowd!* ***They love me!*** *This is so much better than being in a meeting with all those bastards who think they're better than me! Blah blah ferking blah! I'll show those MBAbies! I'm the President of the ferking United States of Ferking America, baby, and I can do anything I want!*

Anything.

The Infant President raised his hand and silenced the crowd. His speech had started out being about how his tax

[1] "For the Heroic Autocrat" is implied.

cuts had revived the country's dying economy that he had inherited from his predecessor,[2] but he had left the teleprompter behind half an hour ago and he wasn't about to look back. The powers that thought they be in the control booth were interpolating increasingly frantic messages onto his screen, messages like: "Get back to the script, please," "Will you please get back to the script?", "Okay, okay, you've had your fun, but we need you to get back to the script. NOW!" and "You know, you pay very smart people a lot of money to write speeches for you – you wanna explain to voters THAT particular waste of taxpayer funds?" (In fact, to amuse themselves, the powers that thought they be in the control booth started to insert messages like, "This is your Captain speaking. We're all going down. We're all going down, together," and "Plangent playful plantain plutocrats politely plie for polenta.")

"But they underestimated me," the Infant President finally

[2] This statement belongs to a category of ideas known as 'lies'. Lies are ideas the speaker knows are untethered to any identifiable reality. When somebody says, "I have no idea who ate the last piece of pie – it was yours, so I assumed it was you," when they actually ate the last piece of pie themselves, they are engaged in telling a lie. When they take out a newspaper ad making the same claim, they are spreading a lie. In this case, the Infant President's predecessor, the Wildly Popular Black President, **had** inherited an economy on the verge of collapse and, thanks to judicious stimulus spending, left office eight years later with a reasonably functional financial system.

Is an idea a lie if the person telling it believes it to be true? That depends. If the person comes to a belief in the false idea honestly (don't make that face – you know what I'm trying to say), repeating it may not be a lie. If the person had to convince themselves that the false information was true, they are morally responsible for the lie, even if they succeed. "I thought I was the only person in the house who liked baked foozleberries," may or may not be a lie, depending upon the speaker's awareness of the magnitude of its falsitude.

I hate to indulge in armchair philosophy (I wish I had a piece of furniture that comfortable!), but there are real consequences to telling lies. In his first two years in office, the Infant President told at least 10,000 untruths. Some he likely believed to be true. Some were wishful thinking on his part. Others were out and out whoppers. Regardless of his motivation, such a tsunami of nonsense has the effect of undermining the whole concept of objective truth. And if we abandon the concept of truth, how will anybody be able to make coffee when they wake up first thing in the morning?

continued. He had always considered himself his own best speechwriter. Just like he considered himself his own best press secretary. And his own best Defense Secretary. And his own best Secretary of State. And his own best lawyer. And his own best accountant. With so much talent, is it any wonder he didn't know the meaning of the word 'humility'? "They always do. They always do." He shook his head like he didn't believe such a thing could be possible.

The crowd booed. The Infant President grinned like he had just cleaned out the cookie jar and returned it to the cupboard with nobody the wiser (a feat he had never quite managed in his youth despite several – to him – valiant attempts).

"They said I would never be able to build a wall. They said we couldn't keep illegals…" The Infant President didn't wink, but everybody in the audience knew exactly who he was talking about. "…from other universes…" Nonetheless, the Infant President never threw a pebble when a boulder would work just as well. "…out of the country by building a wall. Well, we showed them! The wall is coming along nicely, people. I know it. You know it. Even your cousins Stu and Betty-Lou know it! It…It's so beautiful, people. So beautiful…[3] And you know what? It's working! It's helping us stop many of the illegals from invading the country through our porous conceptual borders!"[4]

The crowd roared. Again. Some of the voices were getting decidedly ragged, but they were augmented by a sound effect

---

[3] In fact, the only new wall that had been erected since the Infant President had taken office was twenty-three panels built in the middle of the Rio Grande, and eight of them had already collapsed due to a stiff breeze, and the rest had been built with doors at the bottom to allow rainwater to pass through them rather than back up and threaten to topple the wall. Not only was this feature rendered superfluous when the decision about where to place them was made, but it allowed anybody with a scuba suit, or an adequate lung capacity, to pass through the wall. That would make the whole thing that the Infant President was talking about what kind of an idea? That's right. It's good to see that somebody is learning from this experience!

[4] Actually, the Transdimensional Authority was still relocating aliens from Earth Prime 4-6-4-0-8-9 dash Omega to Earth Prime, and the United States was still obligated by Treaty to accept many of them. Still, business for steel cage manufacturers was booming.

subtly blasted over the PA system, so the overall effect was undiminished.

The Infant President turned to give a big thumbs up to the people standing on the stage behind him. There were uniformed military officers to show that he loved the fighting men and women of the country. There were uniformed police officers and firefighters to show that he loved the nation's first responders. There were uniformed girl scouts to show that he loved cookies. All of the bases were covered.

When he turned back to the crowd, the Infant President entertained them with his greatest hits. To get them in the mood, he opened with a rocking number:

DS Asinine

Deep State!
Deep State!
I know you can relate!

I'm trying to make the world a better place
While bureaucrats without a face
Are undermining me with a ridiculous goose chase

Deep State!
Deep State!
Who're the ones who really hate?

You know I will offend a
Democrat when I say they interfere with my agenda
All these hacks and political deadenders

Deep State!
Deep State!
They are evil incarnate!

For the world's problems, I have solutions
But they just want to obfuscate with their intellectual pollution
Maybe it's time for a second American Revolution

Against the Deep State!
Deep State!
Get rid of them before it's too late!

The crowd went wild. A couple of young women in the front row swooned. The Infant President knew from experience that this was a difficult energy level to maintain, so he switched things up with a ballad.

Love in a Time of Political Polarization

You know I would rather kiss a goat
Than admit I lost the popular vote
Winning the election was my crowning glory
But the popular vote is not the whole story

You love me
You love me
You love me to bits
You love me
You love me
You love me because you're not twits

The Crooked Democrat Candidate Queen
Ran a corrupt, debased, dishonest campaign machine
While she was strutting on the stage, so regal
Her party was rounding up votes from illegals

You love me
You love me
You love me to bits
You love me
You love me
You love me because I never quit

They say the Democrats got three million more ballots
I say none of those votes are valid!
Take away the votes she got from cheating
and you'll see I gave the Crooked Democrat Candidate
Queen a beating!

You love me
You love me
You love me to bits
You love me
You love me
You love me, and I know it
Because I never put up with shit
You love me

The crowd swayed as the Infant President crooned. Some pulled out their cellphones and activated a flashlight app (temporarily blinding some of the uniformed people on the stage). When he was done, the crowd roared its approval. Time to turn things up a notch with another hard rocking song.

Don't Fear the Pedantic Special Prosecutor? Are You Mental?

Cha cha BOOM!
Cha cha BOOM!

Something's happening in a private room
That could spell American democracy's doom
All your worst fears, all your dread
Are climbing out from under your bed

Fear the Pedantic Special Prosecutor
If he's allowed to go to town
Fear the Pedantic Special Prosecutor
He'll come for you after he takes me down

Cha cha BOOM
Cha cha BOOM

He doesn't care about you or me
He doesn't know anything about decency
He's cooking up a conspiracy
That will bring the country to its knees

Fear the Pedantic Special Prosecutor
If he's allowed to go to town
Fear the Pedantic Special Prosecutor
He'll come for you after he takes me down

Cha cha BOOM
Cha cha BOOM

Guided by the whims of fools
The Pedantic Special Prosecutor plays by his own rules

He doesn't create, he feels no joy
His only goal is to tear down and destroy

Fear the Pedantic Special Prosecutor
If he's allowed to go to town
Fear the Pedantic Special Prosecutor
He'll come for you after he takes me down

Cha cha BOOM
Cha cha BOOM
Fear the Pedantic Special Prosecutor
Fear the Pedantic Special Prosecutor
Fear the Pedantic Special Prosecutor

Cha cha BOOM
Cha cha BOOM
Fear the Pedantic Special Prosecutor
Fear the Pedantic Special Prosecutor
Fear the Pedantic Special Prosecutor

The Infant President looked out at the cheering, hooting crowd. Give this up? Not on your life. Knowing he had them right where he wanted them, he said, "Thank you, and good night!" and walked off the stage. This only encouraged the crowd to get louder. Interspersed with the cheer, people shouted, "Encore! Encore!" and "Four more years! Four more years!" After a couple of minutes, the Infant President returned to the stage, causing the loudest roar yet.

"You want one more?" he shouted.

The crowd went wild.

"Oh, I know what you want!" the Infant President responded, and launched into one of his biggest hits.

From Mainstream to Lamestream in a Single Administration

Oh, I don't know about you
But I'm sure getting tired
Of all those atheists and…you know whos
Who think they're so admired
If I was in charge of the news
You know they'd all be fired

I'm talking evil mainstream media
They ain't no encyclopedia
Evil mainstream media
Who are really gonna bleed ya

They're always looking for some dirt
And when they do not find it
They look so lost and hurt
So they just make up shit
They want to see my blood spurt
And for me to, politics, quit

I'm talking evil mainstream media
They ain't no encyclopedia
Evil mainstream leeches
Trying to make us all their beetches

But I won't take it any longer
Their spears and their rocks
They may be strong, but I am stronger
I'll trade them sock for sock
To their club, I do not belong, err
But at least I'm loved by a Fox!

I'm talking evil mainstream media
They ain't no encyclopedia
The people who watch them are sheeple
They're the real enemy of the people!

The Infant President walked off the stage to a standing ovation. It was as if phony Beatlemania hadn't bitten the dust.

Every politician loves the arts. They love film. They love television. They love books...as long as other people are reading them. They love to pretend to love opera. They love to pretend to understand poetry. They love to cut the ribbon at art galleries that they would never actually want to enter. They love to be seen as patrons of the arts...but will they ensure that the arts are funded to a level that allows them to flourish, to contribute fully to the national discussion?

Whatever gave you that idea?[5]

In lieu of adequate funding, politicians show their love for the arts by attending fundraisers.

Fundraisers like the one for the Squelch Moose Centre for the Performing Arts. Named after a famed nineteenth century showman and his penchant for hunting animals that were not native to the area, it had grown over the years to become a secondary source of theatrical entertainment for people throughout Wooden Dentured Founding Father State. Why, just last year, the Squelch Moose Centre's re-imagining of *The Music Man* set in Rwanda had reminded citizens of the continuing relevance of live performance to their lives.

Arts fundraisers are a different breed of animal to political fundraisers: best in show poodles as compared to mangy junkyard dogs. Arts fundraisers are black tie affairs; political fundraisers are strictly 'business casual'. Arts fundraisers hire gourmet chefs to create exotic dishes; political fundraisers hire the hash slinger from down the street to make something edible from bulk food purchases. Arts fundraisers often feature top flight entertainment; political fundraisers invariably feature interminable speeches. Arts fundraisers have an open bar; political fundraisers have a single drink ticket, then you're on your own.

The main difference is that arts fundraisers, which arguably exist for a worthy cause, net far less for their subject than

[5] Don't look at me – that's not one I planned on exploring.

political fundraisers, which arguably do not. The multiverse has a weird sense of humour that way.

Oh, one other difference: political fundraisers are strictly partisan affairs: it is rare for a politician to attend a fundraiser for somebody from a different party. Arts fundraisers, by way of contrast, are non-partisan affairs at which members of any party mingle freely. To not agree to an invitation to one would be to reveal oneself as an uncultured Philistine, and that only recently came into fashion.

The Jovial Republican Senator and The Jovial Democratic Senator were having a...pleasant conversation at a table at the Squelch Moose Centre for the Performing Arts fundraiser. They had both been in the Senate long enough to remember the days of inter-party amity, before hyper-partisanship had placed a wall between their two parties, and, in any case, nobody from the press had been invited to the fundraiser, so there was no point wasting energy. Or ammo.

"You look quite pleased with yourself," the Jovial Democratic Senator commented.

"The economy is booming," the Jovial Republican Senator responded. "Why wouldn't I be happy?"

"Typical," the Jovial Democratic Senator retorted, not uncheerily. "Inherit a strong economy from a Democratic President and claim responsibility for it. Meanwhile, you can read economic reports as well as I can, so you know that growth was slower last quarter than it typically is at this time of year. You can thank your President's disastrous trade wars for that."

"So you say," the Jovial Republican Senator took a swig of his drink. "But there's something you seem to have forgotten."

"What's that?"

"Nobody outside of Wooden Dentured Founding Father and a college economics department reads economic reports."

Before he could sadly agree, a...less than a brouhaha, but more than a kerfuffle...commotion...a commotion broke out in front of the bar. Three aliens were standing there holding trays of hors d'oeuvres, resplendent, if somewhat uncomfortable, in the waiter's uniforms they wore over their exquisite three piece suits.

"You're not s'posed ta eat the appetizers!" the alien in the middle grumbled. "They're for the guests!"

"But Oi'm hungry!" the alien on the right whined, reaching for a puffer fish ball on the tray the alien in the middle was holding.

Balancing the tray on one hand, the alien in the middle slapped the hand of the alien on the right away from the food.

"I said: quit it!" the alien in the middle angrily growled.

"You're always hungry," the alien on the left pointed out.

"I can't help it if I have a fast mebatolism!' the alien on the right groused as his hand snuck back towards the tray his neighbour was holding.

Swatting the hand away, the alien in the middle warned, "If you don't cut it out, you and me'll be mebatolizing right here and right now!"

"Oh? Woise goiy, hunh?" the alien on the right complained. Before anybody could do anything, he had swept his free hand in a motion that upended the tray the alien in the centre had been holding, sending puffer fish balls and shrimp skewers (basically: toothpicks with microscopic bits of fish and vegetables) flying in all directions. Given the level of humour displayed by these aliens, one of the appetizers found a home in the cleavage of a woman wearing a low-cut evening gown, while another dealt a glancing blow to her husband's toupee, which twirled out of proportion to the force of the blow and stopped at an angle that emphasized the hair's artificiality. (This was also around the time the jovial senators became aware of what was happening.)

The alien in the middle did a slow fume. Then, he turned on the alien on the right and returned the favour, sending crackers with colourful adornments flying hither and yon. "Wrroof!" the alien in the middle barked. "Wroof! Wroof!"

"Hey! Cut it out, guys!" the alien on the left admonished. "This is a sweet gig – don't ruin it!"

The other aliens turned to face him. The alien in the centre made to poke him in the eyes with two fingers, but the alien on the left held his hand up in front of his nose, blocking the attack. Unfortunately, this left the tray to its own devices, and it quickly succumbed to the advances of gravity (it fell to the ground – fell hard).

"Nyuk nyuk nyuk," the alien on the right laughed.

The alien in the centre turned towards him. He waved a hand upwards in front of the alien on the right's face.

Mesmerized, the alien on the right lifted its head to watch the hand rise. Then, the hand swiftly came down, mashing his nose as it fell.

"Oww!" the alien on the right moaned.

"Okay, here's what we're gonna do –" the alien in the centre started. At that moment, a severe man in a uniform similar to the ones the aliens were wearing came out and loomed over them disapprovingly. The aliens looked at the floor for several seconds, then, on some silent cue, ran off in different directions.

The jovial senators turned back to each other. "I swear," the Jovial Democratic Senator swore, "the entertainment at these things gets stranger and stranger every year."

"These are the beings your party is staking so much political capital on?" the Jovial Republican Senator smirked. In a friendly way.

The Jovial Democratic Senator smiled enigmatically. "We do things because they're right, not because they're easy."

"Sure you do. Sure."

"Don't get me started. The Infant President – your President – is raking in money hand over fist from his properties. He has put close relatives in positions of power. He gave a trillion dollar tax cut to the wealthy and large corporations – how does that sit with fiscal conservatives? He is a serial adulterer who has said vulgar things about women – how does your evangelical base like **that**? That's like the pot calling the kettle a waster of political capital!"

"I'm not saying there haven't been…hiccups in this presidency…" If the Jovial Republican's response had been any lamer, it would have needed a service ferret to help it get by.

"Yet, you stand by him. Who is the stooge here?"

"If this keeps up, not for long."

"Really? What would it take for you to stop supporting the Infant President?"

"I can't have that discussion this sober," the Jovial Republican Senator said, getting up and heading for the bar. While they disagreed on many things, imbibing alcohol at public functions was not one of them, so the Jovial Democratic Senator followed him and grabbed his own flute of champagne from off the bar.

"Russia," the Jovial Republican Senator replied after they

had both taken healthy swigs.

"Russia," the Jovial Democratic Senator agreed, a little uncertain.

"If the Infant President asked for Russia's help winning an election, I could not in all conscience continue to support him." * swig *

"But he did! During the last election, the Infant President publicly asked Russia to release damaging information on his opponent. Two days later, damaging information about his opponent became public." * swig *

"That's circumstantial." * swig * "It could have been a coincidence. I mean, if it was proven beyond a shadow of a doubt that the Infant President had asked for foreign help in an election." * swig * "That would undermine our democracy in a horrible, horrible, really bad way. At that point, he would have to be stopped." * swig * "Damn! These glasses don't hold as much liquor as they look like they should!" * snatch and swig *

"Hmm. How do your other caucus members feel about this?" * swig *

"Oh, we all have our personal threshold of acceptable behaviour from the Infant President. But trust me, we won't let him get away with just anything!"

In the interest of bi-partisan jollity, the Jovial Democratic Senator decided to trust the Jovial Republican Senator. But somewhere deep down in his soul, he wondered…

Silence is like the guy who packages your products at an Amazon warehouse: you rarely interact with him directly, so you just don't think of him. But, like the Amazon packager, silence has personality. Some silences are thoughtful. Some silences are aggressive. Some silences are oppressive. One difference between silence and our postulated Amazon warehouse drone worker is that the absence of sound doesn't have a name.

Except in the White House. Silence in the White House is named Dewey.

Dewey was a regular presence at dinner time. So, while the Stunning First Lady picked at her garden salad with oil dressing, the Son-in-Law Adviser enthusiastically dug into his steak, the Shallow Striving Daughter Adviser tucked into a BLT and the Infant President ate a hamburder and fries (his third of the day, but when you've got a good thing going, why ruin it?), Dewey did his thing around the table.

Not wanting to offend Dewey, but not entirely comfortable with its presence either, the Son-in-Law Adviser quietly said, "I think I've found a path for peace to the Middle East."

Dewey swallowed his statement whole. That's the thing about silence: it's voracious.

A couple of minutes later, the Shallow Striving Daughter Adviser offered: "Negotiations with China are coming along nicely. I think we're about to have a breakthrough. If so, we may finally get that agreement we've been working towards for the last year."

"They're gonna treat American goods better?" the Infant President said through a mouthful of burder. Special sauce dribbled down his chin. The Stunning First Lady resisted the temptation to roll her eyes, but it proved too tempting. Not that the Infant President noticed.

"They're going to allow my line of accessories to be sold in China!" the Shallow Striving Daughter Adviser enthused. "Do you have any idea how big that market is? We could make a killing!"

The Infant President grunted. He often did that in private. His grunts carried nuances that went far beyond the "Yeah, I acknowledge that I heard what you just said," of most people's grunts. In this case, there was a definite undertone of, "That's my girl!" (If your grunts are unable to express pride in your children, you might want to consider going back to inarticulation school.)

Dewey knew a cue when it heard one and wrapped itself around the dinner table tighter than a woman (or man) who thought her (or his) husband (or wife) was killed while on military duty, only to find him (or her) walking into their home unhurt.

"This ferking thing with the ferking Pedantic Special

Prosecutor," the Infant President muttered. Loudly. He had grown up believing that anything under 80 decibels was a waste of breath. "It's killing me. It's ferking killing me! I want him dead! You hear me! Dead! Who will rid me of this meddlesome Pedantic ferking Special Prosecutor!"

This had been a subject of dinner conversation for weeks. Dewey respected the Infant President's passion on the subject and decided, therefore, not to impose itself on the ensuing conversation. Dewey could be thoughtful that way.

"Daaaaaaad!" the Shallow Striving Daughter Adviser groaned. Unlike Dewey, she was thoroughly sick of the subject.

"What?"

"We've discussed this before, Mister Infant President," the Son-in-Law Adviser tried for a tone of sage wisdom, but, as always, only managed to achieve an immature rodent's squeak. "You cannot tell the CIA to assassinate somebody just because they are investigating you."

"What's the ferking point of being the ferking President, then?" the Infant President loudly pouted.

"Ne morem verjeti, da sem se poročila s tem moronom," the Stunning First Lady grumbled in her native tongue. The Infant President smiled at her, convinced that she was, in her own way, saying something encouraging. He reached out in an attempt to squeeze her hand.

"Noben denar ni vreden tega!" the Stunning First Lady cooed at him. And pulled her hand away from his.

"You have other ways of dealing with the Pedantic Special Prosecutor," the Son-in-Law Adviser argued.

"Yeah, yeah," the Infant President pointed an accusing French fry at him. "The little blue menace at our borders! Create a distraction so the base won't focus on the investigation! I get it! I get it! I just – it's not very honest, is it?"

The Son-in-Law Adviser was shocked that the Infant President had gone there. "Not honest? How so?"

"Well, I want to stop the aliens from coming to America because I hate the little blue bastards!" the Infant President explained. "This makes it look like I oppose them just for the sake of political expediency!"

The Stunning First Lady was also surprised: "To je

prefinjena analiza za tako plitkega človeka."

That's a pretty sophisticated analysis, there, dad-in-law, the Son-in-Law Adviser thought. He knew better than to say anything like that out loud, though: the Infant President was sensitive about his intelligence. And his weight. And his health. And his popularity. And his legacy. And his hair. Talking with him could often be like a walk through a field littered with emotional landmines.

Dewey thought it saw an opportunity, but before it could envelop the table once more the Son-in-Law Adviser, who had learned from bitter experience how to start every piece of advice with a compliment, said, "Mister Infant President, you know how to work both sides of an issue. That's one of your great strengths. So, all you need to do is to let the mainstream media think you oppose alien immigration to distract from the Pedantic Special Prosecutor's investigation, but keep dog whistling to the base that you are with them in hating the aliens."

"Yeah," the Infant President chuckled. "I'm really good at that, aren't I?"[6]

Dewey hesitated. Was this the opening that it had been looking for? As the seconds drew on, it seemed like, yes, yes, now was its moment! Dewey stretched out for a long, satisfying bask when…

"Okay. Message received," the Infant President allowed. "Everybody knows how great my election victory was. You know it. I know it. The man who blows up balloons knows it.

---

[6] You might wonder what happens when people realize that the Infant President is giving different messages to different groups. As it happens, not much. When members of his base discover he is letting the mainstream media believe he is against alien immigration in order to distract them from the Pedantic Special Prosecutor's investigation, they believe he is misleading the press and that pure speciesism is at the heart of his position. When journalists become aware of his speciesist dog whistling to his base, some may try to report on it, but soon enough they will be chasing another story about the Infant President's bromance with the Crazy North Korean Dictator, or his fight with Congress to get funding for his wall, or whatever else he may have tweeped that morning. In political science, this has come to be known as 'the fog of words'. The longer he remained President, the less likely it appeared that anybody would get their morning coffee…

We don't need to repeat that. I mean, I will. Repeat it. Because people need to be reminded of it. But I will get on message. About the Deep Dish State – this ain't no American apple pie, let me tell you! And I will hammer that message home – hammer it! Hammer it! Hammer it home! – until nobody can deny what is obvious. I wuz robbed!"

"Daaaaaaad!" the Shallow Striving Daughter Adviser groaned.

"Kaj sem storil, da sem si to zaslužil?" the Stunning First Lady asked herself.

The Son-in-Law Adviser stifled a chuckle.

And Dewey returned to the dining table, ready for a very long bask. It could afford to be patient – it always got the last word.

The Parable of Political Calculation

You would have thought, given the amount of wealth concentrated in the room, that the food would have been better. But this was a fundraiser, the point of which was to raise funds; if more money had been devoted to the menu, less money would be available to fund Republican candidates in the next election. Talk about defeating the purpose! Besides, bad food at fundraisers was a tradition; anybody who had been to one previously knew to make a reservation at a fine restaurant for later in the evening in order to cleanse their palate.

The Obsequious Invisible Vice President was the whitest person in the room. When he smiled (which he often did), you expected one of his teeth to sparkle. He reminded people of the advertising avatar for a line of cleaning products in the 1960s. He was, in the way of Vice Presidents, mostly invisible to the public, but that didn't mean that he wasn't active.

"This putting aliens in cages thing," the Dour Donor said at cocktails. "I dunno. I mean, they work really hard picking foozleberries at harvest time for half of what an American would demand. But I get that they're evil scum who are undermining our system – I could manage without them if I had to. But putting them in cages? The optics of it could kill us, you know?"

The Obsequious Invisible Vice President gave one of his dazzling smiles. The Dour Donor's wife melted. "I understand what you mean," he said. "Really, I do. But there are higher principles at play here."

"What higher principles would those be?"

"Now that the Supreme Court contains a majority of conservative judges, we may finally outlaw child murder in this country."

The Dour Donor, who considered himself a religious person (not only because he worshipped at the altar of tax cuts), considered this for a moment. "Is there any way the narrative can be...softened so that the caging of these aliens doesn't look so bad?"

"The Infant President is already on it," the Vice President assured the Dour Donor. What he meant was that the Infant President had already started posting outrageous tweeps about 'fake news' being 'the enemy of the people' that would be widely discussed in the mainstream press, thereby diverting the public's attention from the issue of aliens in cages. What the Dour Donor understood by what he meant was anybody's guess, but the Obsequious Invisible Vice President's tone was so reassuring that he decided to give his usual amount to the cause.

Is it influence peddling when a politician believes in the same things as the people who contribute to his party's campaign? Really?

The Provocative Pundit looked straight into the camera and frothingly fulminated, "C'mon, people! The pith, the essence, the very nature of our way of life is at stake, here! This is no time to go soft!"

The Infant President mumbled, "No time to go soft," to himself.

"The little blue aliens may look adorable in their funny little suits, but don't be fooled! They are in the vanguard of an invading force that will turn us into the butt of one of their little jokes if we let them! First, they'll get the gays laughing, but you won't care because you're not gay. Then, they'll get the blacks laughing, but you won't care because you're not black. Then, they'll get the Jews laughing, but you won't care because you're not Jewish. Then, they'll get the atheists laughing, but you won't care because you're not an atheist. Then, they'll get you laughing, and there will be nobody left to defend you! Wake up, people! If you don't, they'll have us laughing all the way to human extinction!"

"Ooh, that's bad," the Infant President muttered. "That's very bad."

"You might feel bad for the aliens when you see them locked up in metal cages the size of the box your fridge came in," the Provocative Pundit continued, relentless. "That's what makes us different from them: Americans have big hearts."

"Big hearts," the Infant President repeated, smiling to himself.

"Don't be fooled. They're not suffering. These aliens are the kind of beings who could be locked in a cage for three months and say things like, 'That's the last time I book accommodations for a vacation online!' or, 'How are you going to put a mint on the pillow on my bed when I don't have a pillow…or a bed?' or, even, 'I hope you realize that I'm not going to be giving this place a positive review on Yelp!' Does that sound like people who are suffering to you? Because it sounds to me like we've thrown the worst at them that we can think of, and these aliens are laughing at us. I tell you, people: they're just not human!"

The Infant President admired the way the Provocative Pundit screwed up his face and raised his voice to a near-squeal when he quoted the aliens. The Infant President had tried this once at a rally, and the next day had to suffer accusations that he was being cruel to disabled people.

Not that he suffered anything for very long. When you're born into enough money, you can pay people to suffer things for you.

"No, don't shed, lean-to or small hut any tears for caged aliens. If they didn't want to be treated this way, they shouldn't have come to America illegally. They should have used every legal avenue that the Infant President hasn't already closed to them. One – and, when I say 'one', I mean 'me' – can only hope that when images of their brothers and sisters in cages reach their home universe, maybe they'll think twice about trying to force their way into our too generous for too long country!"

As the Provocative Pundit faded to black, to be replaced by a tasteful advertisement for a hemorrhoid cream, the Television Intern muted the sound. Everybody in the Oval Office, who knew from bitter experience that woe betide any man, woman or legal adviser who made a distracting sound while the Infant President was watching Far Right News, felt free to start talking.

"Mistuh Infant Pres'dent," the Prejudiced Attorney General stated, "Ah do believe we have a problem heah."

The Infant President, who already had his Foozleberry out, said, "Gimme a minute."

```
@realinfantpresident Aiens laughing at being
put in cages attack our freedom. Don't believe
lib poppaganda - putting them in cages is a
detergent!
#ifnobodyisillegaleverybodyisillegal
```

"Okay," the Infant President looked at something other than a screen. "What?"

"Mistuh Infant Pres'dent," the Prejudiced Attorney General, who looked like a fascist Elmer Fudd and had no off switch for his folksiness, looked over his spectacles as he pointed out, "theah have been complaints that aliens heah legally ah bein' mistakenly caged along with illegals. It's just so damn hahd ta tell them apaht – they all look alahk!"

"So?" the Infant President was genuinely confused. "If caging illegal aliens sends a message, caging innocent aliens should send an even stronger message. Right?"

"That's what Ah'm afraid of, suh."

"We have a plan for that," the Son-in-Law Adviser, whose twelve year-old looking face belied an eleven year-old's understanding of the way the world worked, jumped in before the Infant President could say something foolish, derogatory or both.

"Do tell."

"Vestal recognition software."

The Son-in-Law Adviser explained that, although most people didn't realize it, the exquisite three piece suits that the aliens wore were as unique as snowflakes. There were su –

"Snowflakes aren't all unique," Pedantic Intern interrupted. "That's a myth."

"That's irrelevant," the Son-in-Law Adviser waved her off. "Can we focus, here, please?"

He gave everybody a moment to focus, then continued: "Where was I? Oh, right. Unique. The exquisite three piece suits that the aliens wore contained subtle variations in colour, pattern and weave, making them as unique as…finger prints? Are they unique enough for you? Good. That makes it possible to identify individual aliens by their clothing. You can simply adapt existing pattern recognition software to look for a specific article of clothing – early tests have suggested that the vests aliens wear are the easiest articles to identify."

"How would that work?" the Infant President asked, fascinated.

"Well. Say, illegal aliens were coming across the American border with Mexico. A security camera would capture an image of the vests that each of the aliens were wearing and enter it into a database with meta-information such as where the picture was taken, at what time, and how big the grins on their faces were (as measured on the Reiner Scale of Goofiness). Then, if an alien robbed a bank, we could compare the image of the alien's vest on the bank's security camera with the vests in our database, and capture the miscreant. Neat, eh?"

"What if the vest wasn't in the database?" the Infant President wanted to know.

"It will be," the Son-in-Law Adviser assured him. "When aliens apply for visas or other documents, we can get photographs of their vests. In a perfect world, we will have a visual record of every alien vest in the country."

"Oh, mah," the Prejudiced Attorney General oh myed. "Am Ah thuh only one who kin see a problem with this heah approach?"

"Problem?" the Son-in-Law Adviser responded. "There's no problem with this plan. It will give us complete information."

"But that's thuh problem raht theah," the Prejudiced Attorney General argued. "Look, son, Ah'm not opposed ta yer overall goal of protectin' thuh Murrican people from thuh alien menace. Really, Ah'm not. But this plan smells of massive suhveillance of aliens, even when they'ah just goin' abaht theah lawful business. Iffen we trah this, thuh social justice tahpes will be all ovah us!"

The moment the words had left his mouth, the Prejudiced Attorney General knew that he had made a mistake. The Infant President's eyes narrowed, and he growled, "Ferk the social justice types! This sounds like a fantastic idea!"

"Mistuh Pres'dent, Ah do believe that iffen y'all give the idea just a smidge moah thought –" the Prejudiced Attorney General started. Unfortunately for him, the Provocative Pundit's face had returned to the television set, and he lost the Infant President's attention.

"Ta be –" The Infant President turned to glare at the Prejudiced Attorney General, who dropped his voice to a whisper to conclude, "…continued."

"…ile we're on the subject of aliens in cages," the Provocative Pundit was saying, "I would like to make it clear that American cages are the cleanest and most well-kept cages in the world. You think Iranian cages are as good as ours? Aliens in Iranian cages can only dream of staying for months in cages in the United States of America! You would not believe –"

Without warning, the image on the television changed to somebody wearing a goofy naval uniform and neatly trimmed facial hair.

"Who are you?" the Son-in-Law Adviser asked.

The Infant President moaned. "Das Kapitan Oblivious."

"Actually, I'm Das Kapitan Obvious," the figure on the TV corrected him. "But thank you for making the effort to at least try and remember."

"What do you want?" the Son-in-Law Adviser demanded.

"You know," Das Kapitan Obvious stated, "if you know crimes are being committed and you help the person who is committing the crimes, you can be prosecuted for the crimes as well."

"Ah you a lawyuh, suh?" the Prejudiced Attorney General demanded.

"In this outfit?" Das Kapitan Obvious pointed out.

"Can you get him off the screen?" the Son-in-Law Adviser demanded.

"I'm trying!" the Television Intern responded.

Impatient, the Son-in-Law Adviser grabbed the converter from the Television Intern, pointed it at the set and pressed buttons. A lot of buttons. To no effect.

"Turning off the messenger will not stop the message," Das Kapitan Obvious pointed out.

"I'll just turn off the television, then," the Son-in-Law Adviser advised.

"Noooooooooooo!" the Infant President cried.

A hush fell over the room. Several seconds passed. People looked at each other, not wanting to be the one to break the silence. Eventually, Das Kapitan Obvious said: "Awkward." Several more seconds passed in silence. "I don't want to be the one to say it, but I think somebody is a little icted-adday..." Das Kapitan Obvious tried again. The silence continued to be unspoken. Eventually, Das Kapitan Obvious shrugged and said, "Well, this party is dead."

The Provocative Pundit reappeared on the television set. "...adical liberals welcome the alien invasion because they have never been committed to American freedoms. That's why we need to keep the aliens in cages – to prove how much we love freedom!"

The Infant President smiled and opened Twitherd on his Foozleberry.

Entertainment Interlude 001

Typecasting is not an Alien Concept to Hollywood, And Yet...

by ELMORE TERADONOVICH, Alternate Reality News Service Film and Television Writer

She was a short blue woman with exaggeratedly round features and an exquisite three piece suit with a dream. The woman, not the suit. While it is possible that the suit had a dream, it was unable to communicate that to this reporter, so I have no basis on which to make a judgment on the matter one way or the other. And in any case, what would a suit dream about? Retiring to the Riviera to enjoy a life of endless shots of Febreze and all the steam cleaning it could handle?

But, uhh, yeah. This is not an article about the secret life of womenswear. It is about an alien with a dream: to use her Audi Enz given talent to entertain the citizens of her new home.

"When I was told that I had to leave my home universe and come here," Ghisleyn Jeroboam explained, "My first thought was: what can I do for the people in my new home? After I stopped bawling my eyes out, I mean. I used up so many tampons soaking up the tears that day, let me tell you! And the strangest thing is that people don't have genders on Earth Prime 4-6-4-0-8-9 dash Omega, so I don't even know where they came from! I will say this: with a little bit of imagination, tampons have a million and one uses! Why, you can use them to –"

Jeroboam believed that her facility for walking into walls and over furniture ("And I can do that without even being anywhere near a cellphone!") would make her a natural movie star. She tried out for several parts ("I was offered a role in an Adam Sandler film, but it was one of his occasional serious performances – imagine my disappointment!") when her audition tape was seen by Bryan Fuller.

"I had never seen anybody who could walk into walls with such unaffected klutziness," he commented. "As it happened, I was looking for somebody who could add comic relief to an untitled *Star Blap* series that I was developing at the time, and that's how ensign Andromeda Galaxian was born!"

Fuller left the series, which by then was called *Star Blap: Stochastic* (all the really dynamic ship names had been taken), two days after Jeroboam was signed on. The new producers wanted the series set between *Star Blap: Free Markets* and *Star Blap: Adventuresome*; unfortunately, there were no aliens of her species in the *Star Blap* universe at that time.

"They wanted me to play a Dvorakian Scuttlemonkey!" Jeroboam moaned. "Can you believe that? They're six feet tall and have tentacles instead of arms! That wouldn't have been a bit of a stretch – it would have been an entire rack!"

After lengthy negotiations, Jeroboam was asked to play a character of her species that had fallen through a wormhole and was sent back in time to the period in which *Star Blap: Stochastic* was set. "That's one thing I'll say for science fiction: you can have a backstory that's out of this world!"

Alien immigrants had had minor roles in films and television series on Earth Prime before her (Antonio Bandobrothers, for example, had three lines in the film *Die Hard With a Double Entendre*, while Eloise von Hildebrandt was a recurring background character on the TV series *Friendly Vengeance*), but none were so prominent. More than that, she was the first alien to actually play an alien on the 50+ year-old science fiction series. Did Jereboam feel any pressure knowing this?

"Fifty years? Really? I...I didn't feel any pressure because I had no idea that that was the case," she told me. "But now...you know, I kind of wish you hadn't told me tha – fifty years? I'm the first alien to play an alien character? I...I...I – excuse me."

Jereboam rose out of the seat she had settled into for the interview and headed towards the door of the hotel room where the studio had set up a suite. She caromed off the doorframe and into the hallway.

"Did you see that?" publicist Becky Shaftoe enthused as Jeroboam careened out of sight down the hall. "She'll be fine. She's a natural!"

But will audiences accept an alien playing an alien on a *Star Blap* show? We'll find out on January 32, when the new series premiers on OmniDisney+.

Gianni Verbatim
Well, that's going to be different.

Alannah Voluminous
It's about time they got an alien to pay an alien! They have certainly appropriated enough alien stories! I just hope they're not going to make her a caricature of her species.

Alamo Tendentious
Oh, please! Could you move to another discussion group? Your heart is bleeding all over my shiny Naugahyde upholstery!

Peter the Grape
Having an alien in the cast can only make the show better. When she gets scripts, she can tell them if what she is being asked to do is true to her species or not. I mean, so many Star Blap aliens over the years have acted like humans with funny plastic prosthetix - we could actually get an authentic alien character for a change.

Alamo Tendentious
Seriously?! I watch Star Blap because its got great space adventure. If I wanted politically correct pro-diversity bullshit - which I don't, I would watch CNBC. This is a bad idea! Bad! Bad! Very bad!

Alannah Voluminous
Have you ever watched Star Blap? If you had, you would know that it has promoted diversity since the beginning. Like, the very beginning. In Star Blap: The Original Series, Captain James T. Pompous had the first inter-species kiss…practically every episode! Most of the bridge crews on the ships that came after had more colours than a Benetton ad! Hiring an alien

to play an alien is just a continuation of what the franchise has always done.

Gianni Verbatim
Absolutely.

Alamo Tendentious
THAT'S NOT THE SHOW I REMEMBER! YOU'RE KILLING MY CHILDHOOD WITH THIS POLITICALLY CORRECT FERKING BS! WHEN I WATCH STAR BLAP, I WANT TO SEE SPACESHIPS AND RAY GUNS AND THINGS AND PEOPLE BLOWING UP! THAT'S ALL I WANT TO SEE!

Gianni Verbatim has left the discussion.

Peter the Grape
troll

Alannah Voluminous
troll

Frenchy Tyler
definite troll

Alamo Tendentious
I'm not a troll.

Frank Baradont
troll

Ada Gloveplace
for sure a troll

Hieronymus Tishtosh
the trollest

Alamo Tendentious
I AM NOT A TROLL!

Alannah Voluminous
Really? How can you dis a show you haven't even seen yet?

Alamo Tendentious
I've seen stills.

Alannah Voluminous
Yeah, and what you saw was probably better than

the rubber-bodied aliens of the Original Series, or the CGI of some of the more recent series or the movies. Come on, admit it: a real alien is the best special effect the series could have.

Alamo Tendentious
At least creating the rubber bodies and programming the CGI gave work to real human beings. This alien is screwng people in your own species and you don't even realize it.

Peter the Grape
That may be. But there are also whole industries rising to cater to the needs of the aliens. On balance, their presence here could be creating more jobs than are taken away.

Alamo Tendentious
Yeah, I should know better than to try to talk sense to alien-loving ferkers like you people. Blues will not replace us! Blues will not replace us!

Alamo Tendentious has left the discussion.

Ada Gloveplace
He seemed like a nice guy.

Frenchy Tyler
Think he'll be back?

Alannah Voluminous
Probably.

Peter the Grape
With friends.

Frenchy Tyler
What should we do?

Alannah Voluminous
What we always do: argue about whether the new show will respect existing canon!

CHAPTER FOUR
Squiggles, Not Giggles, or A Pon Too Far

There's an old saying[1] in the Transdimensional Authority: to make love to a Ventrosian Squiggle requires patience and tweezers.

Squiggles from the planet Ventrosia have a basic humanoid structure, but they look like they were drawn by a two year old. Strands of squiggly lines make up their arms, legs, torsos and heads; to some, they look like they are made entirely of pool noodles. Because they are not entirely solid, when they move they tend to sway and lurch, not unlike those twenty foot tall balloon characters you see outside all of the best used car dealerships.

To move amongst humans, Ventrosian Squiggles have developed 'human suits', plastic cases that look like human bodies. However, because of their squiggly appendages, Ventrosians can't manipulate their human body suits to make them look entirely human. Their heads bob at odd angles, their limbs flail at odd times and their movements are just...odd.

Worse: everything Ventrosian Squiggles know about human sexual response they learned from porn movies from the 1960s. "Ooh, big boy! Keep it up!" "Yes, yes, stroke me there!" "But I didn't order a pizza!" are common phrases

---

1 An "old saying" is an idea that may have started out being wise, but, through repetition over a long period of time, can give off an air of wisdom while being utterly baffling.

It is also possible that the person speaking uses the phrase "old saying" to give an air of wisdom to something they just made up. That tactic is a piece of very old wisdom.

uttered by Ventrosian Squiggles when having sex in their human suits. Unfortunately, the phrases are not coordinated with any physical movements, since the Squiggles don't move much during sex. This doesn't make a lot of difference when the Squiggles (which do not have a gender) are wearing the body of a female human, but when they are wearing the body of a male human, sex can be long and frustrating.

Daveen Rasmalai Rapier walked out of the small bathroom wearing nothing but a towel and asked, "Was it good for you?"

The 'woman' lying on the bed, who had given him the name Esmeralda von Stauffenstein (although he knew her name was actually Stauffy van Esmeraldson) flopped on her side (not an easy feat considering how awkwardly put together her body was, and how slick the bed was with the remains of a dozen watermelons), and mouthed an idea that was completely untethered from any identifiable reality, "I haven't had sex that great since Dunkirk! You?"

"You were fantastic," Daveen Rasmalai replied as, neatly sidestepping the Capuchin monkey whose leash had been tied to the radiator by the window, he went over to the bamboo chair in the small, plain hotel room on which his clothes lay neatly folded.

"Was I?" Stauffy/Esmeralda asked with all the eagerness of a cat in a cage being taken to the vet. "Human anatomy has always confused me."

Daveen Rasmalai was supposed to believe that she was human, so he ignored the alienness of what she had said, responding, "Me, too, baby. Me too."

"Hmmm…"

Daveen Rasmalai put on a white shirt and started buttoning it up. A woman's voice in his head said, "Red Rover, Red Rover, is the grossness finally over?"

"Ladybug, Ladybug, was that 'over' part of your question," Daveen Rasmalai sub-vocally responded, "in which case you have more to say, or the signal that you had finished, in which case I could start talking? The protocol can be ambiguous on that poin –"

"You started talking," Ladybug, Ladybug groused (if I may mix my zoological metaphors), "so you must be working on the assumption that it was the signal that I had finished. And anyway, since when have you been concerned with protocol?" After a second, she added, "Over."

"Since you became my field manager," If sub-vocal communication could contain subtle emotions, Daveen Rasmalai's could be said to be extremely amused by itself. "Over."

"Everything okay, honey?" Stauffy/Esmeralda asked from the bed. She had turned to watch him on her stomach; her hips didn't quite line up with her back in an entirely human way. If a human being had said the line, it would have come across as seductive; because she was a Ventrosian squiggle, her tone was as seductive as that of a car driven by a teenager who had never learned how to change gears with a stick shift.

"You know what they say," Daveen Rasmalai, putting on his perfectly pleated black pants, replied: "once you go squiggle, you…umm…"

"Giggle…wriggle…higgle…dy piggledy…" Ladybug, Ladybug unhelpfully helped.

"You'll never do Rob Riggle?" Stauffy/Esmeralda suggested.

"Sure." Daveen Rasmalai had never been impressed with the American comedian's barely suppressed rage shtick (John Cleese had cornered the market on it decades earlier), but this cast him in a new light. A new and disturbing light. Daveen Rasmalai filed that thought away for further consideration. He pulled on the vest – the item of clothing that really made the suit exquisite – and buttoned all of the buttons except the last one.

"Do you have to leave so soon?" Stauffy/Esmeralda asked in a tone of voice that suggested she was asking her accountant why she had such a huge tax bill last year.

"Duty calls," Daveen Rasmalai gallantly commented as he picked the jacket of the suit off the back of the chair and put it on.

"I thought you were on vacation," Stauffy/Esmeralda pouted, although her voice contained all the ennui of a character in a French New Wave film.

"Whatever gave you that idea?" Daveen Rasmalai asked, swatting her bottom. Instead of rippling, it dimpled. "I'm in Caracas for an international conference of textile companies, baby. Because global carpeting never sleeps!"

"You're laying it on kind of thick, don't you think?" Ladybug, Ladybug complained in his head. "Over."

"Thick as shag," he sub-vocally agreed. He figured there was a rude joke in there somewhere, but he left it for Ladybug, Ladybug to find as he untied the Capuchin monkey.

"Will I ever see you again?" Stauffy/Esmeralda asked with all the passion of somebody contemplating the comedic sensibilities of Ayn Rand.

"In your dreams, baby. In your dreams," Daveen Rasmalai said over his shoulder as he and the monkey fled the scene.

"It was like the two of you were playing scenes in different movies!" Ladybug, Ladybug howled, her laughter deep and rich. "I expected a director to walk into the room at any moment to yell, 'Cut!' and ask what the hell the two of you thought you were doing!"

"It wasn't my best work," Daveen Rasmalai admitted. "It didn't help that my co-star was giving…really strange line readings. I found it hard to keep from laughing half the time!"

"I could tell."

"One thing I will say, though…"

"What's that?"

"The sex was great. Fantastic, really. I had never imagined I could get so much pleasure out of a group of sentient pool noodles…!"

Ladybug, Ladybug immediately stopped laughing. "I…I didn't need to hear that," she admonished. "I really didn't need to know."

Daveen Rasmalai laughed, a high, tinkling sound.

The pair were drinking cheap tequila in a dive bar on the top bun of the burger (i.e.: seedy) part of Caracas, the part that tourists never get to see (unless they want an authentic Venezuelan experience, in which case it is the part they intentionally seek out, but there aren't many of…**those** types, and most who do have the authentic Venezuelan experience of ending up in the hospital because their systems aren't able to cope with drinking the cheap tequila don't speak fondly of the experience when they get home). Ladybug, Ladybug was a tall, slender woman with a face whose resting state was 'severe'. Her long, brown hair was tied in a bun on her head, cementing the effect. She wore a colourful peasant blouse. Because girls just wanna have fun.

"Did you deliver the package?" Ladybug, Ladybug asked.

"Did I ever!" Daveen Rasmalai enthusiastically answered as he signalled to the waitress to bring another round. "I delivered it in the living room, then the bathtub, then, finally, the – what?"

Ladybug, Ladybug had held up a squeamish hand. "You know what I was asking about. I don't need…extraneous details."

"Okay. Right. Sorry." But, as new glasses were laid on the table, Daveen Rasmalai's grin suggested that he wasn't sorry. Not even a little bit. When the waitress had moved on, he said, "Yes, Double L, I delivered the package. The one that you're so concerned about, I mean."

The package in question was a sub-dermal patch that contained a tracking chip no bigger than a grain of rice (and, with the right sauce, no less tasty). Daveen Rasmalai's goal was to attach it to the inside of the target's human shell. The only way he could do that effectively was to have sex with the alien. A lot of his assignments were structured in such a way that to be achieved, Daveen Rasmalai would have to have sex with an alien. There was probably a note in a file on a computer at Transdimensional Authority headquarters about this, but if anybody read it, they would have been jealous that independent contractors got perks that regular employees did not.

If sex with a Ventrosian squiggle could be considered a perk. * SHUDDER *

Freeze frame. How did –

"Now, we just have to wait until –"

I called freeze frame. When I call freeze frame, you are supposed to immediately stop moving and talking until I'm done my exposition.

"Oh. Right. Sorry."

Don't mention it. How did –

"I didn't pick up my cue."

It happens to the best of us.

"Before we freeze, can I just…?" Daveen Rasmalai took a big swig of the glass in front of him.

Through gritted teeth, Ladybug, Ladybug quietly said, "I really think you should stop talking, now."

Freeze frame! FREEZE FRAME! FREEZE BLOODY FRAME!

Daveen Rasmalai froze wiping liquid off his upper lip. Ladybug, Ladybug froze doing her best not to roll her eyes.

Ahem. So. As I was saying: how did our heroes come to be in a dive bar in Venezuela talking about planting tracking devices on a Ventrosian squiggle one of them recently had sex with?

Ladybug Ladybug let out an involuntary, "Eww!" The exposition had begun, so I chose to ignore the outburst.

The adventure started, as many do, in a bland office in Transdimensional Authority headquarters in Ottawa. The briefing was led by a man known only by the designation 'M-C'. M-C was ex-military. His spine was so straight you could use it as a ruler. His hair was spiked and short, so short it gave people who met him the sense that it was scared to disobey a direct order not to grow any higher. His speech was clipped, as if he was about to go over his monthly allowance for verbs and he hated being in debt. To anybody. For any reason.

In briefings, Daveen Rasmalai was known as 'The Operative'. He was sitting next to a middle-aged woman who was fit enough for field work; she had laugh lines around her eyes so deep you could fly X-Wing Fighters on bombing runs through them. She was known as 'The Field Commander'.

M-C stood on the other side of a small desk, giving an air of one who felt chairs were for the weak. Or, possibly, that the seat of his pants was allergic to wood.

Without preamble (if we don't count the last three paragraphs), M-C stated, "Aliens are going missing. Across Latin America. We need you. To find out why."

The Field Commander frowned. "What do you mean by 'going missing?'" she asked.

"Not showing up for work. Not showing up for meetings. With government officials. Not showing up for trysts. With co-workers. In seedy hotel rooms. Not responding to calls. Not being at home. When we send field agents. To follow up. On initial reports. That they are missing."

"How many so far?" The Operative wanted to know.

"Eleven confirmed," M-C told him. "Another fifteen suspected."

"This couldn't be another Lyons," The Field Commander inquired. "Could it?"

Four months earlier, twenty-three aliens had disappeared from the French city. They turned up seventeen days later in a forest in the countryside. They had all simultaneously had the urge to mount a production of *The Mikado*, and they had abandoned their lives to rehearse. When the all-alien version of the operetta was performed in London's West End, it was savaged by critics: *The Guardian* called it 'an incoherent mess of an interpretation of a British classic'; *The Daily Mail* wrote that it was 'a competent version of a light musical that was long beyond its best by date'. Taking the hint, the aliens returned to their day jobs.

"No," M-C informed her with the finality of the gravy. "It is not. Another Lyons."

This stopped The Field Commander short for a second. But just a second. "How can you be sure?" she demanded.

"Transdimensional Authority. Data Collection and Interpretation and Technical Support," M-C winced, as if including the last couple of words in the sentence had caused him physical pain. "Analyzed data. For patterns. Aliens disappeared all at once. In Lyons. Aliens disappeared over two weeks. In Latin America. Cases are different. Eighty-three per cent certainty."

The Field Commander nodded. You can't argue with math. "Do we have any idea what's happening to the aliens?"

"No."

"Do we know who is abducting the aliens?" The Operative asked, careful to keep any tone of irony out of his voice.

"No."

"Any clues at all?"

"Yes." M-C leaned over and opened a drawer in his desk (it was the lowest drawer, which doubled him over like the cutting edge of a switchblade almost folded back into its handle; if he had been a more contemplative man, he might have made a mental note to leave important objects in the top drawer in order to ease the wear and tear on his back, but, being a man of action, he accepted the pain stoically), and removed a matchbook, which he tossed at The Operative, who effortlessly snagged it out of mid-air. The front of the matchbook read: 'The Alham-Bar'. The back featured a picture of a grinning devil. Or, possibly a grinning marmoset with horns. The artist (the owner's four year-old daughter) wasn't very good (although she was quite good for a four year-old).

"Eleven missing aliens had one," M-C explained. "Of these. In a pants pocket. In a drawer. In a stuffed armadillo. How we found that one? Don't ask. None of the aliens drank. None of the aliens smoked. Why have a matchbook? From a bar?"

"So," The Operative took a deep breath and summed up, "we go to the bar, see if anybody there is responsible for what's happening to the aliens, find out what they're doing with the aliens and stop them. That about it?"

"Couldn't have put it better. Myself."

"I'll get my pre-packed travel kit."

"I'll phone my husband," The Field Commander stated. "I'll let him know that I have been invited on a tour of carpet-producing facilities in Central America, so I'll have to extend my business trip, but I'll be home as soon as I can."

"Very good." That (not to mention turning his back on whoever was in the room, even though it meant staring at a blank white wall) was M-C's way of telling people that the briefing was over and that they should leave. So, The Field Commander and The Operative left.

The Field Commander (whom I liked better when we knew her as Ladybug Ladybug, so that's what I will call her) was one of the few human beings in existence who desired to fly to Venezuela on a commercial airliner. She was hoping that the Dimensional Portal™s had been booked solid for the next six months with aliens from Earth Prime 4-6-4-0-8-9 dash Omega being strewn across the multiverse like the seeds of a crop of squirting lapel flowers. "In the time it takes to send us to Venezuela on Earth Prime 0-0-0-0-0-3 dash beta," she argued, "and back, you could save three aliens from imminent doom."

The Dimensional Portal™ technician looked at her sanguinely and replied, "Lady, in the time it takes you to lose this argument, I could save **seven** aliens from imminent doom!"

Travelling through the space between universes, a void of ever-shifting geometric shapes and oozing driblets of colour known as 'Pollock', you maintain the position of your body as it went into the Dimensional Portal™. The Operative (which is a tossup with Daveen Rasmalai, but I'll go back to that to keep the confusion to a minimum) ran into the machine, so he drifted through the Pollock in a classic action pose, leaning forward with arms and legs pumping. Ladybug, Ladybug, on the other hand, jumped into the machine, so she drifted through the Pollock looking like she was cannonballing into a swimming pool but never quite reaching the water.

"I hope there will be tequila in our hotel room," Ladybug, Ladybug said through the chip she had implanted in her brain to the chip implanted in Daveen Rasmalai's brain.

"It is better to travel hopefully than to arrive dopefully," he replied.

"I'm pretty sure that's not how that phrase goes."

"Tequila in our hotel room is not how the mission is going to go, so that seems to work out, then."

Ladybug, Ladybug sighed. (She had actually entered the Pollock with a sigh on her lips; this was just a psychic forerunner of the suspiration to come.) "I have explained this to you before," she exasperated at Daveen Rasmalai. "My family thinks I'm a teetotaller. Missions are the only chance that I have to get rip-roaring!"

"Indeed. And I have explained to you before," Daveen Rasmalai retorted, "that I cannot afford to get rip-roaring. My mind needs to have a razor-sharp focus on the mission if I am going to carry it out successfully."

"The mission?" You can't really snort via the chip implant network – it comes across more as a metallic slurpy kiss – but Ladybug, Ladybug tried it anyway. "How many times have you drunk alcohol with a subject of investigation while trying to get them into bed?"

"That was different!" Daveen Rasmalai protested.

"How?"

"That was part of the mission!"

Before Ladybug, Ladybug could remonstrate with him further, the two shimmered into existence in an alley on Earth Prime 0-0-0-0-0-3 dash beta. Daveen Rasmalai took another step and Ladybug, Ladybug fell almost onto the ground before they were swept back into the Pollock. A confused gecko decided then and there to swear off the dew drops.

"You keep your cover for your family?" Daveen Rasmalai gently inquired. "They think you are an international carpet salesperson?"

"It's the best way to keep them safe," Ladybug, Ladybug answered.

"The best way to keep them safe," Daveen Rasmalai gently retorted, "would be to **be** an international carpet salesperson..."

The pair spent the rest of their time in the Pollock quietly travelling hopefully.

Daveen Rasmalai and Ladybug, Ladybug shimmered into existence in an obsolete medium (seedy) bar in Caracas on Earth Prime. For the first time. Even though we've already seen them drinking there. Jesus begesus – whoever invented flashbacks must have had a particularly warped imagination! Daveen Rasmalai's forward momentum caused him to run forward a couple of steps, catching his side on the edge of a table. He swore once, his economy of language overtaken by the depth of his anger. Ladybug, Ladybug fell to the ground with a slight * WHUMP *!

"I thought the whole point o' undercover operations was ta not call attention ta yerself," a deep voice whispered.

Daveen Rasmalai and Ladybug, Ladybug surveyed their surroundings. Dim lighting? ✔. Plain wooden chairs and tables? ✔. A jukebox filled with Spanish language hits, with one exception: "Stairway to Heaven?" ✔. Neon signs? ✔. Advertising American alcoholic beverages? ✘. The neon signs advertised alcoholic beverages of an unidentifiable nature; if the survey ended there, they would have concluded that the bar was primarily for locals. But there were just one or two more details... Half a dozen roughnecks drinking alone at tables scattered throughout the establishment? ✔. All eyes, including the bartender, who had stopped rubbing a glass with a threadbare towel in mid-wipe, on them? ✔. Unfortunately ✔.

"It is," Ladybug, Ladybug urgently whispered back.

"Only one thing to do, then..."

"Umm...what would that be?"

"¡Bebidas para todos!" the deep voice boomed. "Y uno para usted, señor barman, ¡por favor!"

A couple of patrons let out a languid cheer and the bartender grunted. Not much of a reaction, to be sure, but everybody's attention turned from the newcomers back to their quaffable toys.

The man with the deep voice was a tall drink of coffee coloured skin. He waved Daveen Rasmalai and Ladybug, Ladybug towards a table in a dark(er) corner of the bar, where the three of them sat. There were already a bottle of tequila and three shot glasses on the table.

"Felix Heavior," Daveen Rasmalai greeted the man with a grin.

"Daveen Rasmalai Rapier," the man replied, adding a couple of syllables where they didn't belong.

"On this mission, he's known as Red Rover, Red Rover when he's in the field," Ladybug, Ladybug pointed out, reaching for the bottle and pouring herself a glass.

The gentleman raised an inquisitive eyebrow at Daveen Rasmalai, who shrugged. "I've been called worse."

"By yer own people?"

A chug and a shiver later, Ladybug, Ladybug said, "I'm the Field Commander of the operation. You can call me Ladybug, Ladybug. You are?"

"I don't have me no fancy mission name," the man smiled at her as she filled her glass. "Y'all can call me Felix. That'd be Felix Heavior, of the Pennsylvania Dutch Heaviors. I'm what ya call that there CIA Station Chief for Latin Murrica. Your boss honcho got in touch withen my boss honcho and asked fer a little help with thisen missin' alien problem y'all got."

"Does he always talk like this?" Ladybug, Ladybug asked Daveen Rasmalai under her breath.

"Wait til you hear him drunk!" Daveen Rasmalai told her.

Not waiting to determine if he was telling her to wait until she was drunk or Heavior was drunk, Ladybug, Ladybug threw back another shot (which, fortunately, landed on the back of her throat).

"Felix and I go wa –" Daveen Rasmalai started.

"Status?" Ladybug, Ladybug demanded.

"Beggin' yer pardon, ma'am," Heavior charmed, "But I do believe yer podner was about to engage in a bit o' personal exposition."

"There'll be plenty of time for that later," Ladybug, Ladybug assured him as she filled her glass once again. "I'd like to be brought up to speed on conditions on the ground right now."

Heavior looked at Daveen Rasmalai, who lightly licked his upper lip with the tip of his tongue, a sign they had worked out many years before to mean agreement. (Licking his lower lip was a sign of disagreement, while sticking his tongue out of the left side of his mouth meant he was confused and could use some guidance. Sticking his tongue out of the right side of his mouth was an empty slot that was waiting to be assigned meaning at some future date.)

Having been given the green li – err, pink tongue, Heavior explained that he had men stationed at the Alham-Bar – a dumb name for an establishment, one which must have been for tourists because no local would countenance it with their patronage – for the past couple of days. The only person any of them had witnessed expressing an interest in the aliens from Earth Prime 4-6-4-0-8-9 dash Omega was an alien herself – a Ventrosian squiggle.

Ladybug, Ladybug shuddered as she drank her third shot and filled her glass again. Ventrosian squiggles! She had spent some time in that particular uncanny valley, and she didn't cherish the idea of a return trip.

"Did the squiggle give the aliens a matchbook?" Daveen Rasmalai inquired.

"I do believe that she did, yassuh," Heavior told him. "Funny thing about that..."

"What's that?"

"The Alham-Bar don't have matchbooks."

Ladybug, Ladybug halted the motion of the glass to her mouth, just barely stopping herself from executing a spit take and wasting precious fluid. A moment later, certain that she was over the surprise, she mentally said, "Ground Control, this is Ladybug, Ladybug. Do you copy? Over."

"Hi, Ladybug squared," a man's voice replied in her head. "Wassup?"

Ignoring the informality (it was Malcolm – it was just his way), Ladybug, Ladybug (or Ladybug x 2 – Malcolm didn't math as good as you might have thought for a man in his position) asked, "Can you please ask the lab to analyze the matchbooks found in the apartments of the missing aliens? Over."

"Like, put them on a couch and ask about their childhoods?" Pause. "Over?"

"Like, do they contain a tracking device, or are they made of a rare or unusual material that would make them easy to track? Over."

"Track? I field you. All over."

Ladybug, Ladybug winced. It wasn't that Malcolm wasn't funny – it was that his witticisms barely registered as humour. "Let me know if the lab finds anything. Over and out." Ladybug, Ladybug shut the connection and downed another drink. Oddly enough, the alcohol had not made Malcolm seem any funnier. Ladybug, Ladybug considered her empty shot glass. She had already drunk a Passover seder's worth of tequila – dared she risk drinking from Elijah's cup? Sadly, she turned her glass over, done for the evening.

"Now," Daveen Rasmalai told her, "we do reconnaissance."

The Alham-Bar was brightly lit and contained many fancy sconces, sconces that had convinced themselves that they wouldn't be caught dead in a dive bar, unaware of how time can destroy our most cherished beliefs about ourselves. The customers were also bright, many of them already lit though it was early evening; if you listened closely, you could hear a smattering of languages, none of them Spanish. If it hadn't been for the occasional alien, it would be easy to imagine the scene taking place in 1971...or 1921. Time travel didn't always require a special device or a magic spell.

Daveen Rasmalai and Heavior sat at a table within eyeshot of the bar, where a little blue alien with exaggerated round features and no hair wearing an exquisite three piece suit sat nursing a pitcher of cognac. Daveen Rasmalai described the scene sub-vocally for Ladybug, Ladybug, who was in her part of the adjoining rooms they shared at the Overlook Hotel a dozen blocks away. A couple of minutes after the alien sat down, a Ventrosian squiggle flounced up to him (given its physiognomy, it couldn't move any other way). From the description Daveen Rasmalai gave her, Ladybug, Ladybug was able to search government databases to determine that the squiggle was probably Stauffy van Esmeraldson, an operative for the Ventrosian Department of Transuniversal Mischief. Her specialty was transdimensional puppy smuggling; her cover story was that she was an interdimensional carpet saleswoman.

"The nerve of some people!" Daveen Rasmalai joked.

"I know, right?" Ladybug, Ladybug responded. "I've spent years perfecting my cover story, and some alien just waltzes in and claims it as her own! Bitch!"

"Riiiiiight..."

A matchbook was exchanged between Stauffy and the alien. He bit into the wooden object and frowned, disappointed that it wasn't...something. The two aliens talked for several minutes, after which the squiggle walked away. Looking at the almost full pitcher of alcohol in front of the alien, Daveen Rasmalai commented, “And now, we wait.”

Thirty seconds later, the alien had finished the pitcher, paid his tab with a few large bills and jumped off the bar stool and headed for the door. Heavior looked at Daveen Rasmalai, who nodded, and followed the alien out of the bar.

The alien meandered for several blocks, Heavior discreetly staying a few steps behind him. Eventually, the alien threw out his arms and spun around with increased speed until he eventually fell to the pavement.

Heavior ran to him. “Sir?” Heavior urgently demanded. “Are you alright?”

The alien opened one eye and replied, “I’m all that’s left.”

Heavior helped the alien sit up. He didn’t know how to respond, so he did what he always did in such situations: he pulled out his wallet and showed his identity card. “Sir,” he said, “I’m an agent with the CIA, and I sure would appreciate it iffen you would answer a few questions.”

“That is a very official looking wallet,” the alien replied. “Take me! I’m all yours!”

The alien flomped into Heavior’s suddenly very masculine arms. “Sir, we should probably continue this discussion somewheres…more conducive to privacy, if you catch my meanin’.”

It wasn’t that they were attracting attention – people walked around them on the sidewalk like they didn’t want to get the alien or the American on the soles of their shoes. However, Heavior didn’t want to attract the attention of the squiggles, so he helped the alien – who introduced himself as Melchior Adrenal-Rousch – to the nearest establishment: Rick’s Cafe Americain. (The franchise was all over Latin America, although nobody could explain the appeal. Blame Jeff Bezos.) They sat at a table, Heavior ordering them two coffees, and settled in for a long conversation.

“Am I in trouble?” Adrenal-Rousch asked after burning his upper lip on the lukewarm beverage. (Some comic effects you have to work harder at than others.)

“Nossir,” Heavior assured him. “We’re about as interested in you as a polecat is interested in shortin’ airline stocks. No offence to varmints. I'd like to ask you a few questions about the woman you were with."

"Esmeralda von Stauffenstein? A charming woman, even if I found myself wondering how her limbs didn't fly away from her body at strange angles while we were talking. That's very distracting!"

Heavior frowned.

"Or, not," Adrenal-Rousch quickly continued. "I'm good with leaving it at charming if you are."

Heavior had frowned because he didn't think that actually was the Ventrosian squiggle's name, but it sounded too close to what he had been told was her name to be an effective cover. He mentally shrugged: maybe squiggles were just bad at espionage. Although he said he wasn't interested in this alien, Heavior found him kind of…twitchy. Yep. There was definite twitch in the boy. He wondered what that was about.

"Who are you?"

Adrenal-Rousch described himself as a humble salesman for the Imperial Coffee Company. He had been given the territory that included Brazil, Venezuela, Alberta, Ukraine and much of western Europe (except France). It was a challenging job – he hadn't sold a package in six months, and was beginning to think that the route had been created specifically for him to keep him out of the head office – but he had met a lot of colourful characters on his adventures, and –

"What did you two talk about?"

"Hunh! What didn't we talk about?" Adrenal-Rousch took a swig of his now tepid coffee, but fanned his mouth with his free hand as if he had just downed lava. "We spoke of many things. Of shoes, and ships and ceiling wax. Of cabbages and –"

"Okay, I get it," Heavior waved a dismissive hand. "The two of you have a lot of interests in common. Did she talk to you about anything that made you…uncomfortable?"

"I'm usually the one who makes other people uncomfortable," Adrenal-Rousch stated. "It's my religion – it can demand a lot of its believers."

"Mmm, but –"

"Okay, your superior interviewing skills have dragged it out of me!" Adrenal-Rousch dramatically revealed. (Nobody in the establishment paid him any mind – dramatic revelations happened so often at Rick's Cafe Americain that there was a sign at the door announcing showtimes.) "I'm not here on a sightseeing tour of the ruins of ancient used automobile dealerships! I'm here…I'm here – oh, I'm so ashamed! – I'm here…for the sex!"

The only reason Heavior's jaw didn't hit the ground was because he had his stunned reaction wired shut when he joined the secret service. "The sex?" he asked. "The bodies of two people from your universe melt into one. You can't do that here – you – you – you have human bodies which you no longer control on a molecular level."

"What if I told you there was a machine that allowed us to do exactly that?"

"What iffen I told you the moon was made of bleu cheese?"

"I'd ask you for crackers."

Heavior considered this for a moment. "This here gizmo have a name?"

"We call it…The Orgasmatron."

"Course you do. How does it work?"

Adrenal-Rousch explained that the Orgasmatron was created by Rodney Pendleton, the first alien to come to Earth Prime; it was the size and shape of a small shower stall. A human being and one of his people entered and closed the door. The device decohered their atoms and mingled them. After a minute – which feels like an eternity – they are recohered and go about their lives.

"Pleasure on a molecular level," Adrenal-Rousch summed up. "There's no experience like it!"

"Does it have to be a human and one of your kind," Heavior asked, "or can it be any two beings?"

"Ooh, kinky!"

"I'm just trying to understand how this here machine works."

"Of course you are."

"Forget I asked."

"Some experiences in life are unforgettable."

Heavior had questioned hardened criminals and scared children, but he had never had an interview go quite like this. Either this alien had had extensive training on resisting interrogation techniques, or he was a complete idiot. Either way, Heavior decided to bull his way through.

"How did you find out about this?" he asked.

"I received an email about it," Adrenal-Rousch told him. "It told me to go to the Alham-Bar in Caracas, where I would be approached by a Ventrosian squiggle who would give me instructions on where to go."

"Do you still have the email?"

"Naah. It self-destructed after sixty seconds. You know, like those tapes at the beginning of that spy show on television…"

"*Mission Impossible*."

"Oh, don't say that. I'd hate to think I'd come all this way for nothing!"

Heavior wearily rubbed his eyes. "And the matchbook? What is the significance of that?"

"I'm supposed to go home and wait for an opening. Apparently, the Orgasmatron is booked weeks in advance! When I receive an email telling me it's my turn, I'm supposed to come back here and call the Tijuana Taxi Company and ask for a driver named Itsger. When the cab arrives, I'm supposed to give Itsger the matchbook to show him that I made contact with the squiggle. Then, he'll take me to where they're keeping the Orgasmatron."

This didn't make sense. If the aliens were supposed to surrender the matchbooks, why did they still have them in their rooms? "Are you planning on giving that there matchbook to Itsger?"

"Naah!" Adrenal-Rousch looked at the CIA agent as though he had sprouted an extra head. "I'm gonna keep it as a souvenir of my adventure."

"Aren't you worried that Itsger will refuse to take you to the…whatchamacallit?"

"The Orgasmatron?"

"Yeah. That?"

"I'll tell him I left the matchbook in my other exquisite three piece suit. That's totally credible – right?"

Heavior had been trained not to shake his head during an interview (he devoted twenty minutes before he went to bed every night to experiencing the reactions he had been trained not to experience during the day – oh, the stories his bathroom mirror could tell!), but he found it moving to the left of its own volition. He consciously had to stop his head from moving to the right.

"Mister Adrenal-Rousch," Heavior heavily pronounced, "we have reason to believe that this Ventrosian squiggle is involved in some kind of scheme in which aliens from your universe disappear. If you follow through on this, your life could be in danger. I would strongly suggest that you go home and forget all about this."

"Will I get a refund?" Heavior glared at him. "What?"

Heavior caught up with Daveem Rasmalai and Ladybug, Ladybug at the bar. Daveen Rasmalai took the opportunity to pour a drink for Heavior and himself; he offered one to Ladybug, Ladybug, but she declined it. Hevior had a crypto-photographic memory: he remembered conversations perfectly, except for every seventh word. So, while there were odd gaps in his recounting of his conversation with Adrenal-Rousch, they were minor and easily filled in.

"Hmm..." Ladybug, Ladybug hmmed. "That still leaves us not knowing where the squiggles are taking the aliens, or what they're doing with them."

"I know what we can do," Daveen Rasmalai started.

"Could we put a tracker on Adrenal-Rousch and send him in?" Heavior proposed.

"I don't like putting civilians in harm's way," Ladybug, Ladybug responded. "What are our other options?"

"Seriously, I have an idea that would work," Daveen Rasmalai tried again.

"Does the Transdimensional Authority have any agents from Earth Prime 4-6-4-0-8-9 dash Omega?" Heavior vamped. "We could get the matchbook from Adrenal-Rousch and send in our alien – it's not like anybody could tell the difference."

Ladybug, Ladybug shook her head. "Unfortunately, the

Alternaut Academy is a four year programme and the aliens have only been on Earth Prime for just over two years. We haven't had enough time to train one to work well in the field."

"Are you ready for my idea yet?" Daveen Rasmalai cheerfully asked.

"If the Authority doesn't have any alien agents ready," Heavior suggested, "perhaps they could hire a freelancer like Rapier here?"

"I'm not exactly like that any more," Daveen Rasmalai protested.

"To my knowledge, the Transdimensional Authority doesn't have freelance agents of that specific alien race," Ladybug, Ladybug told him. "Besides, you've seen how the aliens act. Would you trust one in the field?"

Heavior shuddered. Nothing needed to be said. The three pursued their own thoughts for a couple of minutes. Eventually, Heavior turned to Daveen Rasmalai and asked, "Do you have any ideas?"

"As a matter of fact…" The Operative looked at Ladybug, Ladybug, who reluctantly waved him on. "Okay. I make contact with the squiggle and get her to spill the beans about where she's taking the aliens."

"Make contact?" Heavior inquired.

"Physical contact," Ladybug, Ladybug explained with distaste.

"Oh… **Oh!**" Heavior, who had been sipping at his drink like it was precious, took a big gulp.

"Your ability to get aliens to talk may be a little exaggerated," Ladybug, Ladybug carped. "But I suppose you could put a tracker on her that would lead us to wherever the aliens are being taken."

"Can you get close enough to the squiggle to place a tracker on her?" Heavior asked.

With pride, Daveen Rasmalai told him: "I can get close enough to a Ventrosian squiggle to place a tracker **in** her!"

Not being able to help herself, Ladybug, Ladybug grabbed back the bottle of tequila, poured a glassful and drank it in a single gulp. Elijah would just have to wait until next year.

"Okay, to make this work," even Malcolm on Earth Prime, with whom Daveen Rasmalai had opened his psychic connection, could hear the gleeful hand-rubbing in The Operative's voice, "I will need an exquisite three piece suit – you should have my measurements on file, Ground Control – a dozen watermelons and a trained Capuchin monkey."

"Does it have to be a Capuchin monkey, Red Rover, Red Rover? Over." Ground Control asked.

"The alternative would be an orangutan, Ground Control," Daveen Rasmalai advised, "but they're a lot harder to keep on a leash!"

"Copy that, Red Rover, Red Rover," Ground Control responded. "I'll get on that right away, but it may be a couple of days before we are able to wrangle a Capuchin monkey. They're bitey. Very bitey. Over and out."

Three days later, the materials that Daveen Rasmalai had requested arrived at his room in the Overlook Hotel. The three piece suit was exquisite, the watermelons were ripe and the Capuchin monkey was so well behaved that Ground Control's admonition seemed unnecessarily cautiou – ooh! Oww! Ouchie! Oww! Bitey! Very bitey!

That evening, Daveen Rasmalai swaggered into the Alham-Bar with all the unearned self-confidence of James Bond. An Egyptian James Bond. He walked up to the bar and ordered a martini. Shaken. **And** stirred. He looked around the room like a Jehovah's Witness stalking its prey. Eventually, he found what he was looking for: a woman who gave the term 'loose-jointed' a whole new meaning. Sweeping his drink off the bar with an economical motion ($3.99 at Walnut-Mart, ordinarily a $4.99 value), he walked up to the Ventrosian squiggle in an unconvincing woman suit and said, "They say you haven't lived until you've seen the puppies of Caracas root through garbage under a full moon."

"Red Rover, Red Rover, worst opening line ever!" complained Ladybug, Ladybug in his head.

The woman turned and appraised him. Taking the loupe out

of her right eye, she said, “You’re not my type.”

Ignoring her, Daveen Rasmalai asked, “What type would that be?”

“Short. Nice suit, though. Exquisite.”

Before she had a chance to turn away from him, Daveen Rasmalai added: “Pity. I have a dozen watermelons that will likely go rotten before I get a chance to use them…”

“How many?” the woman, clearly impressed, gave him her full attention.

“Only a dozen,” Daveen Rasmalai explained. “Too many for my purposes. Perhaps…you could help me find a use for them…?”

“As tempting as that offer is –”

Before she could reject him again, Daveen Rasmalai snapped his fingers. “Oh, wait! Sorry, but I can’t!”

The woman looked unimpressed. “You can’t?”

“I am so sorry.”

“Why not?”

“I promised my sister I would babysit her pet Capuchin monkey.” Daveen Rasmalai made a show of looking at his watch. “I have to pick it up in an hour.”

“Weelll,” the woman said, “I suppose I could make an exception for a man with a Capuchin monkey. It would, of course, have to be in the room with us to ensure that it didn’t chew through its leash and wander off.”

“Of course.”

“Did she just propose what I think she did? Over?” Ladybug, Ladybug wanted Daveen Rasmalai to know how disgusting she found the proposition.

“She did,” Daveen Rasmalai sub-vocalized. Disgusting would not describe his attitude towards the proposition, not unless you antonymed it.

The woman offered Daveen Rasmalai her hand. It flopped in a way that suggested that it was thinking seriously about dropping off its hinge. “I am Esmeralda von Stauffenstein, of the Delhi von Stauffensteins,” she introduced herself.

Daveen Rasmalai took her hand and kissed it. “Bond,” he introduced himself. “James Bond. Of the London, Ontario Bonds.”

“How soon can we get to your sister’s place?” Esmeralda eagerly asked.

"Ah, that would not be a good idea," Daveen Rasmalai demurred. "She's a bit paranoid – cameras everywhere. Not someplace we could get any privacy..."

"How soon can we pick up the monkey from your sister's place and get to your place?" Esmeralda didn't miss a beat.

"Ah, also not a good idea. My condo board is very strict about its no pets rule. If the Capuchin monkey got a little...excited during the night, I would almost certainly lose my apartment. You wouldn't want that to happen, now, would you?"

Esmeralda looked unsympathetic. "What alternative do we have?"

"I could pick up the monkey from my sister's place and meet you at **your** place."

"I don't know..." But there was no enthusiasm in the woman's voice for her denial.

Daveen Rasmalai put an arm around Stauffy/Esmeralda's waist and gave her a passionate kiss on the lips, tactfully avoiding the fact that her face slid a little to the left. This seemed to galvanize the woman. She picked a cocktail napkin off the bar, took a pen out of her purse and wrote down an address. Handing the napkin to Daveen Rasmalai, she said, "Meet me here in half an hour!"

Without glancing at the napkin, he responded, "It may take me longer than that to –"

"Half an hour, or you can find other uses for your watermelons!"

"Yes, ma'am!" As he sped out of the bar, Daveen Rasmalai asked Ladybug, Ladybug how long it would take him to pick up the watermelons and monkey and get to the address on the napkin.

"It depends on the traffic," she told him.

"I'd better get my ass in gear, then, hadn't I?"

"This is going to be a long night, isn't it?" Ladybug, Ladybug groaned. The last thing she wanted to think about was the gears of his ass.

"I would suggest you engage the chip's filters for moaning, groaning, shouting endearments and profanity," Daveen Rasmalai advised.

Okay. That pretty much brings us up to date. Unfreeze frame.

Daveen Rasmalai finished wiping liquid off his upper lip. Then, he waved his arm up and down, working the kinks out of it. "Did that freeze frame have to take so long?" he bitched. "It's tough on the muscles!"

Ladybug, Ladybug had frozen trying to stifle an eye roll. She decided the effort wasn't worth it and let her eyes roll where they would.

"Where were we?" Daveen Rasmalai asked.

Oh. Uhh…that's always the tricky bit of coming out of an extended flashback. Uhh…Daveen Rasmalai met the Ventrosian squiggle in the bar and…was about to convince her to let him go back to her room with him?

Ladybug, Ladybug moaned. "Oh, please, don't make me live through that scene again!"

No, no, you're right. It was the next day – the two of you were talking about what you had learned the night before.

"Line?" Daveen Rasmalai demanded.

Err… "Now, we just have to wait until –"

"Right." Daveen Rasmalai cleared his throat, went up and down a scale a couple of times, and said, "Now, we just have to wait until the squiggle goes to wherever they are holding the aliens, and, once I've verified that the place is, in fact, what we're looking for, Felix can lead a team to raid it!"

"I have to admit," Ladybug, Ladybug had to admit, "that sounds like a plan."

"Now, where can I get an ice cream truck?"

Three days later.

<Meghan Markle.>

<What about her?>

<She was the last nail in the coffin of the British monarchy.>

<Not Prince Andrew, who spent time in the company of a pedophile and his young victims?>

<Please! If **that** was meant to be the cause of the final

implosion of the monarchy, it would have happened centuries ago!>

<Not the racism of Prince Philip?>

<Of course not. At least he was representing his people.>

<What about –>

<No! Meghan Markle is to blame. It's bad enough that Prince Harry married a commoner. Some people might think that was…romantic. But an American? That has only happened once, and the King couldn't be a King after it! But worst of all? **An actress!** I tell you, my friend, the monarchy has no standards any more!>

Cesar was about to protest further when he thought he heard a faint tinkling in the distance. This would be most unusual: Cesar and Manny were guards at the gate of a compound in the middle of a dense forest: there were no tinkling sounds in nature.

<Do you hear that?> Cesar asked.

<Don't try to change the subject,> Manny replied. <You know that what I am saying is tru –>

<Shh! Shh! Shh!> Cesar hushed him. <For Gord's sake, man! Shut up and listen!>

The tinkling got louder, so much so that Manny could hear it. <What in the name of the Holy Mother is that?> he cried.

Cesar reached for the rifle he had casually propped up against the wall of the guardhouse. <I don't know,> he grimly stated, <but it's not a sound heard in nature. Best to expect the worst!>

Manny grabbed his rifle from the wall. Then, the pair waited, anxiously looking through the guardhouse window at the dirt access road that had been cleared out of the forest as the tinkling steadily got louder. Eventually, a small truck drove up to the gate. It had foreign writing all down the side and pictures of Drumsticks, Solar Bars, Fudgsicles, Oreo Ice Cream Sandwiches, Klondike Ice Cream Sandwiches, Creamsicles and more flavours of Häagen-Dazs than you could shake an empty cone at. The tinkling was a short repeating jingle that wafted out of the top of the truck.

<Hello!> the driver of the truck greeted the guards in the guardhouse out of his partially-rolled down window. His Spanish, halting and with atrocious diction, made Cesar wince. <Can you please open these gate for me? I have a

delivery to making!>

<See what he wants,> Manny demanded.

<You see what he wants!> Cesar retorted. <I dealt with last week's disturbance!>

<It was a rabbit! A rabbit brushed up against the fence and triggered an alarm! Ooh, you are so brave to deal with such a terrible threat!>

<It's your turn!>

<I have a family!>

Cesar muttered under his breath as he walked out of the guardhouse and up to the door of the truck. Loosely translated, he said: "Son of a horizontal vegetable crackling hyena!" Some idioms are just too local!

<What do you want?> he miserably asked the truck driver.

Pause. <Shouldn't your line be: "Halt! Who goes there?">

<You, too? Jesus begesus, does everybody in the world feel it their duty to tell me how to do my job?>

Pause. <Sorry. Of course, you are the one with the rifle, so you can say whatever you feel is appropriate to the moment.>

<Good. As long as that is understood.>

Pause. <Understood.>

<Halt! Who goes there?>

Pause. <Ice cream man. Somebody here ordered ice cream.>

Cesar turned back to the guardhouse and shouted, <Manny! Did anybody here order ice cream?>

Manny took a clipboard off a nail on the wall and looked a couple of sheets over. Returning the clipboard to the nail, he shouted back, <No deliveries of ice cream have been scheduled for today.>

Pause. <Been have a rough day?> the man in the truck asked.

<It would make a strong man weep!> Cesar, turning back towards the truck, answered with a sigh.

Pause. A hand emerged out of the window holding a peanut butter chocolate fudge ice cream bar. <I hate to see somebody having a bad day. On the house.> Cesar took the ice cream bar and began unwrapping one end as the hand retreated back into the truck.

<Hey!> Manny shouted. <What about me? I've been having a bad day! A terrible, rotten, no good day! Don't I deserve some ice cream?>

Pause (almost as if the speaker didn't speak a word of Spanish and was being fed his part of the conversation by somebody at a distant location through a communications chip implanted in his brain). <You've been having a bad day? Sorry to hearing it. If you come out, you can have some ice cream, too. What are you think? I have collapsible arms?>

Manny left the guardhouse as Cesar enthusiastically bit into his ice cream bar. The hand emerged from the truck once again, this time offering a chocolate peanut butter drumstick.

<Could I get a cone?> Manny politely asked. <You know, with the swirly ice cream on the top?>

Pause. <Sorry,> the man in the truck told him, <but my swirly ice cream on the top machine is broken. If you don't like drumsticks, I could always substitute it for something else…>

<It's very good,> Cesar enthused, <even if it does smell of halibut.>[2]

After unwrapping it and tossing the paper away, Manny bit into his ice cream. <Mmm,> he agreed. <I see what you mean.>

Pause. <So, if you gentlemen would be so kindly to let me in, your friends can also enjoy some ice cream.>

<Sorry,> Manny replied, <but we can't let you in. Your name is not on the list.>

Pause. <But I gave you ice cream,> the man in the truck protested. <We're friends, now.>

<Was this…some kind of bribe?> Cesar asked.

Pause. <What? Bribe? Pfft! Nooooo!>

<Good. Because we cannot be guarded in our bribe duties!>

---

[2] Ah. Yes. About that. Felix Heavior wasn't able to get an ice cream truck on such short notice. He settled for the next best thing: a truck that sold street fish. Deep battered halibut was its specialty, but it also sold deep battered salmon, poached salmon, scrambled salmon, salmon over easy, and salted squid. It took no time at all to cover the truck with white enamel and paint a menu of ice cream treats on the side. It was even a relatively simple matter of emptying the fridge, hosing it down and replacing the frozen fish pieces with ice cream. However, no matter how often Heavior's crew hosed down the fridge, they couldn't entirely remove the fishy smell from it. No plan is perfect.

<Wait,> Manny protested. <That can't be pickles…>

<Pickle flavoured ice cream?> Cesar counter-protested. <Eww!>

Cesar and Manny looked at each other for a moment, then started giggling. <Allegheny pothole frump frump!> Cesar snorted.

<Glub glub painting warehouse!> Manny responded.

Cesar and Manny dropped their rifles and sat on the ground with their backs to the guardhouse. Cesar stared at the back of his hand as if the secrets of the universe would be revealed on it if only he paid it enough attention. Manny tried loudly counting backwards from one million, but always got confused before he managed to say ten numbers and started again.

Certain that the two men's attention was not on their job, Daveen Rasmalai walked out the back door of the truck. Whistling 'A Happy Tune' (from the Broadway hit *Hannibal: The Musical*), he removed his white jacket and threw it back into the truck, after which he wrestled the uniform coat off of Manny and put it on. Since Manny was a much bulkier man, Daveen Rasmalai almost disappeared into the coat, but he figured that nobody would notice because this often happened with outfitting a mercenary army. He just hoped that the same nobody would notice his red bowtie.

"Thank you," he said to the man who continued counting backwards. Daveen Rasmalai didn't believe the conspiracy theories about the CIA having secret labs where they developed all sorts of nasty drugs, but he was grateful that Heavior was able to supply him with a fast-acting hallucinogen, wherever he had obtained it from.

Daveen Rasmalai walked into the guardhouse and looked around. Control panel. Desk with short-wave radio. Two chairs. Pin-up picture on the wall from the 1950s. He was disappointed that it was such a cliché. Would it have killed them to have a poster of Stephen Hawking and the Event Horizons on the wall instead of the pin-up, or a Gobi desert snow globe on the desk? Not wanting to spend any more time in the guardhouse then he needed to, Daveen Rasmalai pushed a button on the control panel and, walking over the seated guards, entered the compound through the opening gate.

"Okay, Ladybug, Ladybug," he sub-vocalized. "I'm in."

<Far out!> Cesar commented to nobody in particular.

<Nine hundred and ninety-nine thousand, nine hundred and…and…and – dammit!> Manny agreed.

Four squat, single storey buildings stood before Daveen Rasmalai. After explaining the situation to his field commander, he asked, "Where do I go from here?"

"The building that's closest?" Ladybug, Ladybug suggested.

Helpful, Daveen Rasmalai thought. He strode towards the front door of the nearest building and walked in. He found a small reception area, off of which two corridors diverged. He considered asking Ladybug, Ladybug which one to take, but, mindful of her most recent answer, decided he could take the closest corridor without being advised to.

The corridor contained a dozen doors, six on each side, over which were lights with red, yellow and green components. The green light over the third door on his left was on; the lights over the rest of the doors were red. The corridor was actually lit by overhead fixtures. Daveen Rasmalai tried the first door on his right; finding it open, he walked in.

The room contained a chair, a dresser and an odd looking eight foot high black tube with a door on the front and a control panel on its side. Daveen Rasmalai recognized it immediately.

An Orgasmatron.

Daveen Rasmalai's vision went all soft-focus. He remembered being at one end of a field with Rodney Pendleton, the first alien to come to Earth Prime, his charge, at the other. Recognizing each other, they started running across the field in slow motion. Running towards each other. Running. Daveen Rasmalai spread his arms in welcome. Rodney did the same. Running towards each other. Running. Daveen Rasmalai sprouted a big, goofy grin. Rodney responded with a bigger, goofier grin. Still running towards each other. Still running. Daveen Rasmalai skipped through the flowers in the field, giddy with anticipation. Rodney skipped, almost tripping over a tulip, but correcting himself at the last moment; at this point, the mo was so slo, the stumble actually made him appear to move faster. Too much running towards each other? So much running! Just when you couldn't take it any more, Daveen Rasmalai and Rodney met in the middle of the field and embraced...or, tried to, an Orgasmatron suddenly appearing between them. * CLUNK *! * CLUNK *! Fortunately, they were going so slowly that it didn't hurt as much as the sound of crashing into the machine may have led you to believe. The pair threw back their heads and laughed.

Okay, Daveen Rasmalai and Rodney's encounter in the Orgasmatron may not have actually happened this way. And there was no scene in a fancy restaurant where Daveen Rasmalai playfully smeared a little tomato sauce on Rodney's nose, the alien responding by dumping the plate of spaghetti in Daveen Rasmalai's lap. And the pair throwing their heads back and laughing. And they definitely did not go to a farmer's market where Rodney made a generous offer to buy the stool the woman at the vegetable stall was sitting on. And everybody threw their heads back and laughed. People often romanticize romantic encounters. The important thing was that Daveen Rasmalai had known Rodney Orgasmatronically, and, while he may not remember every sexual partner he ever had, he never forgot a sex toy.

Daveen Rasmalai conveyed the scene to Ladybug, Ladybug. Then, he left the room and went to the door marked by the red light. He opened it. He found a room that was exactly the same as the first one he had entered, with a couple of exceptions: the wardrobe door was open, revealing clothes inside, including the vest of an exquisite three piece suit; and, the Orgasmatron was humming, lights on its control panel periodically blinking. Before he could plan his next move, Daveen Rasmalai heard the door of the building open. He jumped into the room and closed the door, leaving it open just enough to hear the conversation of the people who just entered the building.

"Are you enjoying your stay, Mister Burpstein?" a woman's voice said.

"Naah!" a man replied. "This country is too damn hot! If the mosquitoes don't eat you alive, the price of the hotel will! All the drinks at the bar are watered down, and the internet is spotty!"

"But there is one good thing..." a timid, tired voice hopefully suggested.

"Ferk, yeah!" the man replied.

"Some days, the air is barely breathable!" the timid, tired voice said with as much enthusiasm as it could muster.

In the silence that followed, Daveen Rasmalai could hear a door opening.

"Here we are!" the woman brightly said.

"You trying to be funny?" Mister Burpstein bitched.

"It is my –" the third voice started; it was cut off by the shutting of the door.

Figuring the coast was clear, Daveen Rasmalai walked out of the room he was in. A burly soldier with a bushy moustache and squinty eyes had been posted on the opposite door (the light next to which had turned yellow). After a moment of startled silence, the guard asked, <What are you doing here?>

Pause. <Following orders. What are you doing here?>

This confused the soldier. <Following orders.>

Pause. <Carry on,> Daveen Rasmalai ordered and sauntered out of the building. He didn't look back; had he, he would have seen the light next to the door change from yellow to green.

As soon as he was out of the building, Daveen Rasmalai quick walked to the door of the next one. He entered a barn, a large single room, that was dimly lit. At the far end was a glass-enclosed office in which people were moving. Between him and the office, the floor was lined with cages. Six foot high, four foot wide, definitely not handsome cages.

"Are you room service?" a voice, heavy with exhaustion but game, asked. "Because, if you are, I have a complaint about the food!"

"I've been here weeks, and never once came back to my cage to find a mint on my pillow!" a second voice, heavier than the first, moaned.

"I've been here longer," a third voice groaned, "and I never once came back to my cage to find a pillow to have a mint placed on!"

"Red Rover, Red Rover," Ladybug, Ladybug asked, "what the ferk is going on?"

"Aliens," Daveen Rasmalai told her. "A couple dozen at least. All in cages."

He walked up to the closest cage. The alien in it had

sunken features, as if his face had deflated, and seemed too thin for his exquisite three piece suit.

"Hey!" the alien stated with a cough. "You…you're not the concierge!"

"I'm Daveen Rasmalai," the human introduced himself. "I'm here to help."

"Yeah, yeah," the alien remonstrated. "Humans claiming they were here to help are what got me into this mess in the first place!"

"I…I'm a friend of Rodney Pendleton…"

The alien's eyes widened. "You…you know our middle names," he whispered. "You must be here to help!"

"That doesn't really make any sense," Ladybug, Ladybug commented.

Like anything that had to do with the alien culture did? "What's your name?" Daveen Rasmalai quietly asked.

"Michelangelo de la Frathouse," the alien introduced himself. "Pleased to make your –" he started coughing. "Your – kaff kaff – your – kaffity kaff kaff – yeah. Pleased."

"Michelangelo de la Frathouse is one of the names on our list of missing aliens," Ladybug, Ladybug confirmed. "He hasn't been seen for three and a half months."

"What's going on, here?"

Once the coughing fit had subsided, Michelangelo answered: "When I came to Earth Prime, I was employed as a futurist for a research firm in Brazil. A couple of months ago, I went all pon fary all over the place. You know how it goes. I had heard of this company that had a machine that could meld bodies together, so I contacted them and came here to have my needs…taken care of. Turns out, my needs weren't what they were concerned with. Once we arrived, I was thrown into a cage. If I don't perform ten…twelve…fifteen times a day, they won't give me food."

"You did come here willingly," Daveen Rasmalai pointed out.

"You know what they say about the Orgasmatron: the first time is for pleasure; by the sixteenth time, it's become work; by the thirtieth time, you stop feeling anything in the lower half of your body!"

"Okay, that's enough," Ladybug, Ladybug had difficulty keeping the disgust out of her voice. "What we have here is a case of alien sex trafficking. I'm making the call to Felix to send in the troops and shut it all down. My guess is that there will be a firefight – get out of there as quickly as you can. Over."

"Copy that," Daveen Rasmalai sub-vocalized. "Over and out."

"Are you…subvocalizing?" Michelangelo asked.

"Don't worry," Daveen Rasmalai, depending upon your point of view, assured and/or ignored him, "Help is on the way."

"Will it…" Michelangelo huffed.

"Yes?"

"Will it…" Michelangelo puffed.

"Will it what?"

"Will it…come with Grey Poupon?" The effort of making the joke seemed to tire him out; he fell back against the bars of his cage.

"And a mint?" the second voice piped up.

"And a pillow to put it on?"

Knowing that somehow this was going to turn out alright, Daveen Rasmalai left the building with a smile on his face and a bounce in his step. He headed towards the gate, but stopped well short of it.

"Red Rover, Red Rover, is everything all right? Over," Ladybug, Ladybug asked, concerned.

Daveen Rasmalai looked back at the buildings. There were two that he had yet to explore. On the one hand, he was confident that Heavior's team would clean the place up. On the other hand…he had a lot of unanswered questions that he wanted to know the answers to.

"Red Rover, Red Rover, the party is over." Ladybug, Ladybug waited a moment for Daveen Rasmalai to mistake her statement for a sign that she was done talking. When he didn't, she continued: "The tactical team will make sure of that. Get out of there. **Now!** Over."

Shaking his head, Daveen Rasmalai turned and ran in the direction of the third building. He had to know. Thanks to the chip implanted in his head and the satellites in orbit above him, Ladybug, Ladybug knew that he was running in the direction away from safety. "Daveen! What are you doing? Get the hell out of there before the firefight starts!"

"I have to know," Daveen Rasmalai grimly told her.

"You'll know in a couple of weeks when Heavior writes his report! Daveen...Rover! **Red Rover!**"

Daveen Rasmalai entered the third building. He walked into a large reception area with at least 30 chairs. At the front of the area was a counter behind which a glass wall gave a view of an open office. On this side of the counter, three people sat on chairs, clutching small slips of paper that they must have gotten from a small machine next to the counter with a sign that read: "Please take a number and you will be served when your number is called." And indeed, somebody was calling, "Number nine. Number nine. Number nine. Numb –" When a woman's voice broke in and announced, "Number twenty-seven. Now serving number twenty-seven. Will number twenty-seven please bring their ticket to the service counter," he realized that it was actually the muzak playing in the background. And that he wasn't going to find what he was looking for in this building.

Daveen Rasmalai stuck his head out of the door. Seeing that the coast was clear, he strode towards the final building in the complex. Inside, he found a small room in which a big guard sat behind a small desk, watching security footage on black and white televisions. Looking up, the guard asked, <What are you doing here?>

Daveen Rasmalai smiled at him, waiting for Ladybug, Ladybug to feed him an answer. When all he heard were the thoughts rattling around in his head, he sub-vocalized, "A little help, here, please? Over."

<I asked you a question,> the guard growled. <What are you doing here?>

"I am not going to support you in this madness," Ladybug, Ladybug informed him. "This is suicide!"

Daveen Rasmalai's smile broadened as he sub-vocalized: "You think hastening me to my death by forcing me to ignore this guard's question is going to help?"

The guard stood up, a hand on the holster on his hip. <I am going to ask you one last time: what are you doing here?>

Pause. <I've got an urgent messaging for the secure chief!> Daveen Rasmalai gratefully spit out.

The guard looked at him for a moment. <Are you drunk?> he asked.

<I've got an urgent messaging for the secure chief!>

Daveen Rasmalai repeated with greater urgency.

<What is your urgent **message**?>

Pause. <There is an ice cream truck outside the gate, which is opener!>

<An ice cream truck?> If there had been any more disbelief in the guard's voice, he could have been mistaken for Richard Dawkins. <You **are** drunk!>

Pause. <Look at the camera on the gate if you don't believing me.>

Keeping one weary eye on Daveen Rasmalai, the guard leaned over, pressed a couple of buttons and set his other eye on the screen. His eye on the screen registered surprise and his eye on Daveen Rasmalai reluctantly joined it to find out what all the fuss was about. The second eye widened to match the surprise in the first eye. They both turned to Daveen Rasmalai just in time to see the fist that punched their lights out.

Daveen Rasmalai sat the guard in as natural a position as his unconscious body would allow, then pressed a button on the desk which opened the only other door out of the room. As he crept into another corridor with many doors off it, he heard Ladybug, Ladybug say, "Tactical team is expected to arrive in seven to eight minutes. Try not to get yourself killed before then, okay, Red Rover, Red Rover? Over."

"That's always the plan," Daveen Rasmalai smiled to himself.

He stood in the doorway, uncertain what to do next because he didn't know what he was looking for. He may have found it by looking through the rooms one at a time, but he may also have found somebody who would alert security to his presence on the compound. As he considered his options, Daveen Rasmalai noticed an odd aroma in the air. He hadn't smelled that smell for a long time. He had hoped never to smell it again. Could it be…could somebody be smoking a carrot?

Daveen Rasmalai followed the smell to the third door from the end on his right. He raised his fist to knock, then, realizing that politeness was not appropriate in this situation, barged into the room shouting, "P. J.! You bastard!"

"The Bastards of the Universe is my posse," the silver-haired man sitting with his back to the door contemplating the Margaret Keane poster on the wall behind his desk smoothly said. Then, taking a bite from the end of the carrot that wasn't on fire, he added: "What's your excuse, D. R.?"

"I don't do that any more," Daveen Rasmalai told him.

"So I heard. Word is that you work for the Transdimensional Authority now. Really? You can take the boy out of the con…"

"I don't do that any more," Daveen Rasmalai insisted.

"It's freaky, don't you think, how those eyes follow you around the room?"

Despite his best efforts not to, Daveen Rasmalai looked at the print on the wall. The image was of a young girl slithering along the floor in a crocodile costume. The girl had unnaturally large eyes. Daveen Rasmalai doubted that they moved when somebody in the room moved, but now that Pinchus had given him the idea, he would get the feeling that they did. The bastard could get into your head that way.

"Alien sex trafficking," he admonished. "That's low. Even for the Bastards."

Pinchus turned to face him. "We go where the money is. You know that. Besides, the aliens come here willingly. They want to use the machine – they **need** to use the machine."

"Once," Daveen Rasmalai argued. "But you keep them in cages and force them to go through it a dozen or more times a day. You're killing them."

Pinchus rubbed his manfullly stubble-strewn chin thoughtfully. "There's plenty more where they came from."

Daveen Rasmalai glared at him. "I'm going to enjoy framing your mug shot and hanging it in my living room."

Pinchus shook his head and put the flaming carrot stub out in an ashtray on his desk. "People like me don't do jail time," he informed Daveen Rasmalai.

"Because your wealthy backers buy your way out."

"Because evil cannot be easily confined to a single human being. We all have the potential to commit evil acts, and most of us do at one point or another in our lives. Arrest me? You may as well try to arrest human nature. And human nature has a great team of lawyers!"

"Okay, Red Rover, Red Rover," Ladybug, Ladybug urged in Daveen Rasmalai's head, "you've had your confrontation with the bad guy. All that has happened is that you've given him an opportunity to give us his vacuous but somehow plausible theory of good and evil. Could you please get the hell out of there before you over –"

"We're going to stop you," Daveen Rasmalai ignored her. "We've got a team on its way to shut this whole atrocity down."

"Share." Ladybug, Ladybug completed her thought.

Pinchus smiled. He took a deep, satisfying breath and enthused, "I love it when a plan falls apart."

"Because then you have an excuse to blow shit up."

"I don't need an excuse to blow shit up. But yeah, okay, it's easier to explain the whole blowing up thing to clients that way."

"You gonna take the rest of your posse with you when things blow up?"

"They're not here."

"They're not?"

"Naah." Pinchus took a big, fat, orange tuber out of a desk drawer and a cigarette lighter out of a pants pocket. He lit one end of the carrot and took a big chomping mouthful of the other end. "Eustace is in China – they're finding all sorts of interesting uses for the aliens. You've got to hand it to the Chinese – they can be very creative when they want to be. Jessie is advising the British government on how to identify unwanted aliens using nothing more than chewing gum and a network of surveillance cameras. You know how she likes a challenge. And chewing gum – I hear she's working on a model Eiffel Tower out of used wads of –"

"Why are you telling me this?" Daveen Rasmalai interrupted.

"Oh, you know, we're just two old friends catching up," Pinchus casually remarked as he placed the carrot in the ashtray. "Maybe I'm proud of the work my colleagues and I are doing. Do I have to have any more reason than that to talk to you about things that are happening in my life?"

"P. J., you always had trouble with the fine line between banter and revealing too much. It was usually because…" Daveen Rasmalai's voice trailed off.

"Yes?" Pinchus looked him straight in the eye, not blinking

"Don't keep us in suspense, Red Rover, Red Rover," Ladybug, Ladybug said in Daveen Rasmalai's head. "Why would –"

Daveen Rasmalai turned and ran out of the room. At speed.

"Red Rover, Red Rover," Ladybug, Ladybug's voice took on a concerned edge. "Is anything going on that I should be concerned –"

A siren started to wail somewhere inside the compound.

"Red Rover, Red Rover," the edge in Ladybug, Ladybug's voice became a plane. "What the hell is –"

"When P. J. Pinchus overshares," Daveen Rasmalai thought at her, "it means that he has tripped a silent alarm, and that he's keeping you occupied talking while his goons are coming to get you. I learned that the hard way in Sevastopol."

"Red Rover, Red Rover," Ladybug, Ladybug suggested, "if you can get out of the building, I can guide you to a rendezvous point with Felix' team. Ov –" Ladybug, Ladybug was interrupted by the sound of shattering glass, followed by a loud, "Unnggh!" as a body that had just flung itself out a window hit the ground. "Okay, if you can move, get over –"

"To the treeline," Daveen Rasmalai grunted. "Already one step ahead of you."

Several * BLAM * * BLAM *s were followed by several * pew * * pew *s as the gunshots aimed at Daveen Rasmalai's receding back hit the ground around him.

"Daveen, are you being shot at?"

"Not very professional of you, Ladybug, Ladybug." Daveen Rasmalai said with a grin. As he made the treeline, several soldiers ran around the side of the building, one of them shouting orders. Flashlights were trained on the point he had disappeared into the flora, and the gunfire intensified on that spot. "Over."

Daveen Rasmalai wasn't overly worried. The soldiers were Ventrosian squiggles; given the flippity floppity of their limbs, even in their human skinsuits, their ability to hit a moving target was on a par with an Imperial Stormtrooper. Daveen Rasmalai considered slowing his pace and even running through clearings, but he didn't want to be mean.

Then, the sound of the hotline to the President from the film *In Like Flint* could be heard.

"Red Rover, Red Rover," Ladybug, Ladybug psychically increduloused at him, "was that the sound of a ring tone? Did you…take a phone with you **on a mission?**"

"Over?"

"Bloody over!"

"Sorry, Ladybug, Ladybug, but I have to take this."

"Red Rover, Red Rover, don't you dare –"

But Daveen Rasmalai did dare cut the connection between them and answered the phone.

"Rodney?" he asked, definitely flapped.

"Daveen? I have a problem," Rodney Pendleton stated.

"Kinda busy, here, bud," Daveen Rasmalai said as he started zig-zagging through the trees to make it harder for the marksmen to hit him.

"Luuuuuucyyyyyy! conked out! And we're starting to hear that it happened to other hoverboards – it could have happened to a lot of other hoverboards!"

"Sounds like you got hacked," Daveen Rasmalai said, although it sounded more like, "Sounds – gasp – like you – pant – got hacked."

"What can I do about it?" Rodney asked.

"Well…" In the seconds Daveen Rasmalai considered this question, he managed to put substantial distance between himself and the compound. The voices seemed to soften, although the gunfire continued unabated. "Okay. This is what you do. Convene a department heads meeting. Determine the scope of the problem. Find a technical solution. Develop a public relations campaign to assure people that Aboveboard Hoverers are perfectly safe." (Distribute heavy breaths to taste.)

"Can I drink coffee?"

"Expect to drink more coffee in the next couple of weeks than you have in the rest of your life! This will be –" Daveen Rasmalai would never finish that thought, because a burst of automatic gunfire rattled his head and a bullet caught him in the left thigh.

"Everything okay?" Rodney asked.

"Nothing I can't handle," Daveen Rasmalai assured him. But he was thinking: *Lucky shot. Nobody should have been able to hit me the way I was zigging, especially the way I was zagging. Probably a ricochet. One in a million. Ferking ricochet.*

"Are you sure?"

"It's only a flesh wound." Daveen Rasmalai slumped behind the trunk of a large tree, hoping he wasn't visible to his pursuers. He tore the leg of his pants up as quietly as he could to assess the damage. Have you ever seen the film *There Will Be Blood*? There was.

"Okay. If I need help in the future…?"

"Feel free to call me any time." Daveen Rasmalai ripped a strip of cloth off the pants altogether and fashioned a tourniquet out of it. It wasn't runways of Paris fashionable, but saving your own life never goes out of fashion.

"I'm sorry," Rodney continued.

"For what?"

"Here I am, talking about my problems, and I haven't asked about you. How have you been? It's been – what? – months since I last saw you! Keeping busy?"

"You know me," Daveen Rasmalai did his best to keep the wince out of his voice, "as long as there are bad guys to stop, I'm happy."

"How is Noomi?"

Mention of his sister made Daveen Rasmalai smile. "She must be doing something right – talk is she is being considered for a promotion at the Transdimensional Authority."

"That's fantastic! I…have always had the utmost respect for her professionalism," Rodney did his best to sound sober and professional.

Daveen Rasmalai wasn't buying it. "I'm not buying it," he commented. "I've seen the way you look at her hair."

"I can't figure out the mathematics of it!" Rodney blurted. "I'm sure that if I could, I would learn something profound about the universe!"

Daveen Rasmalai was about to respond that, no, Noomi had just gone a little crazy with the straightener when she was younger and, just as their mother had warned her, her hair had stayed that way, when the gunfire behind him intensified. "Listen, bud, I'd love to catch up, but I'm kind of in the middle of a situation, here. How about I give you a shout when I get back home?"

"Wouldn't a phone call be more effective?"

"It's a figure of speech."

"Shouting at somebody standing next to you is considered

rude by humans," Rodney mused. "Maybe if you shouted from another room –"

Over the sound of gunfire in the distance, Daveen Rasmalai could make out the sound of twigs breaking very close by. "We'll talk! Gotta Go! Bye!"

"Good shouti –" Rodney got out before he was cut off.

Propping himself up on the tree as best he could, Daveen Rasmalai stood on his good leg and balled his fist in preparation for a fight.

"Is that any way to greet the cavalry?"

The next day, The Operative and The Field Commander were back in a small room in Ottawa, debriefing with M-C. The five year-old boy in The Operative much preferred debriefings to briefings.

"When The Operative's communications inexplicably gave out," The Field Commander was saying, pausing only to give The Operative a dirty look, "I tracked his position by satellite using his chip implant. It quickly became apparent that he was running away from our men. So, while they engaged with the enemy, I directed Felix Heavior to his –" An eight bit version of the chorus from 'Ode To Joy', the ring tone for a message from The Field Commander's son, rang out in the room. "Sorry, I – I gotta take this."

The Operative gave her a sardinic look (it's like a sardonic look, but with a fishy smell). "Taking a phone into a briefing?" he commented. "How unprofessional!"

M-C glared at her with a ferocity that would have stripped the enamel off her fingernails if she had been paying attention. Realizing that it was wasted in this situation, he packed the glare back in its titanium case and asked The Operative to continue the debriefing. The Operative enthusiastically picked up the tale, describing in detail how he had the situation well in hand and did not need the CIA agent's help.

Mom! the message read, Fraidy is acting weird! Tell her to stop!

What is she doing? Field Commander Mom! asked.

You know what happened with the Hoverboards yesterday?

Been busy. There's been a discovery of a new textile that could revolutionize the international carpet industry.

They were hacked. They all crashed.

What does that have to do with your sister?

She kind of hinted the day before yesterday that i shouldn't use my hoverboard. It's almost like she knew or something.

The Field Commander sighed. It was a sound that hadn't been heard in that room for over twenty years. The room recognized that the sound was unprofessional, but it also acknowledged that the sound was human. It kind of missed that humanity. So, the room learned something about itself: that it was okay with a sigh. In fact, it kind of looked forward to its next sigh…in a couple of decades.

I'll deal with it, The Field Commander wrote. Thanks for letting me know.

If her teenage daughter was involved with hackers, The Field Commander mused, Fraidy would be in over her head. Was she inches from the surface, or a kilometre down? The Field Commander couldn't take the risk: she would be in Ottawa for another couple of days at least to fill out the paperwork, and there may be a follow-up investigation that could take her more time. She had to act quickly to help her daughter!

The Field Commander went through a list of encrypted email accounts that went routed via more than 20 servers, making them difficult to trace. Barumba Aslan. Felicity Huffandpuff. Anders Honshu. Gislaine Rutabaga. Gislaine Rutabaga! The Field Commander opened the account on her phone, clicked on 'New Message' and typed the first thing that came into her head: Dear Wilberforce. Having a wonderful tyme in Merrie Olde Azerbaijan. Wish you were hair. Enjoy the photo of our summer cottage. Love, Aunt Berthetamine.

Then, she looked through a catalogue of images that she always kept on her phone for just such an emergency (doesn't everybody?). Of course, there were no images of Azerbaijani summer cottages – that would have been too easy! She scrolled through a variety of thumbnails, quickly assessing images that included: a kitten adorably biting the tail of a Doberman Pinscher; cars driving on the wrong side of the street (known as ordinary driving in England); an image of the head of the Infant President on the body of a baby with its hand on a red button; a black and white image of an abandoned factory, complete with boarded up windows and graffiti of rocket ships, snakes, snakes coiled around rocket ships and the tag 'Jonez96'.

"Field Commander?" M-C broke through her concern about her daughter. "Field Commander!"

"Oh, umm, yes?" Abandoned factory it was. The Field Commander hastily attached the image to the email and sent it. Then, she pulled her attention away from the phone.

"We're talking. About the…the…sex doohickeys. What'd y'all call 'em?" M-C was telling her?

"Orgasmatrons," Daveen Rasmalai told him.

"Right. Those. Pinchus got 'em. Any idea where?"

Ladybug, Ladybug shook her head. "Before this mission, I didn't even know such things existed. Now, they're going to haunt my dreams for the rest of my life."

M-C snorted. "I seriously doubt that," he responded. "You're a highly trained professional. You don't have dreams. Operative, ideas? Where Pinchus could have. Got his hands. On an Orgasmathingie?"

"Erm," Daveen Rasmalai answered.[3]

---

[3] Ideas can mask other ideas, like the spoonful of sugar that makes the cyanide go down. This isn't lying, exactly, since the speaker isn't directly saying something that they know to be untrue. But it isn't exactly honesty, either.

This one word uttered by Daveen Rasmalai, for example, masked the conversation he had with Rodney as he was lying in bed after doctors had removed the bullet from his leg and cleaned up his wound.

"Hey, buddy," Daveen Rasmalai greeted his alien friend.

"Wazzuuuuuuuuup?" Rodney answered.

Daveen Rasmalai didn't want to know what he was doing with his tongue. Daveen Rasmalai couldn't help thinking about what he was doing with his tongue. Yikes. "I have a question for you."

"Oooh. I have an answer for you: forty-two."

"Un hunh. Find out. It'd be a good idea. Very helpful to the investigation."

"Yes, Sir," Daveen Rasmalai sheepishly agreed.

"Field Commander. Your next move. What is it?"

The Field Commander took a deep breath. "Oh. Uhh, well. We have to assume that if the Bastards of the Universe are

---

"...Okay. Good answer. I'm sure it explains many things. But not the answer to the question I actually want to ask."

"The speed of light plus ten."

"Still not an answer to my question."

"The Taj Mahal on a donkey's back!"

"Okay, now I feel you're reaching."

"Okay, fine, what was your question?"

"I was just in a...facility in Venezuela that must have had at least a dozen Orgasmatrons. You're the only person I have ever known who had one. You wouldn't happen to know where theirs came from, would you?"

"Oh, paper clips!"

"Is that some kind of...alien swear word?"

"I was just trying to help other immigrants!" Rodney blurted.

"How?"

"We still experience pon far, even though we cannot meld our bodies together any more. I had scientists at AlTech reverse engineer the Orgasmatron I made with my suitcase and start producing them for distribution to cultural centres for my people. It was a good thing."

"Buuuuuut..."

"But four months ago, a dozen Orgasmatrons were stolen out of our warehouse. Obviously, I couldn't report the theft to anybody because I don't want anybody to know that I'm making the machines. People might think it was weird."

"Un hunh. And what does this have to do with paper clips?"

"Paper clips is the line item in the annual AlTech budget that I use to fund the production of the Orgasmatrons. I learned that trick from the Infant President, back when he was an Infant Construction Tycoon."

"Of course."

"You won't tell anybody, will you?"

"I suppose not."

"Can I get the stolen Orgasmatrons back?"

"Don't push it." (In fact, they were now the property of the United States government. But it would take months to arrange to have them shipped to the US, and the only scientist who would have any success in analyzing how they worked would be Doctor Alhambra, and he is notorious for hating to share.)

Not lying but not telling the whole truth can be a sneaky bastard!

involved in alien sex trafficking, they must be involved in all sorts of other malevolent behaviours. We should probably put some resources into finding them and stopping them."

"Operative?"

The Operative agreed. At length. Giving The Field Commander the opportunity to complete her task. She clicked on an icon of several different birds jumbled together to open a programme called BlendIt. The programme inserts secret messages into photographs and reads them when somebody else has inserted them. It's simply a matter of comparing the original (first photograph) with the adulterated (second) photo to find the changes that have been made. The Field Commander chose the image (file name: "Cronk007Kite"). Then, she clicked on an icon of the letter a with a double arrow pointing to the letter z and typed: Hey, Sweetie. Are you helping around the house while I'm away? Dad is...high energy, but he can only do so much. Anywattles. Something strange happened yesterday, and I'm worrying just a bit. You kno. Like a mother does. If you have any problems in the future, anything so big that you just don't feel like you can handle it alone, text Dr. Alhambra for help. Yes, that Doctor Alhambra. His private number is: 416-638-444. But it has to be important – HE IS NOT THERE TO HELP YOU WITH HOMEWORK! Okay? Okay. Toodles schnoodles. Mom

The Field Commander frowned. Not her best work, but she was under a severe time constraint. She clicked on an icon of the letter a being slipped into an envelope, then saved the image (which was automatically given the file name "Cronk007Kite_002").

Having completed the message encoding, The Operative reopened the Gislaine Rutabaga email account and typed in the following message: `Dear Wilberforce. Did you receive my last message? The one with the photo of my vacation in Punkton, New Brunswitch? The internetwebz is intermittnet out here, so I'm not sure if you did. Tell you what. I'm resending the photo. Hopefully, one of them went through. Love, Aunt Berthetamine.` The misspelling of the word "intermittent" was her masterstroke; she hoped that, if anybody was monitoring her daughter's email, they would see that word and write Aunt Berthetamine off as a semi-literate crank. She hoped that –

“We’re agreed, then?” M-C cut into her thoughts.

“Sir?” The Field Commander blinked.

“Belgium. You’re going. To find the Bastards.”

“Oh. Umm. Yes, sir. Belgium, sir.”

The Field Commander sighed. Inwardly, this time, so as not to disturb the room. She had to hope that she had taught Fraidy well enough and that her daughter was resourceful enough that she would weather whatever was ahead of her. Duty called, and you don’t ghost duty!

One week later, psychology was busting out all over the place.

“People who have undergone traumatic experiences often use humour as a defence against feeling the pain associated with the trauma,” a small, painfully earnestly helpful man said.

“You say that like it’s a bad thing,” the alien responded.

“Past a certain point, it is,” the small man rubbed a bald spot on the back of his head. “Pain can –”

“If you rub your bald spot hard enough,” the alien inquired, “does smoke pour out of your ears and eventually take the shape of a genie?”

The man looked at his hand, which had not sought permission for its rendezvous with the back of his head; this came as some surprise to him. After a moment, he said, “You see, that is exactly what I mean. I’m trying to explain to you why what you are feeling isn’t healthy, and you divert the discussion with jokes.”

“Why don’t you listen to me talk about my actual feelings?”

“Okay. What are you feeling?”

“Happy.”

“No, you’re not!”

Good listening, Michelangelo de la Frathouse, the alien, thought. Out loud, he said, “I’m going to grab myself a piece of pie. Do you want one?”

"No. Thank you. I'm trying to lose weight," the man, a xenopsychologist employed by the Transdimensional Authority to help victims of traumatic experience put their lives back together, responded. He looked like if he lost any more weight, he would be joining the imaginary (at least, until you rub hard enough) genie in the space under his bald spot, but Michelangelo didn't think it would be polite to say so, so he went into the kitchen of his small apartment (he could afford better, but he had learned a lot from his job as secretary to a financial planner) and took himself a slab of cinnamon foozleberry pie.

Michelangelo returned to the den, sitting opposite the man from the Transdimensional Authority. "You've had a horrific experience," the man said. "You were kept in a cage for weeks, given a minimal amount of food, washed irregularly and forced to have sex a dozen times or more a day. We just want to make sure that, after all of that, you're okay, that you're well enough to get back to your life."

"Muuummf ubn snurf," Michelangelo said through a mouth full of pie.

"I'm sorry, I don't – what?"

"Mumfhububble flibn snurf!" Michelangelo said more emphatically.

"Nope. I still don't –"

Michelangelo turned the spork he was eating with towards the man, jiggling it a little to make it look like it had an independent existence. "What he's trying to say, Nimrod, is that you're barking up the wrong electricity tower," the spork, in a higher voice than Michelangelo, stated. "He is an alien. He doesn't have human psychology because he hasn't lived as a human for very long."

The man was impressed that Michelangelo could speak through the spork without moving his lips, although the alien lost points for the spork's hostility. "I can appreciate that," he responded. "But when you are abused, it has to leave a negative imprint on you somehow. Nobody comes away from such experiences without some bad consequence."

The spork shook its head. "You don't understa – hold on a second. Duty calls."

Michelangelo took the last piece of pie, a big one, and stuffed it into his mouth. Then, he allowed the spork's attention to return to his visitor, bobbing...tines and all. "Look. Humour is not a coping mechanism for Michelangelo's species. It's a religion and a way of life. Have you ever considered the fundamental implication of such a philosophy?"

"I...I'm not sure what you're getting at."

"Course you haven't, pudding for brains! You love your theories so much you don't pay attention to other people's actual reality. Laughter is a judgment on experience. When you laugh, you are saying that what is happening to you is not worth crying over, not worth taking seriously. If you laugh at everything in your life, good and bad and everything in between, you are recognizing that life itself is ephemeral, and that you shouldn't take any of it too seriously. Pain, pleasure – these, and all the other things that sentient beings experience, shall pass."

"I can't believe I'm getting a philosophy lecture from an eating utensil," the man marvelled.

"Tell me about it!" the spork responded. "I used to be a movie star – I shared screen time with a couple of legends. And held my own! Now look at what I'm reduced to!"

Michelangelo swallowed what was left of the pie in his mouth. "Thanks, Sporko. I couldn't have said it better myself. Except that part about being a movie star – man, you've got issues!"

The man shook his head. "Okay, well, honestly, I'm not sure I believe this. You can't go through what you went through without **some** adverse effect. However, if you tell me you're fine, I guess I have to take you at your –"

* BRAAAAAAAP *! "Oh!" Michelangelo apologized. "Well, excuuuuuuuuuse me! I have no idea where that –" * BRAAAAAAAAAAAP *! "I, umm, yeah, is this normal with human bod –"

"Some belching happens to most people at some point, but –"

* BRAAAAAAAAAAAAAAAP *! "What's happening to me?"

"Well, if I had to guess, I would say that even though you are emotionally okay with what you've been through, your human body is reacting to the suffering that was inflicted upon it."

"Can you –" * BRAAAAAAAP *! "**Can you help me?**"

"Of course," the man said, giving Michelangelo a warm smile. "That's what I'm here for." But inside the man, deep inside, a place he was only dimly aware of, a small voice said, "Got you, you bastard!"

Three months later, the Data Collection and Interpretation and Technical Support branch of the Transdimensional Authority sent a report to Albert Abrachnel, the head of the Investigators branch of the organization. Marked Super Duper Double Whammy Top Secret, the gist of the report was that after extensive testing of the matchbook picked up by The Operative, DCITS could conclude with 97 per cent certainty that it was, in fact, a matchbook. It had not been altered in any way.

Xenia Zaifman knew that the case involving the matchbook had been closed two days earlier when The Operative was unable to track down P. J. Pinchus or the other Bastards of the Universe and that, because of this, Abrachnel would put the file in a folder that would be stored in a box six rows across from the Ark of the Covenant. However, she saw every report her department produced as proof that the Transdimensional Authority existed, a kind of bureaucratic 'Kilroy wuz here'. She took comfort in the idea that her thoroughness would stand the test of the ages.

Educational Interlude 003

An alien in an exquisite three piece white lab coat stands at a lectern in front of a large screen on which a slide reads: "Srinivas Smerph Kawasaki, BA, MA, PhD, LDL, IMO, RCM (Pea), TMI, Professor of Alien Studies at the University of Hard Fort Knox, Guest Lecturer, Alternaut Academy." A picture of Professor Kawasaki in an exquisite three piece suit, scuba diving in somebody's backyard pool in the suburbs sits above the text. Professor Kawasaki sports steampunk goggles. In one hand, he holds a laser pointer; in the other, a remote.

"Hello. I am Professor Srinivas Kawasaki. I teach at the University of Hard Fort Knox. I..." Professor Kawasaki turns to look at the screen. He sighs. Turning back, he continues, "But, uhh, you, already knew that. You also know that I teach Alien Studies, which is part of the Inhumanities Programme at UHFK, and that I am currently a guest lecturer at the Alternaut Academy."

Professor Kawasaki presses a button on the remote. The text and image on the screen explode in a shower of coloured pixels that must have dazzled early adapters of computer animation, but now just gives viewers mild headaches for no good reason. In its place, a cartoon of an alien with a big goofy grin on its face, even though the top of its head has been removed and a pair of white gloved hands is holding its brain an inch out of its skull, shudders into view. Under the cartoon is the caption: "Inside the alien mind."

"Today," Professor Kawasaki lectures, "I would like to take you inside the alien mind. Most of you are..." He turns and looks up at the screen. "Oh, come on!" he mutters. "If the slides are going to show everything I plan on saying, what's the point of my being here and talking?"

Professor Kawasaki fumbles with the remote for several seconds; lots of text pops up only to quickly be replaced by different text and, in one case, a picture of a stork in ballet slippers. Eventually, an image of an alien male and an alien female in matching exquisite three piece suits sitting in a motorboat on a serene lake appears on the screen. The man casts a fishing line over the side as the woman proudly holds up a purple fish with three eyes. The caption reads: "I went to graduate school for 9 years, and I'm still expected to catch my own food!"

"Much better." Professor Kawasaki turns away from the screen. "If you have seen an alien from Earth Prime 4-6-4-0-8-9 dash Omega, you have probably asked yourself, 'What the heck goes on in their minds?' Well [INSERT READER'S NAME HERE], today is your lucky day, because I'm here to tell you! Okay, the day may not be as lucky as the day you find out that that lottery ticket you bought three weeks ago and immediately forgot in the bottom drawer of your purse is a sixty-four million dollar winner. But the day is certainly luckier than the day you dug around in your purse to find that lottery ticket you bought three weeks ago and promptly forgot until I just reminded you of it – you're welcome – only to find that not only wasn't it a winner, but a chocolate bar you bought at the same time had melted all over everything.

"Okay, they may be more or less the same, luck-wise. Days can be coy that way."

Professor Kawasaki points the remote over his shoulder and clicks it. The image on the screen shudders with an engine revving sound, then returns to normal. A second later, it shudders more forcefully, with a more insistent revving sound, but returns to normal. The third time, the image roars to life and speeds off the right side of the screen. It is replaced by an image of the alien man and woman sitting across a small table from each other in a romantically lit restaurant, eating a single piece of spaghetti at each other. Only, if you look closely, you can make out that it is a shoelace, not spaghetti. Good thing Professor Kawasaki keeps talking, distracting you from the impulse of looking at the ersatz food too closely.

"Because our bodies are shaped to mimic human bodies when we migrate to Earth Prime," Professor Kawasaki continues to lecture, "Our brains look like human brains. Only, as you can see from the slide on the screen, downsized to fit our smaller skulls. And with an extra fiddly bit. Ah, the story that extra fiddly bit could tell if we lived in a universe where all matter could speak for itself! But we don't, not any more, so it can't, so I will have to speak for it. When we recreate our bodies to live in this universe, we encode our memories in our mitochondrial DNA. That's right – every alien is a genetic computer. **Now do you understand how we can carry 5,000 lives worth of memories inside of us?**"

Professor Kawasaki glares meaningfully at the auditor. Just at the point where the look is about to become uncomfortable...and a few seconds more...he continues, "That extra fiddly bit? That's what reads the memories stored in our genes. Ah, now it all makes sense. At least, I hope it does, because this **will** be on the final exam."

With a click of the remote, the following image appears on the screen:

"So, what goes on in the brains of alien immigrants to your reality?" Professor Kawasaki goes on. "I have prepared some pie charts – mmm, pie! – to represent common patterns in our thinking. The first slide represents the brain content of Rodney ..."

Professor Kawasaki turns to look at the screen. His face drops when he sees what is displayed on it. "Oh, that's not right," he complains. "Who – that's just not right. Umm...okay, that's what happens when you rely on interns, but there's nothing I can do about it now. For the record, the segment of the pie labelled 'Fairy dust' should be switched with the segment labelled 'Conceptual humour'. And, the segment labelled 'pie' – mmm, pie! – is a little on the nose. Otherwise, this is a fairly accurate representation of the thinking of Rodney Pendleton, who, as you probably know, was the first alien to immigrate to Earth Prime."

With a sigh, Professor Kawasaki turns back from the screen. "As you can see, a substantial amount of his brain space is taken up by a certain baked good. This is by no means unusual. Things that would occupy most of the space of a human brain such as work or money or last night's baseball scores were not important to us on our home Earth, and two years after he came here, Rodney still hasn't quite got the hang of what passes for normal in this universe. We will. Probably. Maybe. Given enough time. As you may have noticed, we're a rather unpredictable group, which makes studying our behaviour an especially delightful challenge."

With another click of the remote, the following image appears on the screen:

"As you can see," Professor Kawasaki continues, "different people from Earth Prime 4-6-4-0-8-9 dash Omega give different subjects more or less brain space. This chart represents..." Seeing the blank looks on the faces of the students in the first row, he turns to look at what is on the screen. "That's not – is that...?" He skips back to the previous image. Then, to the new image. Then, previous. Then, new. Previous. New. Previous. New. "Hunh. How about that?"

The new image is left on the screen. "This chart represents the thoughts of Soledad Pushkin, a woman I first met on Earth Prime 4-6-4-0-8-9 dash Omega. In that reality, te was a medical doctor; te helped me recover after a safe fell on my head. Long story – not relevant here. Te drives a cab on Earth Prime. Many of timer fares end up in hospital having suffered a mild heart attack or high anxiety – so the circle is, in some sense, complete."

With another click of the remote, a third image appears on the screen:

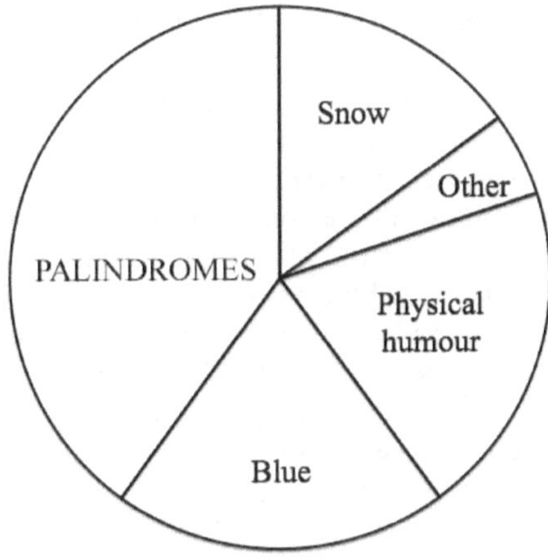

Professor Kawasaki turns to look at it. Previous. New. Previous. Previous. Previous. New. You know the drill. Eventually, he leaves the third image on the screen and turns back to the students.

"These mind pies look suspiciously the same," he allows. "Perhaps it's just the way alien brains allocate thoughts when we take on human bodies, and they will diverge over time. Perhaps it's an elaborate joke played on a humble researcher with more degrees than common sense. Whatever the cause, I believe that there is value in seeing these graphic representations of our thought. We may quibble about the ratio of the subjects aliens think of, but it should be clear that their brains work with fundamentally different processes than those of Earth Prime humans. Because of this, it should be easy to understand why their behaviour is different from that of Earth Prime humans."

As if to prove his point, Professor Kawasaki sticks the laser pointer in his left ear. The red beam comes out of his right ear, illuminating the handle of the door on that side of him. After several seconds, he takes the laser pointer out of his ear, turns it over in front of him a couple of times, and shrugs. "I don't know why I did that," he admits. "Probably to prove a point, but I have no idea what that might have been."

Professor Kawasaki shakes his head in wonder. "In any case…if we drill deeper into the alien brain, we find some surprising facts about the way aliens think."

Professor Kawasaki clicks the remote. The screen starts rotating, getting faster and. faster until it is a blur of colour. Just when you begin to wish you had taken a Gravol, the rotation slows to a stop, revealing a new image: an alien in a shopping mall full of human beings dropping the pants of his exquisite three piece suit. The caption reads: "Relax! This only happens once in a blue moon!"

"They say that you can tell what a race or species values by what it has a lot of words for," Professor Kawasaki continues the lecture. "To illustrate this point, they say that northern Indigenous people have 127 different words for snow. I don't know who 'they' are. Maybe they are snow-cone manufacturers trying to drum up business. Maybe they are precipitation fetishists. I am still trying to get my head around the human concept of theyness. Whoever they are, they are wrong: northern Indigenous people only have seven words for snow. There were so many different regional **pronunciations** of the small group of words that it seemed to early researchers like there were 127. By the time researchers recognized their mistake, it was too late: the myth of the 127 words for snow had been packed into a tight ball and thrown at the academic community, and it stuck there.

"Umm, yes, well, as you can see from the chart on the screen…" Professor Kawasaki turns the laser pointer on and, without looking, points it over his shoulder at the screen, highlighting the alien's left butt cheek. "…the alien race from

Earth Prime 4-6-4-0-8-9 dash Omega has 983 words for acts of humour. They include: 'lavid' (comic social embarrassment); 'mouth malfunction' (spit take); 'eruction eruption' (originally referring to belching, but generalized to any rude bodily noise); 'parlabaloid' (comic embarrassment when one is alone); 'farfetchednugen' (the comic irony of a character not knowing something that the audience knows); 'genuggenugen' (the comic irony of a situation being the reverse of what the audience believes); 'pulling an Ira' (inadvertent physical comedy, small scale); 'pulling a Jacques' (inadvertent physical comedy, medium scale); 'pulling a Buster' (inadvertent physical comedy, large scale); 'blenkenfreuden' (comic misunderstanding among friends); verblenken (comic misunderstanding among nations); Egobooyah (the comedy of an individual or race or species knowing that it is a character or characters in a work of fiction when nobody around them does); 'splunge' (comic sounds); 'hunkahunka' (rude words); and, 'baby's arm holding an apple' (comic lists that end with a recurring non-sequitur that most people won't recognize as a cultural reference). As you can see, the terms can be quite specific. By way of context, my race only has five words for food, which are modified by size, shape and colour, among other descriptive modifiers. Yep. You haven't lived until you've tasted a short brown tube of meat and baked small brown vegetables in a sticky sauce!"

Professor Kawasaki turns towards the screen, then turns back. "As you might – wuuuuuuuuuh‽" He turns back to the screen. "Who put that – that slide isn't supposed to appear until the final lecture of the term!"

Turning back to the class, Professor Kawasaki assures them: "Don't worry. That **will** be on the exam, but it's the easy question." He points the remote ahead of him and, with an audible, "Awwwwww…" the projector turns off and the screen goes black.

Professor Kawasaki looks at his wrist, which is conspicuously bereft of timepiece, and says, "Okay, time for one more point. You may be wondering about alien names. Where I come from, everybody knows everybody else on a molecular level, so we have no need for names. When we want to address somebody specific, we call them 'Bob'.

Anybody or anything can be called Bob. And they are. Somehow, the Bob you intend to speak to knows it is the one, and not one of the ten to the power of 127 other Bobs in the universe. You would be amazed at how much you can communicate with three letters and every atom in your body.

"When aliens of my species first meet humans of your kind, the atoms in our brain communicate with the atoms in your brains so that we may learn your language. Humans that I have told this to have been scandalized about an invasion of something they call their 'privacy'. I would ask you to try and see it from our point of view: when you are able to communicate with every other object in the universe down to the sub-atomic level, privacy is simply not a high priority. And anyway, your species is especially funny when you think nobody is listening. But – ahem – you didn't hear that from me.

"One of the things we quickly learn about human beings is your need to name everything, including each other. So, when we are communicating with the brain of the first humans we contact, we pluck what we hope are names out of their brains and adopt them. In my case, Srinivas was the name of a man who wrote a series of comic books that the human being who first made contact with me had seen on his father's bookcase when he was seven and had all but forgotten. All but. But not all. Kawasaki was the brand of motorcycle that my first contact and his best friend Krieger had seen in an ad in a rock music magazine when they were both fifteen; they pledged to save enough money to be able to one day afford to buy one, but they used their money to buy more rock music magazines instead. All members of my species have the middle name   . No, your hearing hasn't momentarily failed you – it is silent. Our middle name is not Bob, but it is somewhat equivalent in our communications system.

"So, you see, although curious, there is a system to our na – why are you putting away your – is the lecture over already? I'm so glad we had this time together, just to have a laugh and sing a – okay. See you all on Friday. **Live long and nanu nanu!**"

CHAPTER FIVE
Band Age Solutions

Saving the Alien One Song at a Time

by TINA LOLLOCADENKA, Alternate Reality News Service Music Writer

The single-named singer / songwriter Eonayr is the definition of a laid-back pixie chick (which isn't a thing, but could be if the fickle public can be convinced to continue buying her new age heavy metal music long enough for the *OED* to catch up with the term). With the slightly built young woman's pink spiky hair and the dozen or more pieces of metal coming out of her ears, you don't know if you should be asking her if she would like you to buy her an apple juice or offering to help her dispose of the one true ring.

You wouldn't expect her to spearhead the recording of 'We Are the Weird', a song to raise funds for the alien relief effort.

"I can't take the credit for that," Eonayr modestly told us. "It was Wainwright Walsh's baby – I just...changed its diapers and put a little talc on its bum once in a while."

Wainwright Walsh? Wasn't he...umm...you know...that guy...who did that thing...it had something to do with music – you know the one we're talking about... No? Sorry, we got nothing. So, we'll focus on Eonayr, instead.

On the strength of gold and platinum selling albums such as *Auras and Oracles* and *Shot of Enlightenment to the Head*, Eonayr (pronounced: "Yawner," not "Whiner," as her detractors insist, or "Weiner," a term which makes Farcebook reviewers giggle, which tells you all you need to know about how seriously you should take **that** source of music criticism) made a lot of connections within the music industry. As a result, when she saw a report on the plight of the aliens from Earth Prime 4-6-4-0-8-9 dash Omega, her little pixie heart was broken and, being who she is, she had to write a song about it.

"Actually, no," Eonayr tried to correct us. "The person who wrote 'We Are the Weird' was Wainwright Walsh. He was the one who first contacted the musicians who contributed to the song. It was his heart's desire – I just...helped him find the right greeting cards and stamped some envelopes for him."

Why do you keep talking about Playwright Welsh like we're supposed to know who you're talking about?

"It's Wainwright Walsh!" Have you ever seen an outraged laid-back pixie? Her eyes crinkle and she puffs at a stray spike of hair threatening them. "Wainwright Walsh? Lead singer of The Occidental Tourists? I remember when my dad gave me his copy of their single 'Mock It to Mars'. I...I didn't have a record player, so I couldn't listen to it. But I fell in love with the idea of making music from that little round piece of cheap plastic with the hole in the middle. Without The Occidental Tourists, there would be no Eonayr!"

Okay. Guess they were important, then.

"I was watching television with my daughter," Wainwright Walsh told us about his inspiration for the song (which we're still not 100% convinced he wrote, but we don't have the heart to argue with Eonayr about – she's devastating when she brings her pouty A game), "when she asked me who those blue people on the screen were. I told her they were a group of pretentious performance artists and that she should ignore them. When she told me she liked their three piece suits, I had to check it out, because I was pretty sure the people I was thinking of were minimalists who weren't into such fine clothing. That was the first time I saw the aliens and learned of the danger they were in."

And that's what inspired him to write 'We Are the Weird'.

"At first, I felt helpless," Walsh continued, oblivious to our need to move the article along. "What could one singer/songwriter – even one with an unobtainium album – do in the face of such a massive tragedy?"

Use his song writing skills to write 'We Are the Weird', which is a song.

"I consulted friends and family, but they felt exactly the same way," Walsh soldiered on (i.e.: he was stiff and fetishized chain of command). "Hell, I even threw yarrow stalks to get an *I Ching* reading. I should really clean them off my neighbour's lawn – sometimes, I don't know my own strength!"

Finally, after much soul searching, he decided to write a song and invite some of the biggest names in the recording industry to record it with him to raise money to help the aliens integrate after they immigrate.

"Finally, after much soul searching," Walsh finally, after much unnecessary word searching, concluded, "I decided to write a song and invite some of my friends in the recording industry to record it with me to raise money to help the aliens after they immigrate."

We just said tha – gaack! Moving on.

Musicians are not generally considered to be shrinking violets, the incredible shrinking man or prone to shrinking from responsibility. Okay, maybe a bit of the latter. Regardless, we asked Walsh what it was like to work with so many stars.

"We had a bouncer collect their egos at the door," he answered. We started to laugh, but the sound died in our throats when we realized that he wasn't kidding. "Diane Wine. She's very big in the karmic adjustment community. Their egos were dry cleaned and spit polished before they were returned to their rightful owners. They may have grumbled about the treatment, but most of them hadn't seen their egos in such great shape in years!"

So, there was no tension? None at all?

"Weeellll...Keef did try to punch the lights out of a lamp he mistook for a paparazzi," Walsh admitted. "But that's just Keef bein' Keef, innit? Look, we mostly recorded people's parts two or three at a time, so there really wasn't much opportunity for clashes."

Not to mention that all of the participants believed in the cause?

"Goes without saying," Walsh sniffed.

Consider it unsaid.

"Keef?"

"Arrowr. Whozzah?"

"Hey, man. How ya doin'?"

"Ohma ammadef, caff caff, coupla frizzlin har hars. Annu?"

"Can't complain, brother. Can't complain. I –"

"Ha so ha ha innit naw hooha?"

"Wainwright, Keef. It's Wainwright."

"Wayhaha? Youwro uhh uhh uhh cuzu nevahdi?"

"No, that was Johnny. 'Because You Never Did' was the first single from his solo album."

"Ha ha ha. Right tonka tha un!"

"You got that right. I'm Wainwright Walsh, The lead singer of the Occidental Tourists. You remember the Occidental Tourists, right? We opened for you in '84."

"Lotta bandsofor – caff caff – inna ehfour."

"Remember the night we got drunk and trashed a hotel room in Toronto?"

"Lotta bandsrash – caff caff tellroms in Tranna."

"Okay, that doesn't –"

"Wherami?"

"What?"

"Wherami?"

"London, Keef. We're in London."

"Naaah! Nevaherd offa – ha ha – place!"

"Wha – you've lived in London for most of your life!"

"Issadafact? Furreal? Cuz – ha ha – caff caff caff!"

"Umm…yeah. Listen, I'm trying to put together a project –"

"Hava negila tada wid seelyin?"

"No. No, it has nothing to do with sea lions. It's about –"

"Waddya gottagain seelyin? Degotta rights ta – caff – rights ta caff caff – right?"

"I'm sure sea lions are marvellous creatures. It's just that there are these aliens who –"

"Seelyiner ferkin' magbificent neasts!"

"Yeah, you know what, Keef. I think I'm gonna –"

"Hooza?"

"I'm Wainwright Walsh! Rainwright foorkin' Walsh!"

"Yeah? Hunh hunh hunh. Pulludda one – iplays jingerbells! Ha ha ha."

"Yeah. I'm gonna call some other time, okay?"

"Goatfarts?"

"Yeah, you, too, Keef. You, too."

"Sir Paul?"

"Yeah?"

"It's Wainwright Walsh."

"Oh, yeah! Wainwright! Good to hear from you!"

"You have no idea who I am, do you?"

"Not a clue. One does try to be polite, though."

"Lead singer of the Occidental Tourists."

"Was that a sixties waffle band?"

"Eighties. Kind of punkish. Our single 'The World's Going to Hell (And I'm Not Doing So Well)' went unobtainium."

"Mmm…not ringing any bells…"

"Yeah, Pete, our drummer, heard *Tubular Bells* one night and swore off anything outside his basic kit."

"I mean, I can't quite place the name."

"Okay, how about this? Remember when John got into a fight in 1983 with a man who told him that Yoko's installation art was pretentious? He had to have three stitches and buy a new pair of those goofy glasses he used to wear?"

"Yeah! Yeah! Good times!"

"That was our bass player, Johnny Concepcion. I drank his beer while he was going at it with John."

"Of course! Wainwright! It really is good to hear from you, mate! How's it goin'?"

"Good. Good. Listen, I'm trying to put together a band to record a song for charity. Can I count on your support?"

"What's the cause?"

"Alien refugee relief."

"Crikey, Wainwright! You couldn't have picked a more controversial cause?"

"They're in a bad way, Sir Paul, and they could really use any help we could give them."

"Well, when you put it that way…"

"Yes?"

"Did you call Keef before me?"

"What?"

"Did you call Keef before you called me?"

"Whu –? Don't be ridiculous. I never –"

"You did! You did call Keef before me! Of all the bloody cheek!"

"Be fair, Sir Paul – I had to call somebody first! It's not like he even gave me a chance to ask him for his help – you know what passes for communication in his mind these days! So, technically, I asked you for help first. You do appreciate that, don't you, Sir Paul? **Sir Paul?** …Oh, bollocks!"

"Joseph?"

"Is it –? No, it couldn't be!"

"Yeah. It's –"

"Wain-wright ferking Walsh."

"How's it going, Tequila Joe?"

"Wow. Nobody's called me that in ages!"

"Brings back memories, though, doesn't it?"

"Of my liver transplant, you mean?"

"Oh, yeah, I was sorry to hear about tha –"

"Or, maybe you were thinking of the memory of you shagging my wife while I was passed out drunk in the den?"

"Shagging is too strong a term, Joseph. We were just snogging."

"Full body snogging, you mean? The kind that requires no clothes?"

"It…it was just rock and roll, Joseph. Everybody was doing it."

"Well, doesn't that cover a multitude of sins, then?"

"How is Marsha, anyway?"

"Martha, you mean?"

"Yeah, Martha."

"Marsha is great. At least, I assume she's great. She left me…thirteen…sixteen – no, gotta be at least twenty-one years ago."

"I'm sorry, man."

"Yes, but you were a great lay –"

"Come on!"

"–dy's man."

"Oh. Yeah. Okay."

"Waddya want, Wainwright?"

"I have a song –"

"Don't we all?"

"It's about the alien refugee crisis –"

"Aren't they all?"

"I'm looking to put together a lot of name musicians to

record it."

"What, as a charity thing?"

"Yeah."

"Who would be daft enough to agree to something like that?"

"I've been talking to Keef, Sir Paul, some others…"

"And they agreed to be a part of it?"

"They are currently considering it, yeah."

"Working with you?"

"Yeah."

"On a charity project?"

"That's right."

"And you're askin' me to be part of it?"

"Ye-es."

"Ferk off."

"I'll take that as an opening bargaining position."

"I didn't realize this was a negotiation."

"Being part of this will be good for your career."

"What career? **I retired twenty years ago!** I exist on a dwindling bank account, social security and the memories of a small band of fans."

"This could help you recapture the magic of Tequila Joe."

"Whenever my gut feels like it's on fire, I remember the magic of Tequila Joe."

"How about this? If Keef agrees to come on board, will you?"

"Psssht. For a chance to work with Keef, I'll give you half my remaining liver, and it's not like I have all that much to spare!"

"I'll give you the details as we work them out."

"Yeah. Sure. Ferking Keef. Dream on, mate."

"Great talking to you, too."

"David?"

"David is not in right now."

"Yes, you are."

"I am sorry, but David is not in right now."

"David, we've spoken many times. I know your voice."

"…Pardon me for being imprecise. This is David's body. His persona is not in right now."

"Who am I speaking to?"

"Do you mean: 'To whom am I speaking?'"

"Okay, you're too pedantic to be Ziggy Mollusc. Is this the Thin White Drake?"

"I am…between personae at the moment. I find it very peaceful, not being anybody in particular."

"Okay. Sure. This is Wainwright Walsh. I –"

"I recognize your voice. As you observed, we have spoken many times."

"…I'm working on a project that I think David would be interested in. I –"

"I am sorry, but I am not authorized to make decisions on behalf of David."

"**But you are Da** – sorry. Sorry about that. Would you be able to take a message? You know, give it to David when he comes back?"

"I can do that."

"I'm trying to put together a group of musicians to work on a special project –"

"To raise money to help alien refugees."

"How did you know that?"

"The Thin White Drake was talking to Mick, who heard about the project from Keef."

"But I didn't get a chance to describe it to Keef."

"He is much more alert and intuitive than people give him credit for."

"But I didn't give him anything to base an intui – okay. Never mind. Keef is a law unto himself. The point is, yes, I would like to raise money to help resettle the alien refugees. I figure the more stars we get to perform the song, the more money we will raise. It's a great cause, so I was hoping David would want to contribute a couple hours of his time to it."

"That could be difficult."

"Oh, why? Because I asked Keef before I asked you? Can't you put your ego aside to help an important cause?"

"I am persona non-persona. I do not have an ego."

"Umm…yeah. Then, why would it be difficult for him to contribute?"

"David has been working himself sparse over the last couple of years, and he needs to slow down for his health."

"Oh. Ahh. Okay. I'm very sorry to hear that."

"Would you still like me to convey your message to him?"

"Well, yes."

"Your **whole** message?"

"Oh. Ahh. Maybe without that last bit about your – his ego. David doesn't need to know about that."

"Very good, Wainwright. Was there anything else?"

"Well…just…I always assumed that David loved the alien."

"Actually, that was four personae ago. Really, Wainwright, if you want his help you should try to keep up!"

"Wainright?"

"Yes."

"Wainwright Walsh?"

"Yes."

"Wainwright Walsh, lead singer of the Occidental Tourists?"

"You planning on going through my whole resume before you get to a point?"

"Hi. I'm a big fan."

"Un hunh. How did you get my number?"

"We have mutual friends. Wainwright – may I call you Wainwright?"

"Who are you?"

"My stage name is Eonayr. You can call me Susan."

"Who –?"

"Yeah. I've never had an unobtainium album, but I have had two gold albums and one platinum album – that's gotta count for something, right?"

"I'm sorry, but I nev –"

"Hey, do you think we could cut an album together? Our music couldn't be more different – it could be really good for both of us, a real artistic growing experience!"

"Lady, what –"

"Susan."

"Susan. What do you want?"

"Oh. Well. I was talking to Sir Paul –"

"You know Sir Paul?"

"I told you we have mutual friends, Wainwright. Really, this will be so much easier if you pay attention."

"Oh. Umm…sorry."

"No need to apologize. I'm used to it from you people."

"'You people?'"

"You know. Old."

"Old? Let me tell you something, Lady –"

"Susan. Please, Wainwright, call me Susan."

"Fine. Susan. Age is just a number. You gotta lotta ver –"

"Wainwright, please don't get defensive."

"How old are you?"

"Seventeen, but that doesn't –"

"Seven – cough – seventeen?"

"Age is just a number, right? Look, I want to help you with your alien refugee project."

"How can you help me?"

"Well, I thought it was a great idea the moment Sir Paul told me about it. It certainly makes a nice change from talking about pheasant hunting and how unfair the British tax system is – you know how Sir Paul can be. I asked him how I could be part of the project, but he said he didn't know because **he** wasn't planning on being a part of the project. I asked him why, natch. Can you believe that guy?"

"Umm…yeah. It was kind of…childish."

"I know, right? I told Sir Paul he was being a silly old fuddy duddy, that this was a great cause and he shouldn't stay out of it just because you borrowed a couple thousand bucks from him a few years ago and never paid it back."

"Is that the reason he gave you for not agreeing to be part of the project?"

"Yeah. I –"

"**That's** the reason he gave you?"

"Don't sweat it. I reminded him: the life of a musician. Right? It's not like he can't afford it. And anyway, he shouldn't allow a little thing like an unpaid loan to keep him from doing something good for other sentient creatures. He hemmed and hawed and tried to change the subject to his estate, but eventually he agreed. So, he's in."

"You got Sir Paul to agree to contribute to the alien refugee support song?"

"Didn't he call you? He said he would call you."

"No, he didn't call me!"

"I'm sure it'll only be a matter of time before he does."

"Sure."

"I had a talk with Keef, too. It can get...complicated talking to Keef, as I'm sure I don't have to tell you. But he's excited to be part of the project."

"He is? Keef?"

"Or, he was excited about having a roast beef sandwich for lunch. It's hard to tell with Keef. Either way, he assured me that he was in."

"Oh. Umm...thank you?"

"You're welcome. I've spoken to a few of my other friends about the project – they are definitely excited by it. If you have some room, you might want to consider them."

"Friends? What friends?"

"Oh, you know. Elvis. He may sound like a sour bastard on his albums, but he's actually kind of sweet. Lulu – remember Lulu? She's still amazing. Peter – he knows all about what's entertainment. Friends like that."

"Erm."

"So, what do you think?"

"I understand that there are...tensions in the band."

"Not really, no."

"So, you haven't been too...indulgent in the rock and roll lifestyle?"

"Oh, I wouldn't say that."

"But it hasn't been easy, what with all the sex and drugs?"

"There were some problems, but me and the boys worked them out."

"Only, wouldn't it be great if working on this charity gig brought you and the boys back together?"

"I'm telling you: we are together. There is nothing to bring us back from."

"I know you say that, but when the biopic of your life is produced, this is going to be the pivotal moment. In that story of your life, you will have alienated your closest friends, your closest co-creators, as you descend into a destructive spiral of excess. You will want to be a part of something bigger than yourself, no, you will **need** to be part of something bigger than yourself in order to bring yourself back to yourself in a way that will allow you to reconcile with your mates before you die a tragic death."

"Before I **what?**"

"Okay, that dying a tragic death part's negotiable. Maybe…maybe you will find your soul mate and live happily ever after. The point is: you need redemption, and working on this song will give you the perfect opportunity for it."

"But I don't need redemption. This is what I'm trying to tell you!"

"But how will your future biographers be able to create a redemption story out of the raw material of your life if you don't do anything to redeem yourself?"

"I…I don't know how to answer that question."

"Exactly."

Before the conversation could take a rational turn, the doorknocker (in the shape of a man's testicles – I could try and shrug it off by saying it was the eighties, but the combination of too much money and testosterone can spawn an architectural abomination at any time period) thundered throughout the house. "I gotta go."

"So, you'll think about it, yeah?"

"Umm…I guess…sure."

"I'll see if I can interest any screenwriters. Musical biopics are hot, baby! They're smo –"

Ding-a-ling-a-ling-a-ding-a-ling-a-ding-a-ling-a-ding-a-ling!

"Yeah! I'm coming!" Wainwright Walsh shouted after he hung up and ran out of his study. Ding-a-ling-a-ling-a-ding-a-ling! Down the hallway. Ding-a-ling-a-ling-a-ding-a-ling! Down the stairs to the first floor. Ding-a-ling-a-ling-a-ding-a-ling! He threw the front door open.

"Yeah! Puff puff. Whaddya – huf huff – want?" he worked hard to catch his breath.

"Hey!" a woman's voice admonished him. "My eyes are down here!"

There was an alien woman on Wainwright Walsh's veranda. She was blue, hairless and wore an exquisite three piece suit; the only way he could tell that she was a woman was the slight bulge in the chest of her vest. The only thing that made her in any way different from others of her species was the triangle case and silver stick that she carried in her left hand.

"Can I – puff puff – help…gasp…you?"

"Help me?" the alien woman said. "You should look at helping yourself by losing some weight!"

Wainwright Walsh looked at the woman. If he wasn't so out of breath, he would have chastised her for her rudeness. As it was, he was just able to get out, "What?"

"We don't have doorbells where I come from," the alien woman told him. "We always know when somebody is approaching our homes. Interesting concept."

The alien woman reached for the button next to the door. Wainwright Walsh swatted her hand away. "**What do you want?**" he loudly demanded.

"I hear you're getting the band back together. I'm here."

"You were never **in** the band."

"You're not going to hold that against me, are you?"

Wainwright Walsh started to close the door. "Hey!" the alien woman quickly continued, "You want to record a song to support alien refugees. Don't you think it would look better if you had an actual alien refugee on the project?"

Wainwright Walsh reluctantly reopened the door. "That has a certain logic to it," he allowed.

The alien woman held out her free hand. "Tara Raboomdeeh. Pleased to meet you!"

Wainwright Walsh looked at the proffered hand like it was a sheath of snakes. He shook it anyway. "What, uhh, instrument do you play?"

Tara proudly held out her triangle. "I've been playing it for three days! It's not really that hard – you just hit it with varying degrees of enthusiasm. But you know what they say: the simplest tasks take a lifetime to master!"

Wainwright Walsh was only partially listening to her. He was thinking he could get her into the studio to record for five minutes, then bury her part in the mix. That way, he could get credit for having an alien work on the song without the hassle of having the alien actually work on the song.

"Sounds good," he smiled. "Welcome aboard."

Tara smiled. "Yay!"

"How do I get in touch with you to let you know when we start recording?"

Tara stopped smiling. She looked down at the ground, where the big toe of her right foot seemed to be kicking the stone of its own volition. "Yeah, about that," she meekly said. "Can I stay here until we record?"

"Absolutely not."

"I could be very helpful to you. Very helpful." Tara looked up and batted her eyelashes in what she hoped was a seductive manner.

"I don't need any help," Wainwright Walsh coldly responded. Part of him was intrigued, but most of him was repulsed.

"Everybody needs help with something. I could…clean the place."

"I already have somebody come in three days a week."

Tara leaned in and slid a finger over the bench inside the door. After inspecting her finger, she disappointingly said, "They're good. They're very good."

"I know." Wainwright Walsh smiled smugly. Smugled.

"I could be your driver."

"When I leave the house, I use taxis."

"It would be less expensive to have your own car."

"I don't leave the house that often."

"Now that you're recording a new song, you will."

Wainwright Walsh raised his voice in pride. "I no longer own a car. They're bad for the environment."

"But you take taxis every – " Tara had enough sense to know that she couldn't argue with such nonsense. "I could cook for you."

"I cook for myself."

"I'll bet I'm better."

"You'll lose that bet. I've been cooking for myself since I was a kid – it's a hobby of mine, and I'm quite good at it."

Tara put her free hand on her hip and tried to put the hand in which she was holding her triangle on the other hip. Awkward. Eventually, she held the triangle out to Wainwright Walsh and asked, "Can you hold this for me, please?"

"Umm, sure." He reluctantly took the musical instrument, hoping that it wouldn't go off.

With both hands firmly on her hips, Tara could properly say, "You're a hard man to help, you know that?"

Wainwright Walsh ruefully responded, "I have been told."

"Thanks for your help," Tara added gratefully, taking back the triangle.

"If there's nothing else…" Wainwright Walsh was tired of the conversation.

"Look, you want me to stay with you."

"I do?" Wainwright Walsh was pretty sure he didn't, but he was starting to be taken in by the alien's enthusiasm.

"Imagine how it would look if you took in one of the aliens you're writing a song to support. You'd be even more of a hero, you know."

"Well…" This was a new idea for Wainwright Walsh, and, although he could see its appeal, he wasn't crazy about new ideas.[1]

---

[1] Are there any new ideas in the world? They say there are only seven (or thirty-seven, or five) original ideas; everything else is just old ideas dressed in revealing clothing to distract you from recognizing where they came from. They may be right. But even if they are, that doesn't mean that original human thinking stopped some time in ancient Egypt.

Let us say that there are only two ideas: the pleasure of eating and the importance of staying alive long enough to keep eating. These two ideas will require different expressions over time and in different places. In some places, people take pleasure in eating scorpion brains. In other places, Pop Tarts. In a similar vein, not being stung by a scorpion would be part of surviving to keep eating in some places, not going into a coma after being hit in the head by a Pop Tart that was ejected by a toaster a little too enthusiastically would be part of surviving to keep eating in others.

Perhaps there aren't any new ideas in the world. But there are

"Okay," Tara's voice got a little steel in it. It was a steel/honey alloy, which made it dangerous. Very dangerous. "Imagine how it would look if one of the aliens you're writing a song about asked you for support, and you refused to give it."

Imagining how that would look was not difficult. "Come on in." Not difficult at all.

Wainwright Walsh's office was a room at war with itself. On the one hand, he had paid a very expensive interior design engineer various expenses to get an eight page spread in *Better Gnomes and Gargoyles* (The Occidental Tourists had a wildly successful career revival a decade earlier on Earth Prime 0-0-8-2-3-0 dash delta). His desk had been ornately carved out of a single piece of oak; if the 500 year-old tree that had to be felled to make it could talk, it would have enthusiastically approved of giving its life for such a magnificent piece of furniture. The walls were lined with books everybody admired and nobody read. All of the chairs were ergonomically correct. On the other hand, magazine covers featuring Wainwright Walsh or his band had been haphazardly taped to bare spots on the walls (and, in a couple of places, to shelves over books). A small dartboard had been affixed to the back of the door (which had resulted in shards of paper from nearby books having to be cleaned regularly off the floor). The desk had burns from slopped coffee and errant cigarette ash.

In short, the room had seen better days. Like much of the world's royalty.

Wainwright Walsh was rocking back and forth in his state of the art (for a decade ago) swivel chair. Squeak. Squeak.

---

always new expressions of existing ideas. Which itself is probably not a new idea. You really ask for a lot from a lowly old footnote, you know?

Squeak. This was a common behaviour of his when he was talking to My Attorney Bernie (who, just to show how odd the universe can be, was actually an accountant).

"...love your enthusiasm for the project," My Attorney Bernie, who was the spitting image of mid-career Bob Balaban, droned. He gave the impression that the only thing he had ever truly loved was the calculator app on his phone. "Really, I do. But I can't help but wonder if you have fully thought it through."

"I have thought of everything," Wainwright Walsh assured him.

Squeak. Squeak. Squeak.

It had been too many years since the chair had been looked after; it would take more oil than the pan of a Bugatti could hold to silence it.

"Un hunh. Yeah." This was My Attorney Bernie's shorthand for, "That's the way you want to play this? Seriously? Because I can demolish you with a very small number of statements. Hell, a very small number of **words**. Are you sure you don't want to reconsider?

"Umm, I mean, I think I have thought of...most things..."

Conversations with My Attorney Bernie were places where self-confidence went to die. But Wainwright Walsh always talked to him. My Attorney Bernie was the person who advised him to take the money he made when The Occidental Tourists were at the height of their fame and use it to buy MicroSquish stock. Unlike the other members of the band, he had made a fortune over the years through a series of prescient investments, the most recent of which was AlTech Enterprises. Considering how much he owed My Attorney Bernie, he could sit for the occasional discussion that made him feel like a three year-old.

"You've discussed the project with all of the musical contributors, and they agreed to contribute *pro bono*?"

Wainwright Walsh smiled. "That's right."

"And you've had them all sign contracts?"

Squeak. Squeak. Squeak.

"Contracts?" Wainwright Walsh was confused. "We're not paying them anything – why would we need contracts?"

"To prove that you're not paying them anything." The worst thing about My Attorney Bernie was that everything he said was delivered in the same disinterested monotone, as if he had been born on Prozac. Well, one of the worst things. "Look at it this way: what will you do if one of your good friends demands to be paid? Without a contract, you'll likely end up in court. If you think my fees are too high now…!"

"Okay. Right. Contracts," Wainwright Walsh muttered.

"Did you write it down?"

Squeak! Squeak! Squeak!

"Yeah, yeah, I wrote it down!" Wainwright Walsh groused. Then, he wrote it down on a pad he always kept on his desk when he spoke to My Attorney Berrnie, because My Attorney Bernie always insisted he take notes. So, he wasn't being dishonest, he just got his timeline a little confused.

"Good." Did a – was that a hint of disbelief in his voice? Or, was it just Wainwright Walsh's guilty conscience?

Somebody knocked on the door of Wainwright Walsh's study. "Mister Walsh, can I get your help for a second?" Tara shouted through the closed door.

"I'm kind of busy, here, Tara!" Wainwright Walsh shouted back.

"It will only take a second!" Tara insisted.

"I'm on an important phone call! I'll come and help you as soon as I'm done!"

"Okay!" Tara grumbled. "I'm sure I can find the fire extinguisher on my own…"

"Finished?" My Attorney Bernie asked.

"Yeah. Sorry about that. I –"

"Okay. That's a good start, but you're going to need more than just musicians. Have you spoken to a producer and sound engineers?"

Squeak! Squeak! Squeak!

"Making a note of it," Wainwright Walsh said as he made a note of it.

"Have you considered the cost of the studio where you will be recording?"

"I…I was thinking of recording the song at the studio in my home."

"I had a feeling you were going to say that." My Attorney Bernie didn't miss a beat. "Do you have all of the equipment you need? Will you need to be moving furniture to create a Green Room for the talent to stay in while they wait for their turn to record? Have you considered how running the studio for several days will impact your electricity bill?"

Squeak! Squeak! Squeak!

Wainwright Walsh regretted not paying more attention to Tara's emergency. But he took notes. And told My Attorney Bernie that he was taking notes. No use being good if the person you were trying to impress wasn't aware of it.

"Good. Now, when the song is ready, how will you be paying to distribute it? Have you considered the cost of producing a single?"

"We won't be pressing a record, if that's what you're asking." Wainwright Walsh was confident he had thought this part of it through. "We'll distribute the song online."

"Ah. And have you negotiated a fee with the music services you plan to use?"

"Erm…"

"I can assure you, they won't distribute your song for free."

Squeak!Squeak!Squeak!Squeak!Squeak!Squeak!

"We…we can put it online ourselves! On our own web page!"

"I see you have thought this through."

"I have?"

"Somewhat. Have you considered how much it costs to have a web site designed and maintained? And of course, you will have to use a payment system that will demand a percentage of all sales."

Squeak!Squeak!Squeak!Squeak!Squeak!Squeak!

"Making notes!" Wainwright Walsh shouted.

Tara knocked on the door of the study once more. "Mister Walsh!" she shouted with some urgency. "I could really use your help out here!"

"I'm busy, Tara!" Wainwright Walsh shouted back. "I'll come and help you in a minute!"

"Fiiiine!" Tara grumped. "The lions have been fed, so they probably won't be hungry again for a few hours!"

"Wainwright," My Attorney Bernie pointed out, "I'm not telling you all of this to make your life difficult. These are issues you will have to deal with. It's better if you deal with them up front than be surprised about them in the middle of production. Right?"

"Right," Wainwright Walsh sullenly agreed.

"Good. Now, who are you going to give the money you collect to, exactly?"

"To aliens. That's the whole point." Wainwright Walsh found it difficult to keep the "duh" out of his voice.

"Which aliens?"

"Uhh..."

"How much per alien?"

"Uhh..."

"How are you planning on getting the money to them?"

"Uhh..." All he needed was the letter "d" and he would have been duhing himself.

Squeak!Squeak!Squeak!Squeak!Squeak!Squeak!

And so, with all of the financial and legal niceties taken care of, it was time to record. This was the song:

We Are the Weird

It's April First
A time for comedy
A chuckle here
A chortle there
A well slapped knee

But save a laugh
For the other ones
Who cannot gaffe
Or make terrible puns

They are the ones who live in fear
That their universe will disappear
No more grinning from ear to ear
At some wildly humorous feud
Well, tonight thank Gord it's them instead of you

We are the weird
We are the alien
We are the ones who'll disappear if we don't help them
We are the weird
We are the alien

It's April First
A time for arcing spit-takes
For inappropriate behaviour
For mocking the earnestly grave, or
For stepping on rakes

But you don't have to be a lama
To feel the suffering of those who can't ha ha
Comedy can comfort in times of strife
But not when you're looking at the extermination of all life

We are the weird
We are the alien
We are the ones who'll disappear if we don't help them
We are the weird
We are the alien

Laugh at the world
Let them know it's April Fool's again
Laugh at the world
Let them know it's April Fool's again
Laugh at the world
Let them know it's April Fool's again

It was probably the best song Wainwright Walsh had ever written. I leave it to the reader to decide what this says about the quality of his artistry.

"Can I help you?" the woman asked in a tone that indicated it would be happy to help the listener jump into a pit of scorpions or have their tax returns for the last decade be audited.

"Yeah," the old man who looked like somebody had sucked all of the liquids out of his body replied, "Werear ta sinwidda – ha ha – ban – koff koff!"

"I'm sorry," the woman said. "I don't speak Klingon."

"Yeah," the old man with the impossibly thick lips said. "We're with the band."

"I bet you've always wanted to say that, haven't you?"

"Lady, I can't remember a time when I haven't been able to say that!"

The confrontation was taking place at the front door of Wainwright Walsh's mansion. The black woman with long dreads and a little more girth than her frame would suggest she could healthily carry stood in front of the door. Immovable. Implacable. Dark glasses ensured that she remained inscrutable.

A propos to nothing, the desiccated old man said, "Sgunner ain."

The old man with the lips looked up. There were wisps of cloud in the sky, but nothing that suggested that precipitation was imminent. "Look, sweetie, it's about to pour," he told the woman. "Be a pet and let us in before we get drenched."

"Rain, hunh?" The woman was dubious.

"My friend knows things." The man with the lips put his free hand on the other man's shoulder. (They were both carrying a guitar.)

"Oh, fershur – ha ha," the desiccated man laughed. "Ma regler Nosterdammit!"

"I'll be happy to let you in," the woman told them, "but you'll have to leave your egos at the door."

The man with the lips puffed up like a rooster. A small rooster. A rooster who would gum you more than peck you. But a proud rooster despite it all. "Lady, do you know who we are?"

"Mick and Keef," the woman told them.

"Oh. So, you do know who we are."

"Whoosa koff koff brd?" Keef asked.

"Did you just call me a broad?" the woman, offended, asked.

"Naah," Mick defended his friend. "He called you a bird. No…offence was meant."

"I'll beajug ofat – ha ha ha," Keef insisted.

"And, my friend does have a point," Mick smoothly continued. "Who are you to keep us away from the recording session?"

"My name is Diane Wine," the woman introduced herself. "I specialize in karmic adjustment. Wainwright Walsh has hired me as his bouncer for the recording session."

Diane Wine held out her hand, as if expecting the two men to put something in it. They looked at each other, uncertain. When she drew a switchblade out of a pocket of the jean jacket she was wearing, Mick looked in disbelief as Keef offered her his hand.

"Lady, you are **not** doing that to us!" Mick protested as he grabbed Keef's hand and pulled it out of the woman's reach.

"Oh, so you want to do this the hard way?" the woman looked over her glasses at him.

"That wasn't the hard way?" Mick goggled.

Diane Wine looked at the two men for a moment. Then put the switchblade away. "Look," she confided, "for most of you guys, ego reduction would require a massive medical intervention. I'm not doing that. All I ask is a little ritual to show that you're moving in the right direction. Know what I mean?"

"Yeah! Yeah! Yeah!" Keef enthused. "Sackerfi aham ster! Drawer pengrams onnafler wiblud! Tha sorra than – ha ha! Great stuff!"

"Ritual," Mick sneered. "Riiiight."

He unenthusiastically held his hand out to Diane Wine. Keef enthusiastically held his hand out. Diane Wine looked at them for a moment, then spit in her hand and slapped each of their hands once. "You can ask to get your egos back when you leave," she informed them.

Keef rushed into the mansion, giddy. Mick followed close behind, ignoring the tingling in his hand, certain that it was only the result of a hard slap and not some sort of ritual magic. But…just to be on the safe side, he decided to demand his ego back after he finished the recording session…

Tara sat on a chair in Wainwright Walsh's Green Room (actually, recreation room three with all of the pool tables removed and a lot of chairs and serving tables moved in); despite the bustle of people coming and going, she couldn't take her eyes off a short man in a purple suit concentrating intently on making a choice from a cheese tray on a long table in front of a series of vanity mirrors. He was fanning himself with a purple hat with a large feather, which made him feel a little calmer, but did not relieve him of the responsibility of choice. The man must have noticed her in the mirror watching him, because he turned towards her and said in a high but pleasant voice, "Can I help you?"

"You're so…" Tara started to say, but trailed off.

"Yes," the man's chest proudly inflated. "I am, aren't I?"

"So…"

"Yes?"

"Brown!"

"Say what?" the man's chest puffed down even more quickly than it had puffed up.

"I love your skin colour!" Tara gushed. "It's so dark, but at the same time shiny! I could lick it all day long! It's not like everybody's else's skin – so pink, so boring! Your brown colour – oomph! It gives me shivers! Do you think I could get skin that colour? I would **kill** for skin that colour! How can I? Please? Can you tell me how I can get skin that colour?"

The man looked at Tara like she was from another universe; he had to consciously remind himself that, in fact, she was. This meant: a) it was very possible that this tiny blue woman had never met a black person before; b) she probably had no idea of the political and cultural history of black people in America; and, c) she was batshit crazy. Taken in *toto* (whom, let us assume for the sake of argument, had safely returned to Kansas rather than trying to convince the Lollipop Kids to form a union), this suggested to him that the situation be handled with delicacy.

"Yeah, lady," the man responded with a glint in his eye. "Changing your colour is easy."

Tara clapped her hands together, excited. "Tell me how! Ooh, tell me! Tell me! Tell me! Tell me!"

"I don't know. Do you really think you're ready?"

"Tell me! Tell me! Tell me! Tell me!"

"Well…only if you're sure…"

"I have never been more sure of anything in my life, and I'm 978 years old!"

"Okay, then…you sacrifice a chicken, right? Cut off its head…on an altar of 45s of Motown hits. Yeah. Motown is a powerful source of magic. While the chicken is bleeding out, sing along to 'Baby Love' by The Supremes while doing some funky hand jive. The hand jive is the thickener – it'll make your skin a nice creamy colour. Then, bathe in a bathtub full of hot chocolate for three hours, until your skin is nicely pruney. You do that, and I guarantee you'll be a real sister!"

"Supremes Baby…hand jive talkin'…chocolate sister…" Tara was trying to fix the process in her memory. "I…I don't know what half of these things mean!"

"Don't worry," the man assured her. "You can always look it up on the internet. Just search on the phrase: 'How can I make my skin darker?'"

"Thank you, kind stranger," Tara gushed once more. If she had been more regular, she could have been featured at Yellowstone National Park. "Thank you! Thank you! Thank you! Thank you!"

In the face of the alien woman's boundless enthusiasm, the man felt a bit bad about the way he had fooled her. "No need to tha –" he started to say.

"My name is Tara Raboomdeeh," Tara introduced herself. "What's yours?"

"ड," ड told her.

"Cliff?" Tara uncertainly asked.

"No. ड."

"Glyph?"

"No! ड."

"Oh. ड Sorry, I'm not wearing my glasses."

"You were able to pronounce – how were you able to

pronounce my name? I chose it so that nobody would be able to pronounce it! How –?"

"It wasn't hard," Tara assured him, smiling. "I just sneezed in my head, and there it was."

Despite himself, Ꚋ smiled. "You alright, Tara   Raboomdeeh. Did I…did I pronounce the silence properly?"

"You left a silent letter off my middle name, but I appreciate the effort."

"   ?"

"Much better!"

Ꚋ looked pleased with himself. Then, a young woman holding a clipboard and talking into a headset bumped him out of the way in her haste to get to the food. He anxiously looked at the cheese tray, which was sparser than when the conversation had started, but still chock full of milk producty goodness. "So much choice," he moaned.

"Do you want help with that?" Tara asked.

"Do you suffer from cheese choice anxiety, too?" Ꚋ turned back to her.

"No," Tara admitted. "But I am good at finding novel solutions to common problems…"

"For inappropriate behaviour erooooahhhhh – ooo – ooo – eee – ooh – ooh – aaaaaaaaaah!"

"Cut."

"I think I really nailed it on that one."

"It was great."

"You think so?"

"Quintessential Freddy."

"Oh."

"Perfect."

"Oh! Thank you."

"But…"

"But?"

"We would like you to record your line again."

"Again? But how can you improve on perfection?"

"We'd like you to – we need you to…dial it back a little. That would make it…more perfect."

"Did you say you want me to dial it up?"

"No, Freddy. * SIGH * Back. Dial it back."

"Freddy doesn't do dial it back."

"Freddy! It's the middle of a verse!"

"So?"

"So, you're hitting the high too soon. Nobody's gonna remember anything that comes after your line!"

"That's how it's supposed to be – aah aah ah oh aah oh oh waaaaaaaah!"

Freddy stood in the sound booth, hands on hips, looking expectantly at Wainwright Walsh, the producer sitting at the mixing board and the groupies of both sexes and Gord knew how many genders on the other side of the glass. Wainwright Walsh and the producer were heatedly conferring. Freddy maintained his expectant pose, adding a topnote of frustration after two and a half minutes; he had had enough experience with these kinds of consultations that he wasn't really feeling it, but he had an audience, and he didn't want to come across as a due rate donna to his fans.

Eventually, Wainwright Walsh leaned over and pressed a button on the control panel. "Great work, Freddy," he said in an almost positive tone. "We appreciate it."

"You really think so?" Freddy asked, although part of him thought, *Yeah. Of course it was great. A man has to have some standards in this life!* He took a hand off his hip and preeningly slicked back his hair.

"I really think so," Wainwright Walsh assured him. The producer gave him an enthusiastic thumbs up.

"I am the champion," Freddy said to himself as he left the sound booth. If he heard Wainwright Walsh say, "We'll fix it in the mix," he chose not to respond.

₷ was sitting next to Tara in the Green Room. He had taken the alien's advice about his cheese problem: he took two pieces of each flavour that was available. He imagined his plate was the ramp up to the ark of his mouth. The thought made him giggle, but not so much that he wasn't able to enjoy the creamy goodness.

"...happy I found a job and a place to stay," Tara was saying, "but Wainie – his name is Wainwright – you knew that – Wainie is just a...my pet name for him – well, he treats me like a slave!"

₷ spit out a piece of medium cheddar. It was not an especially good spit take – cheese being only twenty-seventh on the list of best things to have in your mouth when somebody says something outrageous – the cheese flew in a straight line rather than a majestic arc. But the airborne cheese was strong and true and hit Keef in the back of the head.

"Salri," Keef said out loud. "Salri, fsier. Allga – caff caff – allga qet!"

"Was that a dinosaur?" Tara innocently asked, showing a more sophisticated knowledge of Biblical exegesis than an alien would be expected to have.

"You know," ₷ complained, "I'm trying to understand your...unique situation. But sometimes you say the rudest things!"

"What can I say?" Tara cheerfully replied. "It's a gift."

₷ shook his head. "Nyuh uh," he told her. "You settle yourself comfortably, girl, because I'm gonna school you on what slavery is really li –"

Before he could finish, the woman with the clipboard and headset walked up to him and said, "Okay, Symbol-boy. You're up."

"Who you calling a boy?" ₷ angrily turned on her.

Clipboard and headset woman shrugged. "When you have a name again, I'll use your name," she said, bored of the conversation before it had even begun. "In the meantime, they're waiting for you in the studio."

"Tell them I'm busy!" ₷ petulantly insisted.

"You wanna keep half the music industry waiting?" clipboard and headset woman stifled a yawn. "Mumph – tell Mister Walsh yourself."

Ƽ looked at her. Then at Tara. Then back at her. Then at Tara again. Frustrated, he held a finger up to the alien's face. "Don't go anywhere," he commanded. "We're not finished." Ƽ stood up, half-eaten plate of cheese in his hand. He gave it to Tara. "And hold this 'til I get back."

"Umm, will you be gone long?" Tara asked.

"Wadda you think, baby?" Ƽ answered, "I rock!"

"...and that's where birthing no babies comes from." Ƽ concluded forty minutes later.

"I...I never knew..." Tara said, awefully. "Where I come from, everybody is the same, so we cannot hate each other for our differences. Oh, sure, three thousand years ago, there was a brief disagreement between the umbrellaists and the hattites but that only lasted for 427 years, and everybody was respectful of each other's opinions. Except for Bertie, but he spent a decade in the shape of a pretzel, so you know what **his** opinion was worth!"

"Umbrellaists?" Ƽ asked. "Hattites? I... I don't understand."

Tara explained that, on Earth in her home universe, large objects frequently fell from the sky. Some people believed that a tiny umbrella held over their heads would keep them from getting smushed by anvils, safes and the occasional giant octopus. Other people believed that hats could contain the same object-repellant properties as umbrellas, but with the advantage of keeping both hands free to eat a hoagie while walking down the street. Hoagies were really popular at the time. Today, nobody really knows why – I mean, sure, they were tasty and all, but there were any number of other sandwiches that could have been used in the example. Still, it seemed a matter of some urgency back in the day. The umbrellaists argued that their solution was more fashionable, and that one-handed hoagie eating was an easy skill to master. As it happened, it wasn't – as the hattites gleefully pointed out, it was messy and wasteful, the sidewalks becoming slick with spilled sandwich guts. Rather than admit defeat, the umbrellaists switched to eating finger sandwiches, which not only hastened the end of the hoagie era, but cemented their case. Now, the umbrellaist/hattite feud is just a distant memory.

"And nobody died," Tara concluded. "Nobody who didn't want to, anyway."

ਤ shook his head. "Yeah, if only it were that simple in this reality."

"Yeah."

They sat with that for a couple of minutes. Sometimes, our inhumanity towards each other can be encapsulated in a single word and some silence.

"Are you enjoying the cheese?" Tara tentatively offered.

"Absolutely! Except for this…" ਤ held up a yellow object he had taken a bite out of.

Tara was about to tell him what it was (he had clearly never seen the inside of a cow), but thought better of it. They had bonded. She felt this obligated her to be more sensitive in her interactions with him. She was about to advise ਤ not to eat anything that didn't taste right to him when he popped the remainder of the yellow object into his mouth and, making a face of distaste, quickly chewed and swallowed it. He took the napkin off his paper plate and gently dabbed his lips. Then, he looked at his plate and realized that there was no more cheese, or cheese-looking objects, on it.

"Guess I better dance, now," he said, standing up and putting his plate on a nearby table.

"It was good talking to you," Tara told him.

"It was good talking to you, too," ਤ responded. Ordinarily, he didn't feel any responsibility for teaching white people about their role in the oppression of people of colour. But this was a special case. She was blue, for one thing.

"I **will** read *Roots*," Tara eagerly assured him.

"I know you will."

As she watched ਤ head for the door, Tara raised her fist and shouted, "Bite the powder!"

Smiling, ਤ walked out.

And that's how the alien Tara Raboomdeeh became radicalized. Small steps, baby. Small steps…

"Well, tonight thank Gord it's them instead of you…"

Wainwright Walsh and the sound engineer looked at each other in the control booth. Then, he leaned over and opened the microphone to speak. "Umm, Irish, that was a…rather laid back reading of that line…"

Irish was a big, bluff man who lilted when he spoke. He was a lilter. He couldn't help it – he was raised that way. When his band broke big, he considered getting speech therapy, but he was worried that it might adversely affect his singing, so he never followed through on it. And anyway, there are worse things in life than lilting.

"I thought it was pretty decent, that take, there," Irish responded.

Wainwright Walsh shook his head. How was it possible that Irish's speaking voice sounded more like a song than his actual singing? "You did hit all the right notes," he agreed. "And you have the tune down. But this is a song about saving the lives of billions of sentient beings, and you had about as much passion for it as if you were singing about doing the dishes."

"There's a lot of soul in doing dishes," Irish insisted.

"Be that as it may, there wasn't a lot of soul in your performance."

"It's the fault of that witch," Irish accused.

"Witch?" Wainwright Walsh asked, uncomprehending.

"On the front door. The one who took my ego."

Wainwright Walsh took a moment. He knew that this was a delicate place in the conversation, and he wanted to be sure that his response to Irish was sensitive and appropriate. Centred in himself and confident, he asked: "What…the hell are you talking about?"

"The witch at the front door took my ego," Irish explained. "My ego is where all my passion is. Without my ego, I may as well be a foorkin' lounge singer!" Even his swearing had no oomph behind it.

Wainwright Walsh pursed his lips. "Okay, umm, Irish. I'm

going to tell you something. But, uhh, I would appreciate it if you would keep it between us, okay?"

"Of course, man. You can tell me anything."

"Okay." Wainwright Walsh took a deep breath. "Diane Wine is…a very talented psychologist. But she…she doesn't have any magical powers, so she can't actually remove anybody's ego from their psyche."

"She can't?"

"She can't. She uses the power of suggestion to convince people with powerful egos to suppress them voluntarily."

"She can be very persuasive."

"Exactly."

"Hunh. Well, isn't that a kick in the nards of fame?"

"Umm…sure?"

Irish considered this for several seconds. He closed his eyes and contemplated for another few seconds. When he opened his eyes again, they were full of fire. "Okay. I'm ready for another take."

And Irish nailed it.

"Liam, you're such an asshole!"

Tara, who had spent several days in the Green Room, found her flagging enthusiasm run back up the flagpole a little. She recognized Eonayr from the photograph that had accompanied the article she had read on the diminutive singer. (Tara mostly read the Alternate Reality News Service for the gossip, which she knew would come in handy at some point in her life – and it had!) She had just flung an asparagus spear at a hulking young man standing in front of her.

Liam mumbled something challenging at her.

"No, I didn't expect a spear of asparagus to pierce your heart!" Eonayr roared. For such a small woman, she could make a fearsome sound. "You have to have a heart to have your heart pierced by asparagus!"

Liam opened his arms in an attempt at an embrace and

mumbled something comforting at her.

Eonayr threw a large piece of brie (the cheese table had been replenished since Ꝺ's day) at his head. Crumbs of it got in his hair. Liam abandoned the embrace and ran a hand through his hair in an attempt to decheesify it. He mumbled something angry at her.

"You're worried about your hair? Your ferking hair‽" Eonayr screamed. She crumbled a handful of Camembert and flung it at his head, tripling the amount of cheese in it. "You cheated on me, asshole! I think that's a liiiittle more important than your ferking hair!"

Liam looked at her in disbelief and mumbled something confused at her.

"Of course we're not sleeping together! That's so nineties! No, I'm talking about the single you recorded with Adele! You promised that your first duet would be with me! With me! Did you think I was never going to find out‽ Did you really think I would never know‽"

Liam mumbled something conciliatory at her.

"What was that?" Eonayr asked. "I couldn't make out what you just said."

Liam mumbled something conciliatory at her louder.

"No, that does not make things better." Eonayr considered the cheeses remaining on the table, then looked at Liam, who was petulantly picking crumbs out of his hair. Believing that the cheese had made its point, she settled on glaring at him and continued: "When your record label told you to record a single with Adele, you could have told them you intended to record a single with me instead. You're Liam. Your band has had hit after hit. They would have done whatever you told them to do!"

Done with the mumbling, Liam returned her glare.

They might be glaring at each other in the rec room that had been turned into a Green Room in Wainwright Walsh's mansion still if a small blue woman with unnaturally round features and no hair wearing an exquisite three piece suit hadn't walked up to them and asked, "Can I help?"

"Are you a trained relationship councillor?" Eonayr asked, not tearing her eyes away from the glaring challenge.

"No," Tara admitted. "But I have a lot of experience avoiding big rocks falling from the sky, experience that has taught me a lot about life."

Not breaking eye contact with Eonayr, Liam mumbled something penetrating at Tara.

"What?" Tara asked. "I…I don't understand…"

"He wants to know what, exactly, your experience has taught you about life?"

"It's taught me to avoid big rocks falling from the sky, for one thing."

Liam mumbled something appreciative at Tara and Eonayr.

"That's the problem with you, Liam," Eonayr responded. "You think everything is deep! Screw this! I'm done – I was only sticking around because I wanted to grab a drink with you after you recorded your part. I'm gone."

Eonayr stormed out. You could almost see sparks fly off her body as she did.

Liam mumbled something admiring at her back.

"What?" Tara asked.

Liam mumbled something embarrassed at Tara.

"I…I really don't –"

The woman with the clipboard and headset walked up to Tara. "You the alien chick?"

Tara made a big production of looking around the room. There were no alternatives. "Umm, yeah," she finally said. Not funny, but accurate.

"You're up."

Tara squeed. It was a long, passionate squeed. Then, seeing Liam's crestfallen expression, she turned to him and said: "Sorry. I've got to go." She squeezed his arm encouragingly. "Remember the falling rocks."

Liam mumbled something grateful at Tara.

The woman with the headset rolled her eyes. "All this sincerity is making me gag. Follow me, please. And try not to gush all over the place – we just had the carpets cleaned."

Tara was so thrilled that she was going to perform that, as they walked out of the Green Room, down the hall and into the studio, she didn't think to point out that she was the one who had cleaned the carpets.

As Tara took her triangle out of its case and tentatively waved the baton over it, a technical assistant adjusted the microphone to accommodate her height. "Alright, Tara," Wainwright Walsh said from the control booth on the other side of the glass when it appeared that everything was ready to record, "this is your big moment. I want you to give it everything you've got."

"I will!" Tara stated, excited. But she didn't.

After several seconds of silence, Wainwright Walsh asked, "Tara? Everything okay?"

"Y…y…y – of course," Tara stuttered unconvincingly. "Been working towards this moment my whole life!"

Wainwright Walsh resisted the urge to point out that, for most of her life, Tara had been working on not getting crushed by a falling rhinoceros. He had to remind himself that she was one of the sentient beings that the charity single was being recorded to help. Forcefully remind himself. "Okay, Tara, what you're experiencing is called, 'stage fright'. It happens to –"

"But I'm not on a stage," Tara interrupted.

"Umm…okay. It's also called, 'performance anxiety'. It hap –"

"But I haven't started performing yet."

"It doesn't matter what you call it!" Wainwright Walsh shouted. He took a moment to breath as Diane Wine had taught him to. "It…"

"Let's call it…swimming?" Tara suggested.

"Sure. Fine. The important thing is that it happens when you get anxious about having to perform in front of other people. Johnny Flextone, the lead singer of the Uggly Fugglings, used to throw up before going on stage."

Tara looked around the small recording space, then brightly asked, "Do you have a bucket?"

"I…am not suggesting you do that. My point is that it is perfectly understandable for you to experience…what you are experiencing. To help, why don't you…turn around and face the wall. Then, imagine that you're in your favourite place –"

"A fryer at Bob So Tasty?"

"…Sure. Imagine it's just you and…fried foods. That should make it easier for you."

Tara turned around and…waited for the technician to reposition the microphone. When that was done and Wainwright Walsh gave her the go-ahead, Tara struck the triangle.

"Thank you," Wainwright Walsh said.

"That's it?" Tara was disappointed.

"I couldn't ask for a better performance."

"I think I could give it more heart."

"Heart, spleen, aorta – seriously, that performance had it all."

"Shouldn't we – shouldn't we do one more take? You know, just for safety's sake?"

"You shouldn't mess with perfection. You went into the recording studio a nobody, and you're going to come out…to be honest, probably not a star, but definitely a more well known nobody. How many of your people can say that?"

Tara grinned as she packed away her triangle. "Not many. Not many at all!"

The Good, The Bad and The Uggly Fugglings of Musical Activism

by TINA LOLLOCADENKA, Alternate Reality News Service Music Writer

We live in trying times. Politicians trying to ignore climate change so that they do not have to interfere with business. Wealthy business leaders trying to pretend that their money doesn't help them get politicians who will look after their interests. Ordinary people trying to convince themselves that the solution to their problems lies at the bottom of the next bottle of beer.

Humanist activists trying to protest the release of a single in the digital age.

The problem started with the release of a celebrity-studded (you would never have believed that one earlobe could contain so many holes!) single, 'We Are the Weird'. All proceeds from sales of the single were slated to go to The Aluminum Sliding Foundation, a non-profit organization started by entrepreneur Rodney Pendleton to help aliens from Earth Prime 4-6-4-0-8-9 dash Omega, a universe that is imminent danger of imploding, adjust to life in other universes.

Well. Those who oppose alien immigration did not take kindly to the release of the song.

"Blues will not replace us!" said Charlie 'White Bred' Breedlov, spokesperson for Humans for Humanity. "Blues will not –"

Yes, yes, we've heard it all before. But what makes you think, even if it were possible for the aliens to replace you, that they would want to?

"Cuz we created the greatest – * BRAAAAP *! – culture the world has ever seen!"

Some people are easier to convince that the solution to their problems lies at the bottom of the next bottle of beer than others.

The problem was that the song was never released on vinyl – it was only ever made available to the public as a digital download. The old method of putting records in a pile and lighting them on fire to show your unhappiness with them was no longer available.

"That's when human supremacist groups get creative," explained Francois 'The Skipper (Because 'The Professor' Was Too Obvious)' Ultime, who has studied speciesist groups for over a decade.

If they couldn't get physical copies of the song to burn, they could get physical copies of the previous works by the man who spearheaded the project and burn them. They had to figure out who it was, first, which required a lot of research because he was no longer well known, but they were nothing if not experienced in the way of internet research.

Three weeks later, they had a breakthrough: somebody came across the name Wainwright Walsh, who was apparently the lead singer for a band called The Occidental Tourists. Walsh…Walsh – why did that name sound so – somebody snapped his fingers. Of course! He was named at the bottom of news articles on the song! He must have had something to do with it!

This line of protest petered out (Paul and Mary were out at the Shreveport Shrooms Festival, so they were unable to comment) when one of the researchers discovered that The Occidental Tourist's first album, *Appetite for Rice Pudding*, was selling on ehBay for over a thousand pounds (which is at least…$157,000 dollars American, and I don't have a big enough scratch pad to figure out what it would be in Canadian). That was more money than all of the chapters of Humans for Humanity combined would raise in the organization's entire existence!

Plan – wait, that was Plan B – so, Plan At Least C was to buy copies of "We Are the Weird" on the Band Age Solutions web site, and then burn their phones. Dozens of human supremacist groups across North America and western Europe, including Humans for Humanity, the Seahorses of Odin and F*rk the Oxford Comma, participated in the action.

How did Walsh feel about this?

"How the hell would I know?" demanded Eonayr, no longer laid back and probably not rocking the pixie look any more. "I agreed to help him out with his stupid song, I'm not his babysitter or anything!"

But you're one of the biggest recording artists of the modern era, and you did contribute to 'We Are the Weird'.

"That's the last time I help out anybody in need!" Eonayr darkly uttered.

Soooo...how did Walsh feel about this?

"Daddy's not home right now," Wainwright's six year-old daughter Fionnoula said. "Please call back later."

Did Walsh worry that a human supremacist, enflamed by the protest, might make good on the death threats that he had been receiving since the single had been released?

"Daddy's not home." Fionnoula insisted. "Call back later."

Was Walsh concerned that the backlash against the single would hurt the cause?

"Daddy raised over ten million pounds to help the aliens," Fionnoula pointed out. "So, f*rk off!"

Wow. The apple doesn't learn three part harmonies far from the tree!

Several days after the release of the single, Wainwright Walsh was sitting in his den, talking to My Attorney Bernie. Squeak. Squeak. Squeak.

"The good news," My Attorney Bernie was telling him, "is that you probably won't be arrested for the riot on Tower Bridge."

Squeak! Squeak! Squeak!

"I had nothing to do with the riot on Tower Bridge!" Wainwright Walsh protested. "A bunch of yobbos got piss drunk and went looking for aliens to throw into the Thames!"

"And ended up starting a fire that backed cars up for miles. When some of the drivers – who were also yobbos, but for a different cause, I suppose – got out of their vehicles to object to being held up on their journey to...whatever yobboing they had planned, fisticuffs ensued."

"How is that my fault?"

"They used newspaper reviews of the charity single as kindling," My Attorney Bernie calmly informed him. "When the bonfire was roaring, they found the tune on the *We Are the Weird* web site and, as it started playing, threw their phones onto the fire. Never underestimate the ingenuity of men gripped by hate."

"How many of them participated in this…event?"

"Twenty of them were arrested – perhaps as many as forty immolated their phones in protest. But that's just one incident in London. Apparently, protests were held all over the world."

"Mmm. So, at three quid a download, they may have contributed as much as 120 quid to the cause?"

"I said men who hate could be ingenious. I didn't say they were bright."

Wainwright Walsh sighed. "Okay," he finally said. "If not getting arrested is the worst thing that came out of this –"

"There is the matter of the death threats…"

Squeak! Squeak! Squeak!

"I had almost forgotten about them," Wainwright Walsh moaned.

"Your best course of action at this point would be to do just that," My Attorney Bernie advised him.

Before Wainwright Walsh could reply, a knock came on the door.

"Wainie?" Tara asked from the other side.

"I'm busy!" he shouted back, putting his hand over the receiver of his phone. Yeah, he was old school like that. "Come back in an hour!"

"The good news is that I found the fire extinguisher!"

"I don't really have time for this!"

"The bad news is that you're going to need a new stove!"

"Really! Come back later!"

Tara opened the door and walked into the room. Over her shoulder, she carried a long stick, to the end of which had been tied a red handkerchief which had taken the shape of a triangle case. "I won't be here later."

"What?" Wainwright Walsh absentmindedly hung up the phone. My Attorney Bernie shrugged when he heard the dial tone at the other end of the line – he was already planning on making the musician pay through the nose so that he could beef up his security.

Wainwright Walsh could afford it.

"I have accomplished what I came here to accomplish," Tara explained. "Playing a musical instrument on a hit record was strangely anti-climactic, but I met a lot of interesting people along the way and I don't despair for the human race as much as I did."

"Now, wait just a minute –" Wainwright Walsh started to protest.

Tara waved it away with her free hand. "No need to thank me. Helping make the world a better place is its own reward."

"What did you do to make the world a better place? You've been cleaning my house for a couple of months, and it's dirtier than it's been in decades!"

"No need to thank me."

"And now I have to buy a new stove?"

"Oh. You heard that. Let's not get hung up on details. Or, for that matter, bogged down on details. Let's not let the details affect us in either direction is what I'm trying to say. The important thing is that I have learned all that I can from this experience, and it's time for me to move on to other experiences. I know it will be hard for you to let me go…"

"Not as hard as you may think," Wainwright Walsh muttered.

"Oh, you're just saying that to make it easier to let me go." Tara walked up to the desk and put her hand – the free one – on Wainwright Walsh's hand. "You did a good thing here. Oh, sure, you may have had selfish motives, but in the end you did what's right, and, even if the observation is too on the nose, it's still true. Anyway, I speak for all of my people – except Chuckie – he can be a bit of a contrarian – when I say that we will always be grateful for what you've done to help us."

Wainwright Walsh almost blushed. He hadn't done that since he was a kid. Rock legends don't blush. It's one of their unwritten rules. He stuttered (rock legends can do that – Roger had proven it): "Oh – ah, well, you know – I was just…I was moved by the plight of people in need, and used what modest tools I have at my disposal to help."

"Of course you did." Tara patted his hand, then walked towards to the door. Before she walked through it, she turned and said, "I actually have nothing to say. I'm just prolonging the moment for an extra few seconds of poignancy. No, don't say anything – it's just the way my people roll." A second later, she was gone.

Wainwright Walsh stared at the back of the closed door. The phone rang. It was probably My Attorney Bernie wanting to know why the musician had hung up on him. He let it ring. Wainwright Walsh wasn't ignoring his accountant, he was just prolonging the moment for an extra few seconds of poignancy…

Elsewhen Press

delivering outstanding new talents in speculative fiction

Visit the Elsewhen Press website at elsewhen.press for the latest information on all of our titles, authors and events; to read our blog; find out where to buy our books and ebooks; or to place an order.

Sign up for the Elsewhen Press InFlight Newsletter at elsewhen.press/newsletter

THE EYE COLLECTORS

A STORY OF

HER MAJESTY'S OFFICE OF THE WITCHFINDER GENERAL

PROTECTING THE PUBLIC FROM THE UNNATURAL SINCE 1645

SIMON KEWIN

When Danesh Shahzan gets called to a crime scene, it's usually because the police suspect not just foul play but unnatural forces at play.

Danesh is an Acolyte in Her Majesty's Office of the Witchfinder General, a shadowy arm of the British government fighting supernatural threats to the realm. This time, he's been called in by Detective Inspector Nikola Zubrasky to investigate a murder in Cardiff. The victim had been placed inside a runic circle and their eyes carefully removed from their head. Danesh soon confirms that magical forces are at work. Concerned that there may be more victims to come, he and DI Zubrasky establish a wary collaboration as they each pursue the investigation within the constraints of their respective organisations. Soon Danesh learns that there may be much wider implications to what is taking place and that somehow he has an unexpected connection. He also realises something about himself that he can never admit to the people with whom he works…

"Think *Dirk Gently* meets *Good Omens*!"

ISBN: 9781911409748 (epub, kindle) / 9781911409649 (288pp paperback)

Visit bit.ly/TheEyeCollectors

DAVID SHANNON

"Un-put-down-able! A classic hero's journey, deftly handled. I was surprised by every twist and turn, the plotting was superb, and the engagement of all the senses – I could smell those flowers and herbs. A tour de force"

– LINDSAY NICHOLSON MBE

Books are dangerous

People in Blanow think that books are dangerous: they fill your head with drivel, make poor firewood and cannot be eaten (even in an emergency).

This book is about Howul. He sees things differently: fires are dangerous; people are dangerous; books are just books.

Howul secretly writes down what goes on around him in Blanow. How its people treat foreigners, treat his daughter, treat him. None of it is pretty. Worse still, everything here keeps trying to kill him: rats, snakes, diseases, roof slates, the weather, the sea. That he survives must mean something. He wants to find out what. By trying to do this, he gets himself thrown out of Blanow… and so his journey begins.

Like all gripping stories, *HOWUL* is about the bad things people do to each other and what to do if they happen to you. Some people use sticks to stay safe. Some use guns. Words are the weapons that Howul uses most. He makes them sharp. He makes them hurt.

Of course books are dangerous.

ISBN: 9781911409908 (epub, kindle) / 9781911409809 (200pp paperback)

Visit bit.ly/HOWUL

About Ira Nayman

Ira Nayman is a debonair humunculus of mystery who leads an exciting double life as an author of humorous *divertissements*. He has self-published 12 books in the Alternate Reality News Service series, the latest of which is code-named Good King Wrenchless (but is really named *Welcome to the Insurrection (We're* **Not** *Sorry For the Inconvenience)*), as well as XBT12 (*Idiotocracy for Dummies*, an omnibus volume containing the first three Vesampucceri books). *Bad Actors* is the seventh novel in the Transdimensional Authority/Multiverse series, the second in the alien refugees trilogy.

Ira has also been assigned a bottom secret mission to promote the 20th anniversary of his web site, *Les Pages aux Folles*, which will take place in the first week of September, 2022. The birthplace of both the Alternate Reality News Service and the Transdimensional Authority, *Les Pages aux Folles'* weekly updates of social and political satire will fill 38 books and comprise somewhere between two and two and a half million words.

Ira was also the editor of *Amazing Stories* magazine for two and a half years, and is past President of SFCanada, the organization of science fiction and fantasy professionals. Or, at least, that's his cover story and he's sticking to it.

www.ingramcontent.com/pod-product-compliance
Lightning Source LLC
Chambersburg PA
CBHW060812190726
48285CB00002B/641

* 9 7 8 1 9 1 1 4 0 9 8 4 7 *